Colors of the Heart

DK MARIE

<u>**Opposites Attract**</u>

Fairy Tale Lies - Book1
Love Songs - Book 2
Taste of Passion - Book 3
Colors of the Heart - Book 4

There is a loose timeline, but this series does not have to be read in order. Each book is a standalone.

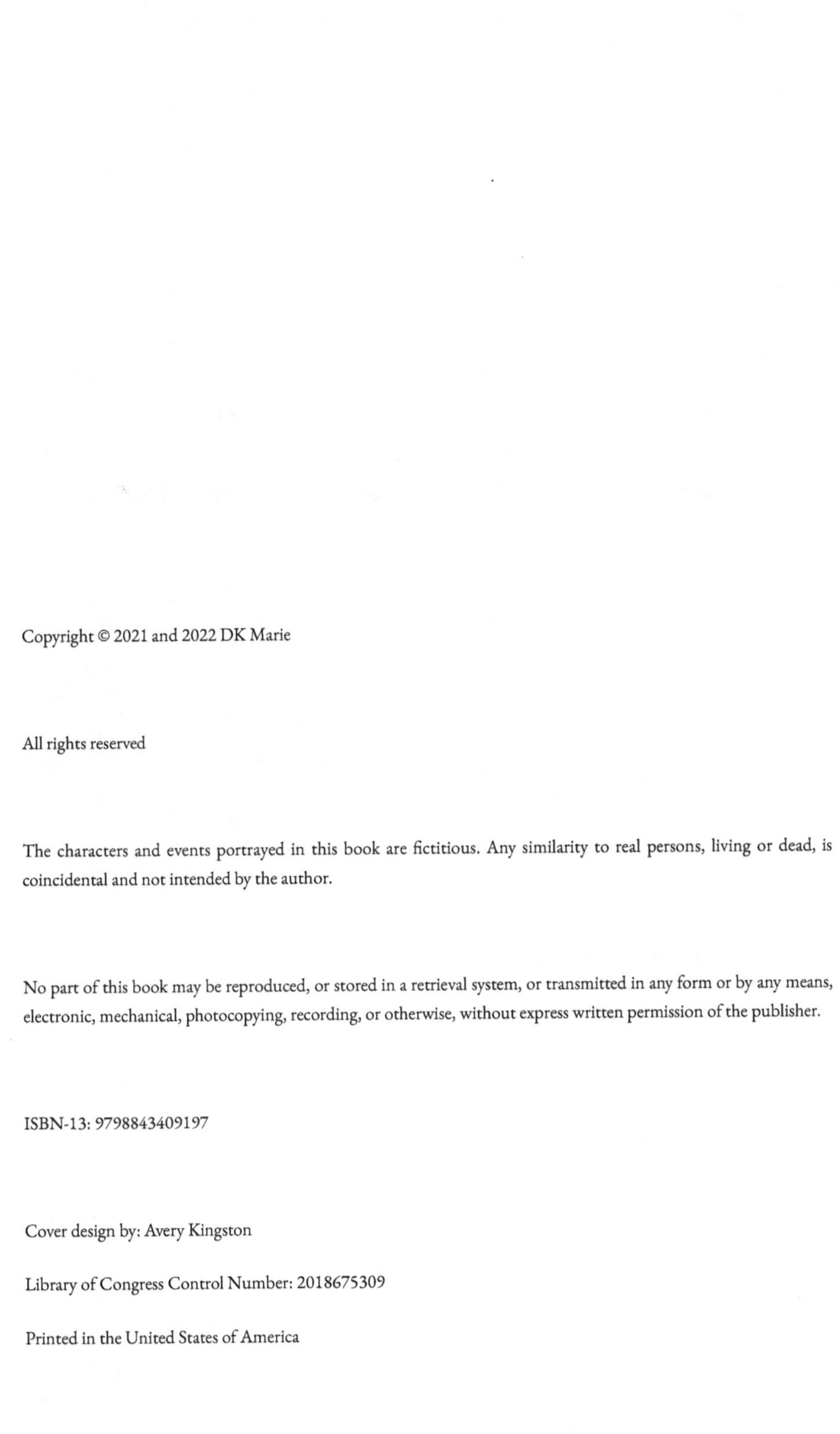

ISBN-13: 9798843409197

Cover design by: Avery Kingston

Library of Congress Control Number: 2018675309

Printed in the United States of America

This book is dedicated to my parents (including step). Thank you for always allowing my imagination to run wild and never stifling it. I know neither of you expected me to use it to write romance. Maybe horror, but not feel-good loves stories. However, they've stolen my heart and given me hope. Thank you for always giving me room to follow my path.

Contents

Chapter One

Lucas needed to get back to the wedding reception, but he couldn't look away. The horse with the bulbous eyes and the demon sitting on the woman's torso, her face a mask of hopeless despair, held all his attention.

This painting, *The Nightmare*, had been him for so long. Until, slowly, life and heartache moved on. The changes were so imperceptible he barely noticed them.

First, he was able to breathe around the sadness. After a while, his laughter began to ring true and his smiles weren't a brittle, false mask. Then one day, he noticed he felt human again.

The click of high-heels pulled his attention from the painting and his musings. He turned to find a woman walking in his direction, her entire focus on the phone in her hand.

She was stunning.

Her black hair was swept into an intricate style matching her fancy dress. A few strands had fallen from her up-do, and she tugged on them with one hand while the other swiped a perfectly manicured thumb across the screen of her cell, scrolling through something.

He recognized her green gown. Like him, she was at the Detroit Institute of Arts for Jacob and Greta's wedding. She was one of the bridesmaids.

She was within a few feet of him but didn't notice she wasn't alone. No surprise. He hadn't moved since spotting her, and it was late in the evening. The DIA was mostly empty. Since sneaking away to the upstairs galleries for a breather, she was the only person he'd seen.

He cleared his throat to let her know he was there.

She gasped, her head shooting up as her phone clattered to the ground.

Shit. So much for not startling her.

He hurried forward, grabbing her cell. Glancing at the screen, he saw a marble statue.

"Sorry, I didn't mean to scare you." He handed her the phone, almost stuttering his words.

He'd caught a brief glimpse of her walking down the aisle during the wedding and thought she was pretty. Seeing her up close, with those gray-metal eyes pinning him, she was striking.

"No, my fault," she said, her quiet, breathy laugh wrapping around him. "I was in my own world and didn't see anyone on my way here." She patted the lapel of his suit jacket. "Are you a guest from the Grimm wedding?"

He nodded, wishing she'd touch him again. It had been light, only lasting a second, yet the warmth of her hand and her nearness was distracting. And entrancing.

Not in a bad way, but definitely different, something that hadn't happened in a long time.

Lately, he'd begun to wonder if that part of him died as so much had on that awful February afternoon two years ago.

"Coming from the same party, I wonder how we managed to miss each other." She gave a brilliant, gleaming smile.

Clearing his throat again, he replied, "I probably left before you. I've been here a while."

She quirked a questioning brow. "Are you avoiding the wedding or your date?"

He licked his bottom lip, his pulse zinging. Was this small talk, or her subtle attempt to find out if he was single?

He ran his thumb along his ring finger. The old, unconscious habit caused him a sliver of pain. His finger was, of course, bare. His wife had been gone for more than two years, and sometime last year he'd made himself remove his wedding ring.

He went with a half-truth. "Neither. I wanted to visit this painting." He pointed to *The Nightmare.* "And, okay, I needed a break from my sister. She talks a lot."

"You came here with your sister?" She lifted a single brow, her gaze running over him.

He wasn't about to get into his reasons for not having a date and shrugged. "Yeah, so?"

"You're handsome. I can't imagine you'd have a difficult time finding a date."

Pleasure warmed his veins. Perhaps she *was* interested in him.

He took half a step closer, her perfume teasing him. The scent was alluring and sensual, matching her perfectly.

"Plus, it makes me feel like less of a loser." She smiled, her enticing full lips twitching with humor. "My mother is my date."

A burst of sharp, surprised laughter escaped him. "Really? You couldn't find someone to bring?"

The woman was hot. All she'd need to do was crook a finger, and men would come running.

"The bride is my cousin, so my mother was already invited. She was the logical choice. I don't have time for a man in my life right now." She shrugged a delicate shoulder. "Why waste my evening with one?"

Her lack of interest in men bothered him more than it should. He wanted to change her mind.

"However," the sexy stranger continued, "if you happen to run into my aunt Sophia, please don't tell her what I said. She's been dropping hints since the wedding invites were mailed that I need to find a man before all the good ones are taken." Leaning in closer, her eyes dancing with mirth, she said in a conspiratorial whisper, "Her other word of advice was to stay away from the groom's side. According to her, they're low-life commoners. She must've missed the memo that we aren't living in the eighteen hundreds."

He snorted. Jacob had told Lucas plenty of stories about his snobby mother-in-law. The man must really love his new bride to be willing to deal with her mother. "Aw, well, that's a shame."

"What is?"

"That you were warned off from the groom's side, and you don't have time for men."

His flirting surprised the hell out of him, and when her smile turned from playful to wicked, his disbelief morphed into something hotter.

"I don't take bad advice. And, I might have time for you." She winked. "If you make it worth it."

Right then, he wanted to make it his life's mission. This woman's boldness and confidence were alluring as hell.

He opened his mouth to say something. What, he had no idea, but her phoned buzzed, snagging her attention.

"Crap," she muttered, reading the screen before returning her gaze to him. "I have to go back downstairs for my bridesmaid duties."

He offered her his arm. "May I have the pleasure of escorting you back to the party?"

She licked her lips. It stroked along his desires.

"The pleasure is all mine," she purred, linking her arm through his. "I'm Harper Marquette."

"Lucas Genezen. Nice to meet you."

• • • ● ● • ● ● • •

Nice was an understatement.

The man was gorgeous with his broad shoulders, thick, dark brown hair, and a charming, quick smile. Plus, their light flirting had been fun.

In a matter of ten minutes, Greta's wedding went from fun to phenomenal.

Harper slid her arm through Lucas's. The smooth material of his suit jacket was expensive and soft under her hand. Even more enjoyable was the surprisingly muscular bicep she was holding tight.

Taking in his warm smile, proud nose and strong jaw, she did her best not to swoon.

He reminded her of an old film star from the black and white movies. She was unable to recall which one, but it would come to her.

The short elevator ride and a brief walk to the wedding reception in the Great Hall wasn't enough time. They hadn't talked about anything important, only how they knew the bride and groom.

He intrigued her, and she craved more time with him. His manner was reserved, yet something told her there was a wildness in him that'd match hers. His moss-green eyes were solemn with an impish glint. She wouldn't mind falling into his gorgeous smile.

As they entered the reception room, she said, "I have to go. Greta's requesting the single ladies for the bouquet toss." She peeked at him through her lashes, suddenly shy. "Will you be out there for the garter toss?"

All his humor seemed to drain away. "No."

"Um-okay," she stammered, rubbing the base of her neck. His fast mood change made her flounder.

He stopped walking. Then, as if forcibly regathering his light-hearted mood around him, he smirked. "With my luck, it'll be my sister who catches the flowers."

Yeah, right. She suspected there was more to it and considered pressing him. However, the flash of pain she caught punching through him before he buried it told her it wasn't a topic he'd discuss.

Instead, she asked, "Okay. Well, what about dancing? Do you do that?"

"If you're asking I do."

Anticipation chased away her curiosity at his odd, sudden mood shifts. She glanced at the gathering ladies, wishing they'd disappear. Wishing the lights were dimming and the band was playing a slow, sensual song.

With difficulty, she managed to keep her smile blasé and carefree. "Let's meet on the dancefloor when this is finished."

"Definitely." His voice promised more than a dance.

Yes, please.

He walked her to the group of women waiting for Greta to throw her bouquet. Some eyed him like they'd take him instead of the flowers.

"See you soon." He dusted his lips lightly over her knuckles before leaving.

His touch remained after she lost him to the crowd of partygoers. With her opposite hand, she ran her fingertips along where his mouth had been, wondering if he was a good kisser.

Taking a spot in the far back, she caught sight of Aunt Kimberley pushing her way to the front. The way she stared at the bouquet in Greta's hands was hysterical. And a little scary.

In the end, her aunt's aggressive maneuvering didn't work. The flowers had landed in her cousin Cindy's open arms as if destiny demanded it.

Hell, maybe it was because five minutes later, the groom's brother, Will, caught the garter.

The two *had* gotten rather friendly with each other during the combination bachelorette and bachelor party at Lake Michigan. Like friends-with-benefits close.

Cindy had said it wouldn't last past the weekend. The way her blue eyes locked with his coffee-brown ones and his hands lingered under her dress, Harper was certain they weren't done with each other.

Eventually, Will finished with the garter, and the chairs were removed from the dancefloor, making room for the band.

The opening chords rang through the Great Hall, slamming against the left side of Harper's head.

She rubbed her temples, sincerely hoping the light thumping pressure wasn't a sign of a horrible oncoming migraine.

Standing on the outer edges of the dancefloor, she tried to decide if she should locate her purse with her meds or find Lucas.

He found her first and offered her his hand, asking if she wanted to dance. She wanted him more than her medication.

Besides, the pain had almost vanished. Perhaps it was only a brief flare-up and not one of her debilitating migraines out to ruin her evening.

He guided her to the center of the dancefloor. His steps were smooth, and he led in a way that had her pondering if he was the same in bed.

Images of him commanding and demanding her pleasure flooded her senses, sending rivulets of desire coursing through her. Her breath hitched, and her cheeks warmed. She sincerely hoped this overwhelming lust for him wasn't stamped on her every feature.

She needed to get her mind out of the gutter. "Do you come to the DIA often?"

"I do love it here, but it's been a few years. What about you?"

"As often as I can manage. I find it inspiring."

He tilted back, appearing intrigued. "You never told me why you were upstairs. Were you wandering, or was there something specific you wanted to see?"

She debated telling him. When they were returning to the party he told her he was a business owner. Something called eco-consulting. Would he scoff and call her passion, her career, a fanciful hobby?

He wouldn't be the first. Hell, even her mother didn't fully understand. She supported her financially and admired Harper's work. However, in the silent spaces and the undercurrent of conversations, her mother's disappointment was heard.

She was a financial manager and a legend in her circle. She'd wanted her daughter to follow in her footsteps, but it was a lost cause.

Harper lifted her chin. "I'm an artist. Mainly a sculptor. I was visiting my favorite statue. *The Veiled Lady.*"

She waited, steeling herself. Would he offer derision, indifference, or interest?

To her immense pleasure, his eyes lit with interest. "I thought that's what I saw when I picked up your cell. It's the small statue by the elevator. Right?"

Him recognizing it warmed her. "Yes. I've managed the technique with clay, but I can't get it with stone or marble. I'm getting closer, and I was hoping visiting it again would offer insight, or at the very least, inspiration." Clamping her mouth shut, she shook her head, mumbling, "Sorry. I tend to get overexcited talking about my work."

He gently squeezed her waist, bringing her closer. "Please, keep going. I find the whole process fascinating. Just don't ask me to draw even a stick figure. It's embarrassing how terrible I am at it." He let go of her momentarily, waving a hand. "Anyway, where do you sell your work? Anywhere I could see it?"

She wanted to answer his questions, but his nearness was distracting and oh-so-delicious. His warm embrace, combined with his sinfully delicious cologne was evoking images of autumn and slow, lazy sex in front of a fire.

As if reading her mind, he leaned in closer. If she stood on her tip-toes, their lips would meet.

Would she kiss a near stranger?

The answer was immediate. Yes.

He didn't bridge the miniscule space between them, and she was too much of a coward to do it. Struggling to calm her rapidly growing desire, she tried to recall his question.

Something about her art...

Oh, yeah. He was asking where I sell my artwork.

"Sometimes, my work is commissioned. Or I'll sell my pieces to private buyers. I'm also opening a gallery. It'll feature my stuff and other local artists. Well, right now it's in its early, infant stage. I'm trying to find the perfect place. I want it in Detroit. In one of those old art-deco buildings. Anyway..." She smiled shyly. "I'm babbling."

He said something, but the song changed to a fast, loud tempo drowning him out. The booming bass shot straight through her skull, making her wince.

His color drained away, and he choked. "Are you okay?"

She blinked, taking in his strong reaction. He appeared close to damn-near panicking.

Waving a reassuring hand, she said, "It's no big deal. I tend to get headaches around loud noises."

"Are you sure it's just a headache?" His voice was a little shaky.

What else would it be?

"Yup, I've been getting them since I was a kid." Tilting her head, she studied him. "Are you okay? You're pale as a ghost."

He ran a hand through his hair. "Sorry, yeah. I'm overreacting."

She stepped from his warm embrace. "I need to find my mother. She has my painkillers."

Leaving his arms bothered her almost as much as her throbbing head. However, ignoring the pain was impossible.

"Do you need me to go with you?" he asked.

She *wanted* him to go with her, even knowing it was a bad idea. Talking would exacerbate the pain.

"No. Enjoy the party. I think they're getting ready to cut the cake. You don't want to miss it. I heard the raspberry and custard filling was heaven on the taste buds."

"I don't mind. Really." He winked. "Cake is great, but I like being around you more."

His words made her lighter, hopeful. He made her feel like she was the only woman in the room who mattered.

Damn, she didn't want to leave him.

Rubbing her forehead, she tried to wish away the pain. It didn't work.

"I'll be terrible company until I get this headache under control. I'll find you when I'm better, okay?"

He nodded, a worry line forming between his brows. His concern made her want to hug him.

She held in the impulse and scanned the room, spotting her mom at the bar. She was talking to a handsome man who was at least fifteen years her junior.

Not that age stopped her. The opposite, in fact. She liked her men young and adoring. From his starry-eyed expression, her requirements were filled.

Since Father left them, back when Harper was ten, to marry his high school sweetheart, mother never dated anyone seriously. Or around her age. She claimed the younger ones were more fun, and that's all she needed from them—a good time.

She caught her mother's gaze. Her smile faded into a worried frown. She said something to her new friend then made her way across the reception room.

"Are you okay?" she asked.

Harper leaned closer as shouting hurt too much. "I'm getting a headache. Do you have my meds?"

Mom pointed to the head table. "Our purses are on your chair. Wait here. I'll retrieve it. Do you want me to drive you home or to the hotel?"

Her heart dropped. She wasn't ready to leave Lucas. "Neither. I'll get it. You stay here with your," she lifted a taunting brow, "friend."

Mom gave an unrepentant smile. "He is spectacular company." She turned serious. "If the medication doesn't help, come get me. I don't want you driving or staying here, suffering in pain."

Harper raised a hand in agreement as nodding hurt too much. She headed for her purse and a quiet corner.

Chapter Two

"Why didn't you bring Valerie?"

"What?" Lucas focused on his sister. He didn't understand her out-of-the-blue question. "Why would I? I'd asked you when I first got the invite."

"I would have understood if you changed your mind and wanted to bring the woman you're dating."

He groaned in exasperation while also wanting to hug Sarah. This was a familiar feeling when he was with his sister. He hated her nosiness, but loved her concern. She was always in his business, convinced he needed what she had—marriage and kids.

He wasn't against it but had also come to terms with the fact it might not happen for him.

He'd tried it once, and it had come close to shattering him.

About six months ago, he'd begun dating again. He'd even met some great women, like Valerie, but there was no real spark.

"Valerie and I aren't in a relationship," he said. "We've gone on two dates. Bringing her here would send mixed signals. Especially since I don't plan to go on a third."

He scanned the room, searching for Harper. There had definitely been a flicker of fire between them. Without a doubt, he wanted more than a few dances with her.

Returning to his sister, he found eyes the same shade as his studying him with open curiosity. *Shit.*

They might have been mistaken for twins many times, though their personalities were opposites She was damn nosy. He wasn't.

Hopefully she hadn't seen him dancing with Harper. The questions would never end.

"Why not?" Sarah asked.

Confused, he stared at her.

She sighed and narrowed her eyes. "Stay with me, big brother. Why aren't you planning on going out with Valerie again?"

He shrugged. "I don't know."

"Maybe you're giving up too soon."

Pinching the bridge of his nose, he grumbled, "What, should I wait for her to grow on me? She deserves better. So do I."

Sarah rested a hand over his on the table, asking quietly, "Are you expecting her, or the others, to take the place of Elizabeth?"

His annoyance flared. "No one will take her place."

"I didn't mean it that way. It's just, she's been gone more than two years. Longer than you two were married...maybe it's time."

"Time for what, exactly?"

"To put more of an effort into dating," she retorted. "All you do is work."

What choice did he have? He'd ignored his company during those endless, dark months, letting Matt run it into the ground. He'd nearly bankrupted Energy Solutions.

There were also the buildings and homes he owned with his brother-in-law. After Elizabeth died, Lucas made Ben shoulder all the work and responsibility for nearly a year. Lucas owed him.

He drummed his fingers on the linen tablecloth, considering what to say. Sarah was unaware of his financial mistakes, and thankfully he'd fixed most of them. He wasn't about to clue his sister in now.

He decided it was safer to stick with the issue of women.

"Listen, Sarah, I'm ready to date again, but it doesn't mean I have to. I don't need someone to warm my bed or eat dinners with me. Alone doesn't mean lonely."

He scanned the room again. There was a tall woman with metal-gray eyes he wouldn't mind getting to know better. Unable to find her, he hoped she hadn't left.

"Are you trying to find the woman you were dancing with? Who is she?"

Damn. So much for assuming Sarah hadn't noticed.

He shook his head. "Woman, you take nosy to a whole new level."

Her smiled widened. "I'm your sister. It's my job. Now, don't change the subject who's the alluring, mystery woman?"

"She's Greta's cousin."

Sarah made a keep going gesture. "Tell me the good stuff. Like, how you ended up dancing together."

"Earlier, when I was wandering around upstairs—"

"Were you staring at the creepy painting again?"

He grinned, draping an arm along the back of his chair. "Fine, let's talk about Fuselie, instead of this Spanish Inquisition you call sisterly conversation."

"No, I don't want to discuss your weird taste in art. Now stop being a drama king, finish telling me about the seductive and sexy..." She waited for a name, and whatever else he'd spill.

He was willing to part with her name. "Harper. Harper Marquette."

"Oh. Even her name is attractive."

He snorted but didn't argue. "Anyway, she was taking pictures of a statue around the corner from me. She's an artist, a sculptor, and needed photos for reference. After wandering into my area, we started talking, and when we returned to the reception, she asked if I wanted to dance when the band arrived."

"A woman who isn't afraid to go after what she wants. I like her already."

So do I.

Lust was part of it. Her seductive smile and bold demeanor called to his dormant desires. Yet, it was more than that. She was his opposite, and he found her refreshing.

His talent was in the business world, but he found her career fascinating. The way she lit up when talking about her art was beautiful. Also, he admired her clever humor. In the little bit of time they spent together, he'd smiled more than he probably had in a month.

"Where is she?" Sarah asked. "She disappeared after you two left the dancefloor. Did you break her heart too by telling her you aren't interested?"

It took a shit-ton of willpower not to roll his eyes or tug on a lock of his sister's hair. His siblings were so damn good at goading him.

"I'm not breaking anyone's heart." He groaned. "Including Harper's. She was getting a headache and went to take something for it."

She had been gone a while. Unease trickled into his stomach.

He tried to convince himself her headache was nothing, but since the sudden and unexpected death of his wife, anything health-related sent his fears into overdrive. The logical part of his brain told him Harper was fine.

He stood, needing to know for sure.

His gaze snagged on a woman who had to be Harper's mother or older sister. She was talking to a guy around his age. No one else was with them.

"I'm going to try and find her. Make sure she's okay."

Sarah nodded, thankfully not giving him a hard time.

• • • ● ● • ● ● • •

Harper wasn't sure how much time had passed as she sat staring at the massive Rivera Court mural, taking in its stunning mixture of hope and despair. Somewhere, in the quiet calm, most of her pain had receded.

Eventually, she noticed the cold seeping into her skin from the marble bench and considered returning to the party. She wanted to celebrate with her cousins.

Finding Lucas also held great appeal.

Gripping the curve of the bench, she tapped a beat against it with her nails. She couldn't decide what to do next. The thumping drums and booming speakers worried her.

Footsteps echoed off the sprawling stone and marble walls, coming closer. She turned toward the sound, and seconds later, the man she'd been thinking about came into view.

The smile that spread when he saw her left no doubt he'd been looking for her. Her heart beamed with happiness, and that feeling of being valued and precious, returned.

It was heady as finishing a sculpture.

"Are you doing any better?" he asked.

Her gaze ran over him as she nodded. The man could wear a suit.

Moving from his jacket and tie, she took in his handsome face. Something about the dip in his top lip and aristocratic nose was familiar. Reminding her once again of an actor from the old black-and-white movies.

She tilted her head. "You remind me of someone..."

He stopped and blinked once, slowly. "Um. I'm Lucas."

She laughed, wincing when it amplified and bounced around the cavernous room. "I know. I meant you remind me of someone from TV or the movies."

"Ah," he dipped his chin. "People tell me I look like Ethan or Gregory Peck."

Snapping her fingers, she said, "Yup. That's it. Shave off some years, and you are Gregory from my mom's favorite old movie, *To Kill a Mockingbird*."

"Ah. Well, she has good taste in films." He sat next to her. "If you're better, why are you sitting here?"

"My head doesn't feel like it's being twisted in a vise anymore, but I worry the music will have it returning with a vengeance."

"Do you want me to leave? Will talking aggravate it?"

She stared at his beautiful mouth, offset by a strong jaw with a hint of evening scruff. *I wouldn't mind being alone with you in a not so public place.* Swallowing her impulsive desires, she said, "Sometimes, although probably not now. I'm mostly on the mend. I'll be fine."

"You sure? I don't want to cause you any pain."

His sweet concern melted her heart while his soothing touch warmed other parts.

Many women were enamored with bad boys. Not her. They could have them.

She found his attentive thoughtfulness freaking hot.

"I don't think that's possible. Anyway, I'm going to hang out here a bit longer. But as impressive as the mural is," she waved in its general direction, "I understand if you'd rather be inside, partying."

"I'd rather be here with you. I hope I'm not being too forward."

Her stomach fluttered as a spark of anticipation ran through her body. "I want that as well," she admitted.

After a couple ticks of comfortable silence, he said, "Don't get me wrong, I don't want you to leave, but I have to ask. If you're stuck here, away from the party, why don't you go home?"

"Jacob and Greta got everyone in the wedding party rooms at a nearby boutique hotel. We arrived here together in a limo. We'll leave together after the party ends."

"The reception is going to last at least another two hours. Are you going to sit outside the entire time?"

"I don't mind. I have you to keep me company. And if you grow bored with me, I'll wander around. Exploring the DIA isn't exactly a hardship."

He shifted, his thigh almost touching hers. "I suspect, even if I had the whole night with you, I'd never be bored.

Images of what they could do if they had until the small hours of the morning flashed through her very imaginative mind. The way his eyes dilated told her his thoughts matched her impure ones.

She drifted closer. His lips were less than an inch from hers. Close enough, she tasted the peppermint on his breath.

A sudden, close peal of laughter stabbed at her fragile relief and shattered the desires caressing them.

She winced, sitting straight.

"Let me take you to your hotel."

Whoa. Her mouth dropped open a little. *And he thought he was forward earlier?*

She wasn't sure what to say.

Okay, a big part of her wanted to grab his hand and leave. Her reasonable side said to slow-the-hell down.

"Oh, shit. That came out wrong." His cheeks and neck reddened. "I meant because you aren't feeling well. I'll drop you off. I, um, won't come inside you—with you." If possible, his blush deepened. He leaned forward, clutching his head with his hands. "I'm going to shut up now."

She laughed, rubbing the back of his neck. "Wow, you're smooth."

He tilted his head, chuckling. "Now are you surprised I'm here with my sister?"

"You still have the whole Gregory Peck thing going for you. Play that angle. Try not to talk too much," she teased.

"Smile and look pretty. Got it." He straightened. "Okay, let me try again. This time I'll do my best not to sound like a lecherous creep. Would you like me to *drop* you off at your hotel? That way you won't have to wait around until the end of the party."

She wanted to say yes. Sitting on the outside of such an awesome wedding was depressing. Plus, extending her time with Lucas was a definite bonus. "What about your sister?"

He pulled his cell from his inner jacket pocket. "I'll text to let her know I'm dropping you off at your hotel. She won't mind, she knows Jacob and a few others."

Harper's pulse thrummed and raced for reasons she didn't want to study too closely. "If you don't mind, I'd be grateful."

"I don't mind."

He typed a message. Immediately his phone dinged in response. His cheeks reddened, stroking her curiosity.

"What did she say?"

"That she's fine with it."

"Nothing else?" She tried to see the screen, but he'd slid his phone inside his jacket.

"Basically." He stood, offering her his hand. "Ready?"

She looped her arm through his. Oh, yes, she was very much ready.

Chapter Three

Lucas parked his car at the curb of her hotel. "Wow. Nice place."

She agreed. The gorgeous 1900's redbrick home converted to an inn was stunning. She'd been here earlier with the wedding party and knew the inside was as striking as the outside.

Everything was updated and converted without sacrificing the original design. What she adored most was the lovely wraparound porch.

She took a chance. Suppressing her galloping nerves, she asked, "Do you have to go back to the party right away? It's a nice night. Want to sit on the porch?"

His gaze flew to her face, but he didn't say anything. She'd spoken in a rush. Maybe he hadn't understood. Or worse, he'd found their easy conversation boring and was wishing he'd never left the party.

Embarrassment flooded her. She gave him an easy escape. "I'm sorry. I forgot your sister—"

"She left."

"Left?" Harper parroted, confused.

"Yeah, I guess her husband found a sitter for the kids and wanted to meet her at some new bar for drinks. She told me not to hurry back because she was going to leave with Austin."

"So…" She refused to repeat the question.

"Oh, yes," he said quickly. "Sorry, I was lost in my mind for a second."

She'd love to get a glimpse of what was going on inside that handsome head of his. How could a man so good-looking be completely lost with the nuances of attraction and seduction?

Does he not date? She rechecked his left hand.

Nope. No ring or obvious tan line.

Not that she truly thought he was married. When she'd been dancing with him, Cindy had given them a thumbs up. Lucas was good friends with Jacob and Will. If he was a married man playing single for the night, Harper's cousins would have told her.

Whatever. Maybe he was shy. She grabbed the car's door handle.

"Wait. Let me help you. My car is low to the ground, and the curbside parking can't be easy for your dress and heels."

The shyness was cute. Him being a total gentleman was hot.

Coming around, he opened her door and offered his hand. He didn't let go until they were on the porch.

She sat in a wide, cushioned wicker chair. He took the one next to her.

Breathing in deeply and rubbing a kink in her neck, she sighed. The night air smelled lovely, like summer with a hint of July flowers, mixing with food from nearby restaurants.

The quiet surrounding them was also a nice surprise. They were in a quasi-residential neighborhood, but a block over were businesses and skyscrapers.

"Are your shoulders sore?" he asked, his voice low and seductive.

"A little bit." She pointed to her tight up-do. "All this hair sitting in one spot with a thousand pins and a gallon of hairspray doesn't help."

"Come here." He opened his glorious thighs and patted the cushion between them.

She was curious and more than willing to sit on his lap.

He must have taken her hesitation as reluctance because he raised his hands and said, "I'm not hitting on you. I'll rub your shoulders. My mom gets headaches, and this usually helps."

She smirked. "Well, I'm hoping your motives aren't completely altruistic."

"Oh, they aren't. A big part of me wants you between my legs." His face flushed an adorable deep red again. "Wow, way to sound super creepy. I'm terrible at this. What I meant was, I like when you're close to me."

She wouldn't mind being encased between his strong thighs. Or perhaps, her straddling them as she rode him.

Whoa. Cool it, girl.

Her hungry, lascivious side wasn't in the mood to listen, it wanted to play. She wiggled her brows, gazing at his slacks before returning to his eyes. "A big part, huh?"

He managed to turn even redder.

She decided to rescue him. Rising from her chair, she moved in front of him, nudging his legs wider with her knees. Turning, she settled between his thighs He was deliciously warm.

Forget the pleasant fragrance of the night air. His scent was pure ecstasy—earthy and all male.

It took every ounce of her willpower not to face him and bury her nose in the sexy hollow of his neck. Or to burrow into his heated, solid body.

His hands moved to her hair, and a gentle tugging followed.

She twisted to see him dropping bobby pins into his open palm. "What are you doing?"

"You said it was bothering you."

"Yeah, but my hair is going to be an awful mess."

"I bet you'll still look sexy."

"Aren't you smooth."

He snorted. "Hardly. Have you already forgotten all the stupid shit I've said throughout the night?"

She laughed. "Nope. I like your fumbling ways."

"Um, why?"

"It makes your words feel sincere. Like you aren't playing games."

He chuckled. "Yeah, it's because I have no game."

Her hair fell from its up-do, and the relief was immense. He was right. She needed those pins out.

"Thank you." She moaned, shaking her head. The long locks hit her shoulders and back.

"My pleasure." His hands slid into her hair, and strong fingers massaged her scalp.

Tingling decadent shivers melted into her flesh. Her head dropped forward, and a groan of pleasure slid from her lips.

"You're talented." Her whole body hummed. "Your hands are pure magic."

He moved to her shoulders, and when he spoke his voice was raspy. "Yes. I do know how to use them."

His comment prowled down her, coiling like a kiss between her legs. Had he meant his words to sound like an innuendo? She peeked over her shoulder at him. There was nothing chaste about the lust swirling in his eyes.

The heat behind his gaze heightened everything. His touch not only eased her kinks and knots but became a seductive caress. His soft exhales tickling her neck were now feather kisses.

"Is this helping?" he asked in a near whisper.

His deep voice stroked her every intimate desire.

"Um, hmm," she hummed, licking her lips, wanting to taste him.

She turned away. Her visceral reaction to him was slightly embarrassing.

His fingers found another knot. She arched as the pain became pleasure. "Yes. Right there. Harder, please."

His strangled curse made her replay her words.

Oh. My. God.

"Sorry. I sound like bad porn. Next, I'll be making high-pitched mewing noises and screaming for you to give it to me good, Daddy."

He laughed loud, holding on to her shoulders. "Wow. That was oddly specific."

She shrugged, loving his deep laughter. "What can I say? The internet is a dark, weird place. Some things can't be unseen...Or so I've heard."

"Uh-huh." He chuckled. "I'd love to take a peek at the search history on your computer."

"You'll only find cooking recipes and sewing tips," she replied innocently.

"Sure. Sure. I believe you." His tone said the opposite.

Her smile grew. Lucas was fun.

"Anyway." She wiggled her shoulders, silently asking him to continue his massage. "I apologize. I'll keep my porntastic words to myself."

He shifted. His mouth a lick from her ear. "I never said I was bothered. Please, continue your sweet torture."

The low rumble of his voice and hunger behind them made it difficult to think, much less form words. So, she didn't and relaxed into him, her body contouring into his front.

His arms wrapped around her and the happy sigh she heard melted away the last slivers of anxiety.

Perfect lips brushed her earlobe. When he reached her neck, she tilted, giving him more access.

Taking it, he kissed her fevered skin. Stopping at her ear, he nipped it. The gentle bite shot desire throughout her body.

She gripped his thighs, digging her nails into the fine wool of his slacks while twisting around and seeking his lips. Finding them, she tasted carnal bliss.

Holy hell, the man could kiss.

He didn't plunge, trying to conquer her with sloppy lips and an artless tongue. Instead, he played and teased, in an almost chaste way, yet he tasted of sinful satisfaction.

Needing more, she shifted sideways. Wrapping her hands around his neck, she deepened the kiss.

A growl rumbled from him, sounding like he wanted to devour her.

Everything in her wanted to be his meal.

His hand skimmed up her side, cupping her breast and swallowing a needy moan escaping from her. Pressing into his touch, he ran the pad of his thumb over the thin fabric of her dress, circling her nipple.

Fireworks of lust exploded through her as a car door nearby slammed shut. Laughter floated on the night air, filtering through her lust. She broke the kiss, peering toward the voices.

They were in the shadows of the porch, but what she wanted from him couldn't happen here. It was time for her to decide if she was going to be reckless or responsible.

Stop and get his number, taking things slower. Or invite him to her room.

The smart answer was simple. She liked him, wanted him for more than a fling. They should get to know each other first.

Her body wept at the thought of him leaving her unsatisfied.

In the end, temptation overruled prudence. Tonight was for pleasure. Tomorrow for consequences.

"Do you want to stay the night with me?" she whispered against his lips.

"Yes." He said it like she'd answered his prayers.

Standing, she picked up her purse from the side table, then entwined her hand with his. They didn't talk as they walked to her room, yet the silence wasn't awkward. For some reason, she was comfortable around him in a way she wasn't with most people.

It didn't hurt either, that her room was on the first floor, and they were inside within minutes of leaving the porch. Flipping a switch, a tall brass lamp next to a light-yellow upholstered chair illuminated the room.

There was a stone fireplace that spoke of romantic winter nights. Off to the right was a small sitting area with a round walnut table with two cushioned chairs matching the massive king-sized poster bed.

There was more in the quaint room, but right now, all she cared about was the enormous bed and the tempting man whose desires teased and played with her erotic dreams.

She tossed her purse on to the bed as he came around and kissed her. He was more hesitant than on the porch. He almost seemed to be asking if she wanted to continue.

With her lips, she told him she was more than okay. Running her hands up his toned stomach and chest, she slipped them under the shoulders of his jacket. He shook it off, letting it fall to the floor.

His lips moved along her jaw, to her neck, and when he hit the sweet spot below her ear, she gasped. She felt his smile against her skin.

In a voice laden with sex, he asked, "Did I find a spot you like?"

She nodded, unable to speak. He teased her with the tip of his tongue before kissing and nipping the area. Need spread over her skin, hot and wanton.

While his mouth was busy melting her with desire, his hands worked the back of her dress. The tiny hidden zipper hissed as he trailed it to her lower spine. When he let go, she stepped from his embrace, letting the silk pool at her feet.

"You're gorgeous," he breathed. His gaze devoured her lacy strapless bra and matching panties. He ran a finger under the beveled edge of lace before cupping her breast.

He tried to bring her closer, but she stopped with a palm on his chest. She needed to get him out of his clothes.

She started with his shirt, working on his buttons, losing focus when his palm skimmed into her panties. His seeking, expert fingers made her legs weak with pleasure. She kissed him, clutching his shoulders to keep from collapsing.

While one hand worked its magic, the other slid off her panties. She shimmied out of them, leaving them on the floor.

Wrapping her in his strong arms, he walked backward toward the bed.

Part of her wanted to return to his shirt, needing to know if he was as firm as he felt, yet she was growing impatient. Instead, she worked on the belt and zipper of his slacks. By the time they reached the bed, they were past his thighs.

She wrapped a hand around his erection, anticipation vibrating through her.

He moaned and thrust, stoking her flames. They'd only begun exploring each other, but she needed to have him. Now.

Letting go of him, she pushed his shoulders. He let out a startled grunt, falling onto the bed.

She straddled his waist then grabbed her purse. Finding a condom, she held it between two fingers.

Slightly embarrassed at her aggressiveness, but refusing to look away, she asked, "Want me to put it on?"

"Yes. You taking charge is incredibly sexy. Don't stop now." The fire in his eyes told her he meant every word.

After rolling on the condom, she kissed him hard and deep. He ran his fingers through her hair, tugging slightly.

She loved the bite of pain alongside his thorough exploration of her lips. Although her ache for satisfaction demanded release, she didn't rush.

Her body needed to adjust to his size. She also wanted to savor him, inch by glorious inch, burning this moment into her mind and body. Their first time.

His fingers traced her spine, stopping at the clasp of her bra. Unsnapping it, he tossed it aside, his focus on her. His gaze was so hot it warmed her like a torch. There wasn't room for shyness or insecurities.

When he rose and kissed the underside of her breast with a hungry groan, all thoughts of savoring the moment crumbled.

She gripped the back of his head in a rough caress. He moaned, devouring her with his mouth as he sat the rest of the way up.

She wrapped her legs around his hips. He moved slow and deep, stroking her everywhere.

Pleasure gathered around her, promising bliss. She was greedy for it now and told him with her body and whispered words.

The coil of need that pulled and tugged since he'd begun his innocent massage, let go, showering her in exquisite ecstasy. It rocked through her.

She muffled her scream in the crook of his neck as his body stiffened, his release chasing hers.

They stayed wrapped in a tight embrace until their breathing returned to normal. He traced lazy circles around her spine while she breathed in his masculine scent as it mingled with their desire.

"I'm sorry," she said, embarrassment wrapping around her contentment.

He chuckled. "Um. Why? I came so hard I freaking saw stars."

"Because I damn near attacked you."

"Honey, I'm not complaining."

Her heart fluttered at the term of endearment. Loosening her embrace, she ran a fingertip down his shirt, noticing she'd only managed to get three buttons free. "I didn't even let you get undressed."

He dipped, kissing one of her nipples. "You're undressed. Which is infinitely more important to me."

She exhaled a laugh. "Well, it is a tragedy for me."

Shifting onto his back, he propped himself on his palms and watched her unbutton his dress shirt. Once open, he slid it off, then removed his T-shirt.

Whoa. The man was fit and fine.

He had abs begging to be licked. She rubbed her palm on his torso, loving the way his tight muscles flexed at her touch. "Tell me again, what do you do for a living? An athlete, or maybe a lumberjack? Something to explain this gorgeous body."

He laughed. The sound wrapped around her.

She felt him kick off his shoes, as he said, "Nothing so interesting. I have an eco-consulting business and own a few rental properties."

He removed the rest of his clothes, and she relaxed. He didn't plan on leaving.

"I'll be right back," he said, standing.

She took in his glorious backside as he made his way to the bathroom.

A few minutes later, he was striding toward the light switch. She took in his tall, athletic frame in all its naked glory. Lust tugged low and heavy in her stomach.

Before flicking off the lamp, his gaze roamed her body. His eyes burned with need. It took her from smoldering to a blazing fire.

"Your look tells me I'm in for a long," she glanced south, taking in his growing erection, "hard night."

He smirked. "Sorry, honey, we can cuddle, but soft and sweet around you is impossible."

She smiled, sure it held the same wicked intent as his. Opening her arms, she said, "Snuggle later. Right now, I need to explore every inch of your delectable body."

Giddy anticipation raced through her. For the night, and for what she already felt for this man.

• • • ● • ● • ● • • •

Lucas woke, sucking in a vicious gasp. The remnants of the nightmare clung to his brain, wrapping around his throat.

He couldn't fucking breathe.

In the dream, he'd lost everything he loved. His family. His heart. Along with optimism and excitement for the future.

The warmth of Elizabeth's body against his back, with her arm draped over his waist, gave him comfort. The combination helped to slow his racing pulse.

He noticed a dark fireplace and an old-style chair. He didn't recognize either.

Where the hell am I?

This wasn't his bedroom in his quiet Grosse Point neighborhood.

Reality it hit him with the force of a cement truck. He hadn't woken from a bad dream. He was living it.

Tears welled, threatening to fall as his shredded heart broke again. His life had been a nightmare. One in which he lost everything on a brittle February afternoon.

Depression and hopelessness had owned him for more than a year. He'd finally clawed his way out, but apparently, they were trying to drag him back into their arms.

He sat on the edge of the bed, gulping for air, trying to find the peace and happiness he had when falling asleep.

It had vanished, and he was falling apart.

Slipping from the sheets, he felt around in the dark for his discarded clothes. He found them draped on a chair then slid into his slacks.

The evening and night had been incredible. It was also his first time with a woman since his wife's passing. Apparently, that shit messes with a man's head and dreams.

He needed air, to get his head on straight. He didn't want Harper to wake and see him like this. A fucking mess.

"Damn it," he mumbled, shoving his arms through his shirt sleeves.

There's no way he'd fall back asleep, and he wasn't about to sit at the tiny round table like some creeper until she woke.

He'd leave, call her in the morning. Try to explain.

Grabbing his shoes, he quietly opened the door. The firm click of it shutting behind him was a hard tap on his brain.

Fuck! Damn it! I don't have her number.

He had two shitty options.

Knock and wake her from a sound sleep to explain why he'd left. *Hell no.* He wasn't going to explain his freak out to her at three a.m.

So he went with the other choice.

Wait until morning. Get her number from Jacob. Harper was Greta's cousin. It shouldn't be difficult. He'd talk to her. Hopefully, she'd understand.

Turning with a stomach as heavy as his heart, he left.

Chapter Four

"Do you want to go with me to Greta and Jacob's barbeque, next Saturday?" Cindy asked Harper.

"Depends on who'll be there," she hedged, glad they were talking on the phone since her expression was always a dead-giveaway.

"Are you hoping to avoid or run into someone?"

Damn, even without seeing her face Cindy knew something was off. Harper hated to say anything. Her curious cousin would have a million questions.

She decided to ask. The alternative was worse. "Will Lucas Genezen be there?"

"Will's friend?" There was a pause, then Cindy muttered, "Oh, crap."

That didn't sound good. "What?"

"Um, a few weeks ago," her cousin paused, "okay, maybe a tad longer—anyway, Jacob called Will right after the wedding, asking him to ask me if I was okay with giving your number to Lucas. Greta wouldn't do it since she wasn't sure of the situation. I'd meant to ask you, but kept forgetting."

Something close to relief filled Harper. Maybe she wasn't just a hit-and-ditch.

Her comfort was replaced with annoyance. "It's September. The wedding was *two* months ago, yet this is the first I'm hearing of it. Why?"

"I forgot. I'm so sorry," Cindy pleaded while also laughing. "At the time, I found it hilarious. All very high school-ish. We'd planned to meet that day, and I was excited to hear the gossip. Then shit hit the fan with Will, and you helped me get drunk. It sort of slipped my mind."

"Fine. I get you forgetting for a day or two, but two whole months?" Harper huffed, although she wasn't surprised.

Cindy was cutthroat, talented, and damn smart, yet at times she played the part of the ditzy blonde to perfection.

"From the tone of your voice, you'd have wanted to know. It almost sounds like he means something to you."

Harper heard the questions in her cousin's statement. She wanted to know everything. Not happening.

Lucas might have tried to call, but it didn't change the fact he'd snuck away during the night without even bothering to leave a note.

She recalled waking in the big king-size bed, a little sore, and a lot satisfied. And alone. The humiliation had nearly choked her.

Close to two months had passed, and the kiss-off still stung. Cindy was her cousin and closest friend, but Harper didn't relish sharing her mortification.

He did try to get your number, whispered her bruised ego.

"Um, no, he's nothing to me." *Liar.* "But will he be there?"

"Probably. He's friends with Jacob."

Harper tried to squash the excitement humming through her suddenly heated skin. Thankfully, her voice sounded even, almost unconcerned as she said, "Either way, I don't care. I'll go. I haven't seen Greta since the wedding."

Cindy's soft laughter told Harper she wasn't as convincing as she hoped. "Shut up, cousin," she muttered.

"Fine, I'll wait. You'll tell me. Eventually."

She was right, but not today. It was time for a change of subject.

In a sing-song voice, she said, "Tell me, how are you and Will? I figured from the way you two kept staring starry-eyed at each other at the lake house during the wedding party, a weekend wouldn't be enough."

"It's nice. Actually, damn near fantastic." Cindy sounded so bewildered it made Harper laugh.

"Why are you surprised? He seems like a great guy. Hot too."

"Because when I first met him, I couldn't stand the man," Cindy stated bluntly. "I thought he was hot, but a total asshole."

"One day you'll have to tell me the whole story of you two."

"Sure. Right after you spill with what's going on with you and Lucas."

She smiled, shaking her head. Her cousin was relentless. "Do you want to drive to Greta's house together?"

Cindy's laughter filtered through the phone. "Smooth topic change. Sure, let's do that. I'll pick you up."

"Perfect. See you then."

After they disconnected, Harper tried to bury her eagerness. It didn't matter if Lucas would be there.

Telling herself the lie repeatedly wasn't working.

Try as she might, she was unable to forget the way he made her laugh. Or how he'd looked at her as if she was the only woman in the room.

The way he'd given her pleasure like she'd never experienced was also impossible to forget.

Their first time had been rushed and intense, fueled by a need that hadn't allowed either of them to go slow. Later, before she'd fallen asleep in his arms, he'd explored every inch of her body with determined focus and blissful expertise.

He'd gifted her with multiple orgasms, as well as with a deep sense of happy contentment. In the morning, alone in the big, cold bed, she'd tried to convince herself it didn't matter.

They'd both enjoyed themselves immensely. It wasn't like he'd promised more than a night.

It was her own damn fault for reading too much into his kind smile and pleasant words.

He tried to get my number.

The reminder sent fireworks ricocheting in her chest. Maybe he did want more than her body.

It made no sense. Why would he leave without a word in the middle of the night like a thief, only to reach out and try to contact her the next day?

She sighed and stood, needing to let go of Lucas. The barbeque was in a few days. They'd talk and either continue or end what they started.

Right now, fresh clay and a new block of marble was waiting for her. Her hands and imagination itched to get to work.

Chapter Five

Jacob was telling Lucas about his honeymoon in Iceland. It sounded amazing, yet he found it impossible to pay attention. His ears were focused on the gate to the backyard and patio door. When either one squeaked, his gaze jumped in the direction of the sound.

Greta had told him Harper would be coming to the barbeque with Cindy. Ever since, he'd been watching all the entrances like a damn overeager puppy.

How had this woman he barely knew manage to burrow inside him so deeply?

Nearly two months had passed since the wedding, but memories of their night were seared into his mind. They snuck up on him during the quiet or idle moments of the day. He needed to know why Harper never called him. Was it a lack of interest or because she couldn't forgive him for the way he left?

Forcing himself to return to his conversation with Jacob, he asked about Iceland's volcanos. However, he kept glancing around the yard. The place was packed with people, except for the person he wanted there.

It didn't help that he was one of the first to arrive, helping set up the tables and prep the food. The couple of scotches he drank to keep cool and tamper his whirling thoughts probably weren't a great idea either.

Jacob asked if, back when Lucas was a teenager and had visited the UK and Ireland with his family, if they'd also seen Iceland. He opened his mouth to answer, but the squeak of the gate's hinges snagged his attention.

He caught sight of Cindy's blonde hair first, gathered in a perky ponytail. Right behind her was Harper.

He'd forgotten Jacob was even next to him, let alone his question.

Both women were stunning, but Harper stole his breath. She wore peach, loose-fitting pants that rippled in the light breeze, with a simple white tank top showing the barest hint of her breasts. Her hair was unbound, shimmering against the summer sun, flowing to the middle of her back.

Jacob tapped Lucas's shoulder. He reluctantly turned from the two women, finding his friend studying him.

"You're distracted today. You okay?" Jacob asked.

Lucas swirled the ice cubes in his glass. "Yeah. I'm fine," he lied. "I think the heat and too much scotch is making me wonky. I should get some water."

Jacob nodded, his gaze sliding past him and snagging on someone. A soft smile formed on his usually hard features. The change was startling, something Lucas didn't often see on his friend. Twisting around, he wasn't surprised to find Greta walking toward them.

She kissed Jacob's cheek before saying, "Your brother is asking if we have extra platters for the ribs. Did you get them from the basement yesterday?"

"Yup, I shoved them between the fridge and toaster oven." Jacob stepped around Lucas.

"I'm heading that way." Lucas said, stopping him. "I'll get them."

Someone turned up the radio, and Jacob shouted his thanks, taking Greta's hand and moving to the makeshift dancefloor. They held each other, swaying to the music. The contentment radiating from them said they had everything they needed.

Sadness tugged at Lucas's heart. He had that kind of happiness once.

He took a hefty sip of his scotch, hoping it would burn away his pity party. He'd been given two wonderful years with Elizabeth, and even with the soul-crushing pain that followed, he wouldn't trade them for anything.

Hell, maybe he'd even find love and contentment again. If he was willing to risk it.

The fear of loving and losing ran fucking deep with him. Still...

He scanned the backyard, stopping on Harper.

She was watching him. Her cheeks reddened, but she didn't break eye contact. Would she talk with him? He pointed with his chin toward the house, silently asking her to meet him there.

She quirked a shoulder, in a maybe gesture. He smiled at her stubbornness.

Fine. He could be stubborn too.

He'd get Will his trays then Lucas would find her, and they'd talk.

To his relief, when he returned to the backyard, by some miracle Harper was sitting alone. He took the spot on the outdoor loveseat next to her, handing her a glass of wine.

"I remember you having white at the wedding," he said.

Taking a swallow of a scotch he didn't need, he sincerely hoped it didn't come off as weird he'd remembered her drink preference. He was never good at the nuances of dating, and it'd been a while since he truly wanted to impress a woman.

His worry dissolved when she thanked him, her smile widening and her eyes warming.

She sipped her wine, her gaze roaming over him. He got the feeling she was waiting for him to start the conversation.

Worked for him.

"You never called," he said.

She lowered her drink to the table. "You snuck away in the early hours, and I only learned a few days ago that you tried to get my number."

His brows rose as surprise ricocheted through him. "A few days ago, are you joking me? I called Jacob the next day."

She relayed Cindy's excuse, sounding exasperated. It matched his mood.

Seriously, she'd met or talked with her cousin countless times between now and the weeks since the wedding, and it wasn't until Harper asked if he was going to be here that Cindy finally remembered. *Christ.*

There were so many questions he wanted to ask. He settled on the easiest. The most important. "Were you hoping I'd be here?"

Harper sighed, focusing on her nails. "I don't know. We clicked at the wedding. I knew we were moving fast, but everything felt right. Nearly perfect." Her blush bloomed, yet her demeanor was determined. "And I mean everything."

He nodded, wholeheartedly agreeing.

"But you left without goodbye or even a note. I was humiliated. I assumed you'd wanted more than my body." She looked at her hands again. "Like I did with you."

He scooted closer. "I did. I do."

She raised her chin. Skepticism was etched on every beautiful feature. "Pulling a Houdini act while I slept tells me different."

Now came the tricky part. Unloading his baggage on a woman who was a near stranger was difficult. What if it scared her off?

He wasn't a man gifted with the grace of words. What if his reason for leaving sounded weak, or stupid? Shit—or crazy.

Not like he had a choice. If he didn't explain, she wouldn't give him another chance.

He did his best to keep it simple. "I woke from a nightmare of sorts and was confused. I didn't want to wake you, but I needed air. It wasn't until after I stepped out of your room that it dawned on me I didn't have a key. I wasn't about to bang on the door at three AM. I left, figuring I'd get your number from Jacob or Will."

"Yeah, they wanted to check with me first." She rolled her eyes. "Thanks, Cindy."

Harper's easy smile and the way she leaned toward him, relieved him. This wasn't as bad as he'd feared.

"Do you normally have nightmares after mind-blowing, great sex?" she teased.

"Mind-blowing, huh?"

"Settle your ego, big guy." She laughed. "I was there as well. I helped with the overall fun and pleasure."

"No, doubt." His mind replayed some of the erotic bliss, even managed to come up with a few new things he'd like to do with her.

"What were you dreaming about?"

So caught in kinky proclivities, he almost missed her question. When it registered, he wished he could skip answering it.

"Huh?" he asked, stalling.

She repeated the question.

There was no way in hell he was going to tell her he woke thinking he was in bed with Elizabeth, realizing seconds later he wasn't and how it had fucked with him big time. However, lying wasn't an option either.

He gulped his scotch. It burned going down, churning in his gut. He really didn't want to have this conversation.

"Um. My wife," he blurted.

Harper shot back as if he slapped her. He replayed his words.

Shit.

"No, no. I'm not married. I'm a widower."

She blinked rapidly as if none of this made any sense. It didn't to him either. People aren't supposed to die before their thirtieth birthday.

"How old are you?"

"Thirty-one. She, my wife, Elizabeth, was twenty-eight when she died of a cerebral aneurysm. Maybe she was born with it. Maybe not. The doctors aren't sure. All I know is she was fine when she left for work. A few hours later, I got a call saying she collapsed while carrying in a box of printer paper. She was rushed to the hospital. Died that night. Fine one day, gone the next."

His words were quick and curt, still managing to cut him. He'd come to terms with losing her, but it didn't mean the pain vanished. Learning in a heartbeat, everything that truly mattered could be lost to him was terrifying.

"When?" Harper asked in a strangled whisper.

"Two years, last February."

"I get it. I was an itch you needed to scratch." She raised her hands, palms out. "It hurts a little, but I understand. You love her, but the body gets lonely."

"No. Listen, it wasn't like that. I wasn't after a physical release. I talked to you, flirted," he grinned, "okay, *tried* to flirt. As you know, I'm terrible at it."

"Nooo…," she teased, and it encouraged him.

"I went to your hotel because I wanted more time with you and not just your body. I like *all* of you."

She sipped her wine, smiling over the rim of her glass. He relaxed, relieved he fixed the misunderstanding between them.

So, of course, he had to keep talking and fuck everything up. "Don't worry, I'm not prone to night terrors or anything. The nightmare was probably brought on because that was the first time I had sex since Elizabeth died."

Harper choked on her drink. Lucas closed his eyes, mentally kicking himself in the mouth. Why did he have to keep talking when his brain stopped thinking?

He swore a shield slammed around her, cutting him off. He'd screwed up. Again.

Before he could try to recover the ease they shared moments ago, she spoke. "I like you too." Goodbye was in her every word. "But we shouldn't date."

"Why?" He turned his whole body to face her. His knees touched her legs, yet she might as well be on the other side of the yard. Hell, the other side of Michigan.

"I've got a lot going on in my life right now. I plan on opening a gallery in the next year. I need to concentrate on my art."

Anger and disappointment bloomed in his chest. "That's a bullshit excuse."

She didn't bother denying it.

Standing, she looked at him. Regret seemed to ooze from her. He wasn't sure if it was from seeing him or walking away.

"Goodbye, Lucas."

Chapter Six

Lucas's footfalls echoed off the soaring tile and concrete walls as he made his way to the elevator. In his gloved hand, he clutched paperwork for the building's code compliance while scanning the area, making mental notes of things they'd need to check.

He loved buying and restoring Detroit's older art deco buildings. The challenge of making them ecological was an added bonus. However, this building was his and Ben's most significant undertaking. Ten floors for offices and the main one for shops and small restaurants. The sheer size and work needed was exhausting.

Back when he was married, his brother-in-law, Ben, suggested the three of them pool their money and buy a few homes and small businesses. Elizabeth loved the idea. Already a business owner, Lucas had been less thrilled but reluctantly agreed when the two siblings promised to take on most of the work.

The decision was now costing him a slice of his sanity. There was no denying Ben and Elizabeth had a talent for finding profitable properties. G&D Investments had grown rapidly. They'd been struggling to keep up when his wife was alive; now they were drowning.

Add that to nearly a year of busting his ass day and night, to win back Lucas's clients at his eco-consulting firm, and his mental space to juggle both businesses was non-existent. Something needed to give.

Yet, he was stuck. G&D was Elizabeth's legacy of sorts. Plus, he couldn't bail on Ben now. Not until the stubborn man agreed to take Lucas's and Elizabeth's shares.

Stepping from the elevator on the top floor, exhaustion weighed on him as he gripped the iron handle of G&D and opened the door. The building in the heart of Detroit might be old, but their small office was all modern with its large windows, open space, and sleek office furniture.

Ben was hunched at his desk, flipping through a pile of papers. The top of his short military haircut was the only part of his head visible.

He stuck a finger in the middle of the stack and looked at Lucas. "Hey, hi. Do you have the code paperwork?"

Lucas held up the folder. "They're happy with the progress we've made, but we aren't done. We have a shit-ton more to do."

Ben nodded. "Yeah, I figured as much. We'll get there."

Glad he's confident. To Lucas, scaling the outside of the building with his bare hands would probably be easier.

"Where do you want me to put this?" he asked, indicating the file.

"I'll take it." Ben held out his free hand. "Do you have to leave right away?"

Lucas held in a groan. Ben was going to have him do landlord crap. "No," he admitted. "I have a meeting this afternoon. A possible job for Energy Solutions."

Fixing buildings was stressful and satisfying in equal measure. Checking on tenants, talking with people behind on rent, those sorts of things sucked the joy from life. He'd rather have a root canal. On all his teeth. Still, G&D was his too.

"How is your business going?" Ben asked.

"Getting better. I'm slowly rebuilding my reputation and getting more contracts. I'm hoping to pay off the business loan by the summer."

Ben let Lucas use G&D as collateral to take out a loan to save Energy Solutions. Yet, another reason he owed the man. "Things are going pretty good here, so no hurry."

It didn't matter. The whole situation made Lucas feel shitty.

"Anyway," Ben continued, "I need to visit a few of our rentals across town. Would you check on two businesses leasing space on the main floor? An art gallery and local clothing store I think sells men's suits. Make sure they aren't knocking down any walls or doing stuff not in their lease. I'll give you some paperwork I need them to sign. That way your visit will come off less intrusive. Hell, you could play the friendly landlord offering some of your eco suggestions."

"Sure. Fine. Where's the paperwork? I'll head there now," he replied, frowning.

His distaste must have managed to slide through because Ben smirked. "Don't let your enthusiasm overwhelm you."

Lucas smiled, not bothering to answer. They both knew he hated this part of the business.

Taking off his gloves and shrugging out of his coat, he changed the subject. "I love Michigan, but it sucks in March."

"Yeah, it's such a tease. Last week was sunny and fifty-five. Today it's drizzling a mix of snow and rain." Ben closed his laptop, sliding it and the papers he was leafing through earlier into a messenger bag. "I'm dreading making these runs. Coming here this morning, my balls damn near froze off. Now I have to leave this nice, warm office to visit one guy who's two months behind on rent and another who's a complete asshole."

"Today is brutal," Lucas agreed. "Though, I'm not surprised. No, what floors me is you're the one still hounding delinquent tenants. Don't you have enough to do? Hire someone."

"I plan to. I need to. Now that we have this place, I can't keep up. Oh." Ben paused in the middle of putting on a wool hat. "I forgot. The company that wanted to rent one of the offices below us changed their minds. I remember you toyed with the idea of moving Energy Solutions here. It would be a better location than where you're at now."

"Maybe," he hedged, unsure. "It might be more space than I need. Plus, I'm considering Ann Arbor, since it's a city that would embrace my company."

"True, but even with property values skyrocketing here, it's still less. Also, Detroit is working to surpass Ann Arbor with your eco-stuff."

His argument made good business sense, but Lucas wasn't sure if it was a good idea on a personal level. Ben was a great friend and business partner, but there was a new, underlying strain between them.

It might be because he was in the office way more than in the past, and they needed to adjust to it. Yet, he suspected the problem wasn't with workspace, but him dating. He believed Ben didn't like that Lucas was moving on with life after Elizabeth.

Keeping his beloved sister front and center in his heart was possible. On the other hand, Lucas must shift her to his past, or he'd never enjoy his future. He could love and miss her, but as a memory.

Not that he went out much. Work took most of his free time, and he never found the interest to go on a third date with any of the women he met.

Harper's smile and curves flashed through his mind. Over eight months had passed since Jacob and Greta's barbeque, yet Lucas couldn't forget her.

She was the one he wished to take out on a first date. He was positive he'd want a second and third date with her as well. Hell, as many as she'd give him.

He shook his head. It wasn't happening. Too much time had gone by. She'd never called nor passed along her number.

Ben handed Lucas two folders. "Do what you want, but let me know soon. If you don't want it, I'll need to re-list it."

"Okay. Let me check my financials and contracts. I'll get back to you by the end of the week."

Lucas left the office, deciding to visit the clothing store first. It was closer to the elevators, and he needed a new suit.

He learned the owner wasn't arriving until later in the afternoon. Nevertheless, it wasn't a wasted trip. The man working behind the counter took the rental papers for his boss, then showed Lucas some suits on the racks, letting him know they also offered custom tailoring.

After going through the fabrics and cuts, he decided to have one tailored. Before leaving, he made an appointment to return the next day and have the owner take his measurements.

His next stop was the art gallery. Preoccupied with thoughts of fabric and cuts, he stepped inside.

Then halted as if hitting a wall.

Not because the white walls were covered with stunning paintings and photographs. Or because the wood floors sandblasted almost white held every size and manner of breathtaking statues and sculptures.

No, what held his attention was the equally surprised woman behind the counter staring at him.

Harper.

He blinked a few times, wondering if she'd disappear. He'd been thinking about her less than an hour ago. Maybe he dreamed her.

Hell, she was a hot fantasy in a fitted black dress. It was high-necked, long-sleeved, stopping right above her knees, hugging all her curves.

"Lucas," she breathed, a slight frown tugging on the corners of her full mouth. "What are you doing here?"

Instead of answering her question, he said, "I see you found a home for your gallery. When do you open?"

"Three weeks." Pride and elation wrapped around her words.

He came closer, stopping when he caught sight of a man in the center of the room. *No, wait.*

Squinting, Lucas took in the wings sagging from the back of the guy's tweed jacket. Not a person, an incredibly detailed and stunning statue.

Drawn to it, he shifted directions. The ancient man was the same height as Lucas, wearing corduroy slacks, vest, tweed jacket, and yes, wings. They weren't open and hung low, still managing to be regal and proud.

What Lucas loved most was the old man's expression. His wrinkled face angled toward the heavens, mouth slightly open in wonder. There was a twinkle in the man's eye, as if he had all the answers and loved what he'd learned.

"Damn," he whispered. "Is this yours?"

"Yes. It's mine," she replied softly, drawing his focus back to her.

His focused shifted from her art to her, and he was slammed with a different sort of appreciation, one that filled him with desire, frustration, and longing.

It didn't matter that months had passed, he wanted her as much, if not more than the night they met. The way her gaze dropped to his mouth and stayed a few beats said her interest hadn't faded either.

He came toward her. "It is astounding. Breathtaking in its mix of reality and fantasy."

"Thank you." She ran a palm over her silky hair. He noticed her hand shook a little. "I created it after my grandfather died. He was religious and..."

She trailed off when he reached the counter. She was holding on to it like a drowning woman would a life vest. Noticing her white-knuckle grip, she let go and placed her hands on the glass top, tapping her nails in a staccato pattern.

"Why are you here?" she asked.

"I have papers for you."

She took one of the folders, scanning the copies. Looking at him, she tilted her head in question.

"There were changes to your lease."

"I know. What I don't understand is why *you're* giving them to me."

"I own the building."

Hurt flashed through her eyes before her lips pulled tight. "You told me you own some sort of consulting business. Why would you lie?"

Hating the counter between them, he came around the side. "I didn't. Energy Solutions is mine. The rental thing is a side project."

"This," she pointed to the massive hallway of the ten-story building, "is a side project?"

He rested a hip against the counter, laughing. "One that has gotten out of hand. My partner, Ben, is excellent at what he does. He finds the property and does most of the landlord crap. I make them as eco-friendly as possible and play his errand boy when he needs it." He pointed to the paperwork he'd given her.

"Is your consulting business here as well?"

"No. It's by Wayne State." A beat of silence fell between them. He filled it by asking what he really wanted to know, "Are you dating anyone?"

"N-no," she stuttered.

"Good."

She gave him a once over, delight dancing in her eyes. "Well, aren't you cocky."

He came closer. She didn't move away. "I'm a man who knows what he wants."

She licked her lips. "And what do you want?"

"You."

She stilled as if shocked by his boldness. Then a slow smile formed, telling him they weren't finished.

"Go out to dinner with me," he said.

• • • ● ● • ● • • •

"Harper?" called Patricia from somewhere in the back.

An odd mixture of annoyance and nervousness slithered through Harper. She wanted Lucas all to herself, but also thought it was better if he left.

She gave herself a mental shake. No. Definitely the latter.

The man's baggage was too heavy for her to carry. Was he still dreaming about his wife?

Plus, he was her freaking landlord. The last thing she needed was the other shop owners gossiping, speculating how she was paying her rent. In cash, check, or on her back.

Most of her family and friends believed she was mooching off her mother to fund her 'hobby job.' She didn't want people here believing the same damn thing.

Patricia strode from the backroom. "Why didn't you answer me? I—" The clicking of her heels stopped, and she took Lucas in from head to toe, drinking him in like a fine wine.

Harper squashed the urge to shout, "He's mine!" reminding herself, he never was or would be hers.

Patricia offered her hand, introducing herself. He did the same. His smile was polite but distant as if he also didn't want to be interrupted.

"Are you renting one of the shops?" she asked.

"Nope." His phone dinged, and he apologized, saying he needed to answer the text.

Lucky him. It saved him from Patricia's prying questions.

Although Harper got the sense, he wouldn't have given much away. He didn't seem to like to talk about himself. He doled out information on a need-to-know basis.

Patricia was the opposite, and her favorite pastime was getting into other people's business. Therefore, it came as no surprise when she nearly jumped on Lucas again when he slid his phone into his pocket.

"If you aren't a renter, were you window shopping..."

The corner of his mouth twitched. "Nope." Glancing at his watch, he said, "Damn. I'm going to be late for a meeting."

Disappointment washed through Harper. She smothered it and said, "It was nice seeing you again."

"Oh, again?" Patricia interjected.

Crap. They'd been friends since elementary school, and next to Cindy, Patricia was one of her closest friends, but she could be judgmental. They had completely different ideas of what constituted a good boyfriend.

Not that Lucas was ever, or would be, one.

"I'll see you tomorrow," he said.

His words caught her and Patricia's attention, and they both parroted, "Tomorrow?"

"I'm ordering a suit from your neighbor. I made an appointment to get measured tomorrow at ten." He smiled, and it melted parts of her she was trying to freeze when it came to him. "Plus, you haven't answered me yet. Think about it. Let me know if our wants are the same."

Her cheeks heated. Patricia's curiosity was radiating off her. The barrage of questions would begin the minute Lucas left.

Harper should tell him goodbye. It'd make everything easier.

Instead, she said, "What if they aren't?"

He leaned closer. "Your eyes tell me different."

She was never good at schooling in emotions. Seeing him before her, a dream turned reality, had elation and anticipation thrumming through her.

Yes. She wanted him. Even if she shouldn't.

His gaze blistered her with hunger and promised to give her everything and not stop until she was satiated with sensual satisfaction.

She licked her lips. They were starving for a taste of him.

He blinked. Then took a step back, severing the moment. He wished them a nice day and was gone, pushing through the gallery door.

The whole encounter was surreal. She'd blame it on her overactive imagination, if not for the fact her friend was already peppering her with questions.

"Who is he? How did you meet? Is he—"

Harper held up a hand and settled with the easiest to answer. "He's a friend of Jacob Grimm. We met at his and Greta's wedding."

Patricia's nose wrinkled as if smelling something slightly rotten. "I'm still shocked Greta married him. I mean, he *is* sexy. That body and face...yum. But how does she stomach going from a massive estate on five acres to a little bungalow here in Detroit?"

Harper's jaw tightened. Most of the time, Patricia was kind and generous. This side of her was less than marvelous.

"You know Greta never cared about such stuff. She was happier in her tiny college apartment than she ever was living in her mother and stepfather's ginormous house."

Unlike her friend's expensive taste, who loved the material gifts more than the men who gave them to her.

She made a sweeping motion with her hand, clearly brushing aside Harper's comment. "Anyway, what do you and Mr. Handsome both want?"

Damn it. She hadn't told anyone about her and Lucas. Best to keep it vague. "He probably wants to take me to dinner."

"Oh, I saw the way he was watching you." Patricia ran her tongue across her teeth. "He doesn't want to take you to dinner. He wants *you* for dinner."

Harper blushed, muttering, "Whatever. You're hallucinating."

"Uh-huh. If you don't see it, you're blind." Patricia glanced toward the door Lucas exited through. "He is handsome, but if he runs in the same circles as Jacob..."

Annoyance bloomed and thrummed through her. "Oh, for god's sake, you act like Jacob is panhandling on John R instead of owning a successful business on that street."

"He obviously doesn't make enough for Greta to stay home."

"She doesn't *want* to stay home. I'm the same. Even if I were married to freaking Bill Gates, I wouldn't want to give this up." She opened her arms wide, indicating the gallery. "Greta feels the same about her career."

"Well, a man with some money wouldn't hurt. He'll take care of you and your art."

Ouch.

"Thanks for the vote of confidence. I'm hoping to support myself."

Patricia patted Harper's hand resting on the counter. "Oh, honey I didn't mean it like that. I know this place will be a success. Eventually."

"I am paying you to work here," she huffed, even though they both knew her mom's name was on the loan for the lease and the upfront cash to pay Patricia's salary.

At least her friend was kind enough *not* to point out that fact.

"There's nothing wrong with wanting love and money." Patricia ran perfectly manicured nails through her white-blonde hair. "Beauty is expensive."

"True, but I'd rather pay the bill and find a man who doesn't want a trophy wife."

"Why? It's a win-win. They get to show off their pretty wife, and she gets treated like a princess."

Because beauty fades, I want a man who looks deeper, finding more to love. Hopefully.

This was an argument they had before, and she didn't want to repeat it, so she merely shrugged.

"Anyway, how did Jacob's friend end up here, in the gallery?" Patricia asked.

"A huge coincidence. He apparently owns the building."

Patricia's eyes widened. "Really? Well that certainly changes things. Does he have more than this property?"

"I have no idea." Harper sighed. She hated this side of her friend. "I didn't ask for a financial dossier. All I know is he has a partner named Ben. It sounds like he does the heavy lifting because Lucas is busy with his eco-consulting firm. I think that's where his passion lies."

"Wow. Two businesses." Patricia rested a hip against the counter, nails tapping on the glass top. "Did you accept his dinner invite?"

"I never answered him."

"I'm sure when he comes back tomorrow, he won't leave without an answer. What will you say?"

"I don't know. I should probably refuse. I need to focus on the gallery. Not to mention, he's my landlord."

"So?"

"What will the other renters say?"

"Who cares."

"I care."

"Okay, fine," Patricia said, studying Harper slyly. "If you aren't interested, do you care if I go after him?"

Jealousy shot through her, hitting like a bullet to the gut. She pictured Lucas laughing and smiling with Patricia. Him touching her. Kissing her.

Her friend didn't notice the bitterness boiling right below Harper's skin, and kept talking. "Good-looking and has money, yet single. Why do you think that is?" Patricia smirked. "Perhaps he's lacking in other areas."

Memories of Harper's night with Lucas flashed through her. The man lacked in *nothing*. She broke eye contact as the warmth of her resentment switched to a different heat.

Patricia's perfectly sculpted brows rose. "Why do I get the feeling you might know the answer?"

"Well..." Warmth crept along her neck, making its way to her cheeks.

"Shut up." Patricia stood straight. "When? At the wedding?"

Harper nodded.

"Why didn't you tell me?"

She shrugged.

"Cat got your tongue," Patricia teased. "Or maybe Lucas swallowed it when he kissed you."

"Ew," Harper laughed. "Gross. I've dated men who kissed like they were trying to eat my face."

"Was he one of them?"

"No. He's a phenomenal kisser. As for dating him, I have no idea. We only had the one evening."

"Why? Is a night all he wanted? If so, why is he asking you to dinner?"

"Maybe because I'm that good," she joked, then said, "Anyway, the sex was fantastic, but we'd never have worked out, so I said no when he'd asked."

Patricia rocked back on her heels. "Woman, are you nuts? He's gorgeous, has money, and good in bed. Why in the hell would you say no?"

Because it's a smart decision, even if I regret it every day.

"I don't need his money."

Her friend waved this away. "Fine. Whatever. What about the other two rather important qualities?"

He had them too. As well as being sweet, a gentleman, and interesting. What the hell was she thinking, turning him down?

Recalling the humiliation of waking alone the morning after the wedding, combined with the devastating disappointment of learning why, reminded her.

The second part was almost worse than if he'd only wanted her body. Instead, he genuinely liked her, yet she'd never measure up to the memory of his wife. It would eventually crush her happiness.

Elizabeth was the love of his life, tragically taken from him. There was no way Harper could compete.

In those situations, people remembered all the good, forgetting the bad. Elizabeth would forever be the perfect wife.

"He's a widower, and I'm pretty sure he isn't over his wife. I won't be his rebound."

Patricia clutched her throat, her voice softer when she asked, "Oh...when did she die?"

"When we met, I believe he said it was around two years ago."

"Eight more months have passed. So at least three years. How long was he married?"

"I have no idea."

"Well, I doubt it was decades. He's close to our age, right?"

"Thirty-one," Harper supplied while thinking his wife was their age when she died.

"Also, it has been nearly a year since he's seen you, and he hasn't forgotten you, wants to take you out. That has to count for something."

Patricia had a point.

No. Lucas was a bad idea.

"It doesn't matter. Like I said earlier, he's my landlord." Before Patricia could repeat herself, Harper said, "Besides, this gallery *has* to be a success, and to make that happen will require all my attention. I want to pay off the loan from my mom, get everything in my name. Now isn't the time to start something with a man."

"Fine. If you're not interested, I am."

"No." Harper crossed her arms over her chest.

Patricia smiled. "That's what I thought."

She laughed. "Okay, fine. I admit it, I like him, but it doesn't change that I don't have time for dating. Nor do I want a man who's probably still in love with his perfect wife. I don't want to be someone he settles for because she's gone."

"Damn, for someone who's never even gone on a single date with the guy, you seem to have him figured out."

Guilt trickled into her. Earlier she considered Patricia quick to judge. Yet, here she was doing the same with Lucas.

"Fine." She held up her hands before running them through her hair. "You've made your point. *If* he stops by tomorrow, and *if* he asks, I'll accept. A night out would be nice."

Especially with Lucas.

"Good. Glad that's settled." Patricia handed Harper a slip of paper. "This was the reason I'd come out here. A man from some art program called. Said something about you volunteering to teach pottery to the elderly tomorrow. They need you to confirm."

"Oh! I forgot. I thought it started next week. Did you tell him yes?"

"Um, no. I wanted to double check, in case he had the wrong person. You don't have time for pet projects."

"I'll make time." She read the phone number while reaching for her cell.

"I don't get you," Patricia huffed, shaking her head. "I have to harass you into going on a date with a gorgeous man, but you jump at the chance to spend your evening at the senior citizen center."

She gave a half shrug. "I admire the elderly. They are interesting, and some are a hoot—"

"Oh my God, you're even talking like an old person now."

"Be quiet." Harper laughed. "Most of my childhood was spent with my grandmother. She was my best friend."

She smiled, recalling the older woman's husky laughter and sparkling eyes. Memories of trips to the Great Lakes, and two magical vacations to Europe, never failed to tickle her heart.

"When I was a kid, I'd spend my summers with Grandma Marquette. She told these crazy, captivating stories about growing up in the forties. Her time era wasn't ready for her." She waved a hand. "Anyway, she was so much fun. The woman was classy and fearless. I wanted to be her when I became an adult. Hell, still do."

"Best friend, huh. That is both sweet and sad," Patricia teased.

"Whatever. I'm beginning to suspect your grandma didn't hug you enough." She poked her friend in the ribs before turning for her office. "Anyway, I better give the senior center a call before they close."

"Yes, you better hurry," Patricia said in a sing-song voice, laughter lining her every word. "The streetlights are on. It's nearly bedtime for kids and old folks."

Harper chuckled, walking away. Entering the quiet of her tiny workspace, she admitted to herself the other reason she was willing to teach but hesitated with Lucas.

The seniors wouldn't hurt her. He'd probably break her heart.

She had a bad habit of giving herself to men who offered little of themselves in return. She wanted someone who'd give her all his heart. Lucas couldn't because he'd already given away his to Elizabeth.

Chapter Seven

Lucas gripped the tray with three coffees in one hand, using the other to open the door to Harper's gallery. She was at the counter again, sitting on a tall stool, the heels of her black boots hooked on the bottom rung. She was sexy as hell in fitted gray wool slacks and a snug red sweater, typing and staring fixedly at her laptop.

After leaving yesterday, unease chased him for the rest of the day. First, old ghost memories of despair had tried to haunt him. Those he managed to squash. There was no sense worrying about love and heartache or how he would handle the fallout from them.

More bothersome was the second-guessing. He'd worried about coming on too strong or reading signals wrong?

He was nearly positive the flash of joy and desire he'd seen spark in her eyes wasn't imagined. Then again, it had been a while since he was in the dating game. Even longer since he was truly interested in a woman.

The chime of her door alerted her to his arrival. Her gaze met his, and her warm, genuine smile disintegrated his hesitations.

He held the tray higher. "I hope you like coffee."

"I love it. Plus, your timing is perfect. Not only was I running late this morning, but I forgot to set my coffee machine last night." She came around the counter, her grin growing. "Please tell me the three of those are mine?"

He laughed. "Mind if I have a few sips of one, just enough to warm my frozen insides? I can't believe it's the end of March and it's this damn cold."

"It has been a cold spring," she agreed. "Cindy and I were in Spain last month. I'd give anything to be back on those beaches."

"I bet." He handed her a coffee. "How is Cindy?"

"Pretending like everything is great. How is Will?"

"The same."

Their breakup surprised Lucas. Will hadn't been this happy or content in years, if ever. The two of them were opposites yet somehow made it work.

Well, for a little while, anyway.

Maybe nothing was meant to last forever.

Harper broke the sad silence. "Did you happen to grab a few creamers when you got the coffees?"

Lucas shifted the carrier, showing her the spot without coffee filled with packets. "I also brought two kinds of sugar and sweetener."

"You're my hero." She took one from the tray.

The woman must love her java. The sincerity in her voice ran deep, and her moan of satisfaction after taking a sip was damn near orgasmic.

He leaned closer, wanting to hear it again. "Good?"

"Um-hmm."

Hell, her hum was almost carnal, and his dick responded. He shifted, moving behind the counter, not wanting her to see how much something as simple as drinking coffee was turning him on.

He needed to prove to her he wanted more than her body. Standing before her with a hard-on wasn't going to help.

After taking a cautious sip of his coffee, he asked, "Have you thought any more about having dinner with me?"

Indecision played over her alluring features. It bothered him how much the answer mattered. How had this woman he barely knew managed to capture his attention so completely? Sure, she was gorgeous, but it was more than her beauty.

"When?" she asked.

He promised his sister he would babysit his nieces tomorrow evening. The following day, he was driving up north for the weekend with Ben. They owned a few small cottage rentals they needed to check on.

Afterward they'd bike a few trails, if the snow stayed away. "What about tonight?"

"I can't."

He tilted his chin and frowned. "Do you mean this evening, or any day of the week?"

"Today. This evening I'm teaching a pottery class to seniors a few blocks away. It's a cool place, a non-profit that sells the pieces made there, in their store. The money goes to feed the homeless." Her gaze darted toward her laptop. "In fact, I need to map the address. Tonight is my first class. I have no idea how to get there."

"What is the place called?"

"Art and Aid."

"I know where it is. It's a ten-minute drive from here." He swirled the coffee in his cup, deciding to try one more time. "I could go with you. Be your driver and pottery assistant."

A tentative smile bloomed on her perfect lips, making him very happy he'd suggested it.

"Really? You'd go?" she asked.

"Yes. I'm busy the next couple of days, but I want to spend time with you. Besides, it sounds like fun…if you promise not to laugh at any of my creations. Hell, I can barely color in the lines of my niece's coloring books."

Harper laughed. "Yeah, okay, having an assistant would be nice. We have to be there at seven. Does that work for you?"

"Sure. I don't have to go to my other office. I'm helping Ben today and checking out an open space on the ninth floor."

"Oh, planning on starting another business? Three's the charm," she teased.

He chuckled. "Hell no. Two is too many. I'm considering moving Energy Solutions here."

"To this building?"

"Yup. Going back and forth is a pain in the ass, and finding someone to rent the old space will be easy."

He wasn't able to tell if she liked or hated the idea of him being closer, so he shrugged it off. In the end, he'd make his decision based on convenience and what was best for his business, not his heart.

He'd let his broken emotions dictate his life for too long after Elizabeth's death. As a result, he'd nearly lost Energy Solutions, caused a rift between him and Ben, and alienated his friends and family.

All of this reminded him he needed to leave. If he didn't get moving, he'd never get everything done and be ready to go with her this evening.

"Okay, I'll be back here at six-thirty," he told her.

After a brief hesitation, he kissed her cheek. Her soft skin and scent had him lingering.

She didn't seem bothered. In fact, he was confident she wouldn't mind another one, maybe even on her lips.

He decided not to press his luck and started for the door instead. "See you tonight."

•••••••••

"I take it you said yes to dinner," Patricia said.

Harper squeaked in surprise, spinning around to face her friend. "Are you trying to give me a heart attack? Why are you skulking?"

Patricia quirked a brow, amusement pulling at the corners of her mouth. "Defensive much? I was bringing you these." She held two glass figurines from a local artist. "Also, I wanted to ask if you sent the accounting stuff to Warren."

"Oh, crap, I forgot." She opened her email while indicating with her chin, "You can set those there, on the metal shelf."

"Where's Lucas taking you?"

Harper tried not to smile. "Why are you certain he and I are going somewhere?"

Patricia rolled her eyes, setting the small statues on the black iron display pedestals. "Um, I saw both of your faces after he kissed you. Who knew something so chaste could give off an R-rated vibe. You two have proven that wrong."

A shiver of want passed through her, but she managed to sound indifferent. "Whatever. It was an innocent kiss on the cheek."

"There was nothing virtuous about the lust on your faces."

Harper blushed. There was no denying she ached to grab him by the lapels and taste more of him. All of him. She'd wanted to wrap herself around his body, needing to know if he was as hard and fit as she remembered.

She mentally shook herself from the reverie of him. "He's going with me tonight. To the pottery class I'm teaching."

Patricia's jaw dropped. "Wow. He must really be into you."

Harper warmed at the assumption. "Why? It's fun."

Her friend snorted, somehow managing to make it sound feminine and cute. "Oh, yes, nothing says a fun Wednesday evening like partying with old people and playing with clay."

Hands on hips, she tried to hide her smile as annoyance and amusement tugged at her. "The elderly *are* fun. They've witnessed and experienced so much more than us and because of it have the best stories. The ones who want to learn and try new things seem to know the secret to a happy life. Maybe their wisdom will rub off on me." She narrowed her eyes. "And if you disdain art, why are you working here?"

"I enjoy spending time with you." Patricia winked. "Plus, an upscale gallery is a great place to husband hunt."

Harper choked on a laugh, shaking her head. "You don't need a man. You're smart, and doing a fantastic job helping me open this place. Without you and Warren's friend doing the accounting, I'd be drowning in the business end of things, unable to finish my sculpture. And I *must* have it done by opening night. You'll always have a place here."

Patricia's warm smile said she was touched. Her family was old-school. They expected her to grow their already massive bank account by marrying a well-off man, verses becoming a success on her own. Harper liked to remind her friend she was worth more than her pretty face.

"I can't lie, it is exciting, seeing you give it a go as an artist and businesswoman. However, for me, my paycheck barely covers my hair and nails, let alone my apartment or the gas to drive here every day."

Harper took a sip of her coffee. "Well, you're the one who has to live in a ridiculously huge apartment in Beverly Hills. Detroit has some great places. They're closer, less money, and many are on or near the water."

"I want to be close to my family. Also, if it's so great, why don't you live here? Aren't you the one who told Greta she was crazy for moving to the 'hood?'"

"I was wrong," she admitted. "Before researching rentals, I didn't come here often. As a kid, I only heard about the bad stuff. The most we'd done was drive in for a show at the Opera House or one of the theaters, leaving right after. The city has changed a lot since those days."

"This is true," Patricia agreed before zeroing in on the cups of coffee. "Why do you have two?"

Harper handed her friend one. "It's for you. Lucas got them for us. Anyway, as for living here, I would if I didn't have another year on my lease. Once it ends, I'm moving. The commute is a pain."

Patricia took a sip of coffee then set it down. "I like your man."

"He isn't mine." Although she had to admit, at least to herself, Harper liked the sound of him being hers.

Her cellphone dinged. Warren's name and a message flashed across the screen. She read it aloud to Patricia, telling her he planned on stopping by later with lunch and the accounting files.

"When you mentioned him earlier," she said, "I wanted to ask, why didn't you let your mother's accountant handle it?"

"I need to cut the apron strings. I'm thankful for my mother's support, but I want the gallery to be in my name. I'll pay her back for the upfront costs, and find my employees and such, without her help. I'm a big girl."

"I'm willing to bet your mom has never worn an apron." Patricia laughed, then sobered. "Anyway, are you *sure* Warren's the right choice?"

"I trust him. If he says this woman is good, I believe him."

Patricia snorted. "He probably wants to get in her pants and is loosening the buttons with your account."

Warren was a bit of a slut, but their friendship had to mean more than a quick lay, right? Harper shook her head. "No. It'll be fine."

"I hope you're right. Oh, when he does stop by, I wouldn't mention Lucas."

She tilted her head to the side. "Um, Why?"

"He won't care for your guy."

"So what? He never likes anyone I date."

"True. Though the problem with Lucas is Warren will see the man as true competition. Even more than Edward."

Revulsion and shame rolled through Harper. She'd wasted years on a man who found her lacking, allowing him to take what he desired and getting the rest from other women.

She was the pretty, perfect pedigree woman to introduce to his parents and clients, yet not a best friend and lover. No, he had his buddies to drink and play golf with and a string of women to fulfill his darker, carnal needs. Meanwhile, all she got was campaign dates, boring vanilla sex, and constant criticism.

She shook her head, returning to Patricia and her comments regarding Warren. "There is no competition. He's not even in the race. We're friends."

"He wouldn't mind more."

She scoffed. "Are you kidding me? Remember, high school? I crushed on him our whole sophomore and junior year. He wasn't the slightest bit interested."

"That's because, much like now, he wanted to screw every woman who smiled his way. When he's ready to settle down, he'll expect you to be waiting."

"Patricia, I love you, but you are delusional. Besides, even if that's his plan, it's not mine and not happening. I refuse to be anyone's plan B."

Harper had been Edward's, and damn it, she'd rather be alone.

Finishing her coffee, she tossed the paper cup into the recycling bin. "Anyway, I don't have a lot for you to do today. The one art dealer who was supposed to stop by, canceled. We have no artist or deliveries today, so I'm going to change and head in the back to work on the clay design for the project I have at my mom's."

Her favorite material was large stone or marble, but she didn't have room at her place for the materials. Not to mention, her neighbors would complain about the noise.

Luckily, she was able to work on the small designs in her tiny room here at the gallery and her condo, saving the sculpting and carving of the large pieces for when she was at the art studio at Mom's house.

"Okay, I'll update the gallery's social media accounts, then probably take off after Warren brings us lunch."

Harper nodded, only half listening. Her mind was already far away, plotting and crafting the piece waiting for her.

Chapter Eight

Lucas spotted Harper leaning against the floor to ceiling window in front of her gallery, reading something on her phone. She'd changed from business clothes into a pair of tight black jeans and a loose-fitting burgundy shirt. She was still exquisite.

"Were you waiting long?" he asked, trying not to ogle her shapely legs.

She met his gaze. "No. Besides, waiting gave me time to stalk you on social media. Not that there was much to find."

He laughed as she turned her cell to show an old photo of him. It wasn't even his account. Someone else posted it and tagged him. "I have a website for my business and an Instagram account I never use. That's it for me."

"Wow. I have business accounts for my art on five different platforms. Managing them is nearly a fulltime job." Her gaze roamed from his oxford shoes to suit jacket. Moving closer, she hooked a finger in his vest. "You're a bit overdressed to play with clay."

"Had I known my evening plans, I'd have brought a change of clothes."

She tilted her head. "Besides Greta's barbecue, I've never seen you out of a suit. Even then you'd worn khakis and a fitted polo."

"You have most definitely seen me out of a suit..." he noted, referring to their incredibly hot night together in July.

Judging by the way her cheeks flushed a sexy pink, she'd caught the reference. He loved that she didn't drop his gaze. Even better, was the little flicker of heat in her eyes.

"I mean, I've never seen you in casual clothes. Smartass. Do you even own any?"

"I run or go to the gym most mornings. You're welcome to join me. Then you'll get the chance to see me in old, ratty clothes, covered in sweat."

"Tempting, and it explains why you look so damn good out of your suits."

Now it was his turn to blush. He loved how she was always willing to play, to smile. He needed someone like that in his life.

Need.

Needing a person sent a light panic scratching at his nerves. Last time he'd cared for someone, it had ended in soul-crushing depression.

He shifted, trying to shake off his foreboding. "We better get going before we're late."

Nodding, she walked toward the parking lot. "Yeah, that'd be rude. Arriving late for my first class. Do you want me to follow you in my car?"

"Nah. We'll go together in mine. I'll bring you back afterward. Finding a parking spot might be difficult, let alone two. Plus, I can drop you off at the door."

It'd also mean he'd have more time with her.

"Okay." Her smile said she was pleased, and it invited him to come closer.

He placed a hand on her lower back. The soft fabric of her shirt and the warmth of her body was temptation under his palms. It reminded him of when he'd run his hands over her naked flesh and the sounds she made when he caressed all her favorite spots.

He needed a distraction. "Where'd you hear of this class your teaching?"

On the way to his car and the short drive to the senior citizen center, she told him about the program and why she volunteered. His admiration for her grew. She was a busy woman but made time to give to the community.

He soon learned she was a fantastic teacher. She had an ease with the elderly in her class, and with the way she explained things, everyone caught on quickly. After a few simple demonstrations with the potter's wheel, everyone was able to create a small, basic bowl.

Well, everyone except him. He couldn't work the potter's wheel for shit. All he managed to do was splatter clay on his slacks, arms, and shirt.

The class found his ineptitude hilarious, and he couldn't remember the last time he'd laughed so hard. Everyone made different suggestions on how he could improve, each one becoming crazier and crazier. The final one was a woman saying it might help him if he and Harper recreated the pottery scene from the old movie, *Ghost*. After which, her friend chimed in, giggling, telling him he had to do it shirtless like Patrick Swayze.

Harper laughed and winked at him before telling her students maybe she'd give him a private lesson later. They hooted and cheered, while he turned three shades of red, loving every minute.

Her students had left a while ago, and he was helping clean and line the bowls outside the kiln for someone to fire tomorrow. He glanced in her direction and caught her watching him, a soft smile on her lips.

He grinned. "Are you worried my two left hands will wreck your students' creations?"

Setting aside the rag she was using to the wipe counter, she came to him and kissed his cheek. "Thanks for coming. You made those ladies' night."

Resting a hand on her hip, he asked, "What about yours?"

"Oh, yes, definitely mine." She stepped closer.

Their bodies were a breath away. He was close enough to count the darker flecks of blue in her gray eyes.

He ran a hand up her arm, to the back of her neck. She sighed as if in relief, tipping her lips to his.

Right before they met, there was a rap on the door. Harper startled in his embrace, and they broke apart.

A stout woman with chin-length gray hair smiled indulgently at them. "Sorry to interrupt, but you're the last class for the night. I need to lock up."

Lucas cleared his throat, trying to swallow his desire. "Do you need me to walk you to your car?"

"No, thank you, young man," the woman said kindly. "My husband is waiting for me."

They waved goodbye as she left, then he asked, "Are you hungry?"

Harper rubbed her stomach. "I'm famished."

"There's a place around the corner that has the best shawarma sandwiches. I was going to stop and get a few on my way home. Want to come with me?"

She rubbed her stomach through her coat. "That sounds way better than the bowl of cereal I was going to eat before collapsing in bed."

"I can't have that. After I came with you to help and instead destroyed nearly everything I touched, the least I could do is make sure you eat real food."

He helped her into her coat before grabbing his vest and putting on his suit jacket. He offered her his arm and she took it, just like the night they met in the upper level of the DIA.

• • • ● ● • ● ● • •

Harper snuggled into the heated seats of Lucas's car, her belly full from the delicious chicken pita sandwich, her mind wandering through the fun evening. The man didn't have an ounce of finesse with the potter's wheel, but his good humor was better than anything he could've created.

She'd also enjoyed it when he rolled his sleeves, exposing thick tendons and veins running through his strong arms as he tried to master the wheel. The end result was messy, and somehow, incredibly erotic.

Perhaps it had something to do with the way his deep melodic laughter filled the room each time he'd destroyed another ball of clay. The sound caressed her heart and warmed her desire.

Glancing at his slacks, she smiled. The dark brown material was splattered with small specks of clay. Leaning over the center console, she picked off a dried spot close to his knee with her fingernail.

Although she barely touched him, he jumped. Delight flashed through her.

"Did I discover a ticklish spot?" she asked, gripping him above his knee.

He sucked in a sharp breath, shooting back into his seat. "Yes," he squeaked. "Unless you want this car wrapped around some road sign, I wouldn't do it again."

She moved her hand higher, no longer gripping, only resting. "No way, this Tesla is too pretty to mangle."

He chuckled, flicking on the blinker and turning into the parking lot of their building. She was bone-tired, yet part of her didn't want the evening to end. To say goodbye to Lucas.

At the restaurant, he told her about babysitting his nieces tomorrow and his out-of-town trip for the weekend. Unless he visited her at the gallery, she wouldn't see him until who-knows-when.

The following week was the opening. The chances of her having a free second were slim to none.

The idea left her a little hollow, even knowing it was for the best. She had a terrible habit of diving into projects, people, and passions that captivated her, forgetting to be clear-headed and responsible.

Lucas definitely ignited her ardor and fascination. She didn't want to rush things with him.

"Thank you for dinner," she said. "I didn't realize how hungry I was until I smelled the food."

He smirked, putting the car in park and turning it off. "Yeah, the way you annihilated your sandwich was impressive."

"Hey," she laughed, scooting closer, running her hand back down his leg and squeezing hard.

He jumped high enough his head nearly hit the roof. Snagging her wrist, he moved it to his thigh. Humor danced in his eyes. "Damn, woman, you take no prisoners."

"Nope. Although I'd like to note you finished your food before me."

"True, but you saw me at your class tonight. You already know, I'm not fit to bring around friends and family."

Her smile widened, laughter bubbling in her chest. "Well, at least not if food or art is involved."

He let go of her hand, clutching his chest. "Ugh. You wound me."

"I'm kidding. I had a great time."

More than great. She was unable to recall ever having so much fun with any of her former boyfriends. Even the times they took her to fancy parties or on expensive vacations.

"Me too. Thank you for letting me tag along."

"If you're free next week, come back. I believe a few of the ladies will be heartbroken if you don't return."

So would I.

As if reading her thoughts, he inclined his head closer to her. "What about you?"

"I want you there," she breathed.

"Good." He bridged the distance between them, his lips meeting hers in a soft kiss.

Her hand resting on his leg slipped under his jacket. He gripped her neck, burying his hand in her hair, kissing her with more hunger.

She responded with equal need, clutching his side and internally cursing the car's console between them. She was tempted to climb over it and onto his lap.

When they broke apart to catch their breath, he growled, "You taste so fucking good."

His voice was low, gravelly, and the way he said 'fuck' melted and pooled between her legs.

"You just like the lingering aftertaste of my sandwich," she teased, hoping a joke would ease some of her near-painful ache for him.

It didn't.

"Hmm. I'll need another taste to be sure."

She savored his lips before he nibbled and sampled her jaw, working his way to her ear. Once there, his warm breath fed her cravings.

He whispered, "You are a dessert, tasting of temptation and passion."

She'd give anything to be spread before him, letting him make a meal of her.

It was on the tip of her tongue to invite him to her place for a sweet treat. She needed to put on the brakes.

She moved away, settling into her seat, one hand on the door. "I better get home. I have an early appointment with the bank." Her voice sounded as weak and pathetic as her will.

He nodded, opening his door. "Let me walk you to your car."

She appreciated the way he listened and didn't push. However, the distance, the lack of his heat, left her cold. She wanted his hands and lips back on her.

He came around and opened her door. She stepped out, smiling. "This isn't necessary. You parked right next to me."

"It's late and dark." He wrapped an arm around her waist. "Plus, I want another chance to kiss you."

Yes. Please.

"You're quite confident you'll get another," she teased.

He ran his irresistible lips along her neck, stopping at the spot that made her melt into a puddle of need.

How had he found it so quickly? Most men skipped the secret spots going straight for the obvious ones: boobs, butt, between her legs.

As they reached her car, she wrapped her arms around his waist, pulling him tight against her. His mouth made his way to her lips, and this time there was nothing gentle about his kiss. It was pure, carnal lust.

His erection pressed in against her hip. She gripped his ass, trying to bring him impossibly closer, knowing they'd never to be close enough unless he was inside her.

She wanted to wrap her legs around him. Or yank him into the backseat of her Mercedes. The car wasn't big, but she'd make it work.

Someone's horn blared, and a guy's voice shouted, "Go for it, man! Take her against that sexy car!"

She giggled as embarrassment raced through her. Why wasn't she able to control herself around him?

Lucas rested his forehead against hers, their laughter mingling. She didn't try to leave his embrace or remove her hands from his backside.

He brushed his mouth lightly over her lips, back and forth twice. "Sorry. That was supposed to be a quick, sweet kiss goodnight."

"Why are you apologizing? It wasn't like I was a passive passenger on this ride." To prove her point, she squeezed his firm, tantalizing butt, before sliding her hands to his lower back.

He smiled. "Yes, but my plan is to show you we're good together as a couple. Grinding against you, losing myself in your touch is proving something else. Something we both already know."

That was the problem. The chemistry between them was off the charts. When he was near, control was damn near impossible. It took control. Thinking became impossible, let alone differentiating between right and wrong.

He kissed her cheek, then said, "There's no doubt I ache to have you naked and underneath me again, but I want more than your nights and your body. I'm greedy. I want your mornings and mind as well."

Wow.

She loved that he didn't play games. She had enough of those with her ex. Still, Lucas was asking a lot. He was basically saying he wanted a relationship with her. Taking that step was scary. Her record with men was terrible, and he came with a lot of baggage.

"You're right. We should take things slower." She decided to be honest and direct without getting into her ex and various insecurities. "I tend to dive into things without restraint, and I suspect you could do some damage if things fell apart between us. I need to be sure before I get in too deep."

"I'll go at whatever pace you need." He cupped her cheek, stroking it with his thumb. "You, Harper, are worth the wait."

With one simple sentence, he stole a sliver of her heart.

Chapter Nine

Lucas shut off his laptop at five. Earlier, he'd checked G&D's planner and found it clear. So, when the buzzer on the door rang, he jerked, startled.

Had Ben forgotten a late meeting? He'd been in a rush to leave when he called, asking Lucas to cover the phones for a few hours and review a possible rental place on Lake Michigan.

Grumbling under his breath, he waited for the person to enter. A woman turned slightly away from him, came inside. Her shoulder-length black hair obscured her face. She closed the door behind her, and when she came toward him, he was surprised to realize she was Harper's mother.

He'd caught a brief glimpse of her at the wedding, but she wasn't someone people forgot. She was stunning like her daughter and oozed confidence. It shouted she was the master of her world. No one told this woman what to do. She was everyone's boss.

She offered him her hand. "I'm Victoria Marquette. My daughter and I are renting the art gallery on the first floor."

"Nice to meet you. What can I do for you, Mrs. Marquette?"

"*Ms.* Marquette," she corrected with a smile that could only be described as sensual predatory. "My daughter mentioned the shop next to hers is closing. I wanted to know if it's possible for us to rent it and knock down the wall for more gallery space."

He was confused. Harper asked him about this last week, and he told her he'd find out. Ben was looking into it. The matter was tricky because the building was registered as historical. Therefore, there might be restrictions and not possible. Didn't mother and daughter talk?

"Yes, Harper mentioned it. I'm happy to take your number and send you both the information. Do you have an email or card with your contact info?"

Ms. Marquette stilled for half a second as if surprised he called her daughter by her first name. He suspected Harper hadn't mentioned him to her mother.

Victoria offered him her business card. When he went to take it, she held on tighter, resting a hand on top of his. "I see you're leaving. Would you like to go to dinner with me?"

Lucas rubbed his chin, opened, then closed his mouth. Was she hitting on him?

"To discuss the lease?" he asked, fishing. "Until the city gets back with me, I don't have much to tell you."

Her gaze raked him before settling on his mouth. "We could talk about other things..."

Uh-oh.

"I know your daughter," he blurted, flummoxed.

She let go of her card. "How?"

"You were both at my good friend's wedding. Jacob Grimm."

Tilting her head, Victoria said, "Yes, I thought you looked familiar." She brushed aside the information. "So, are you hungry?"

The way she said *hungry* told him food wasn't what she was craving. He'd be flattered if the circumstances were different. Instead, he was mildly flustered.

He tried for subtlety, not wanting to embarrass her or Harper. "Um, I was the one who drove your daughter to her hotel when she wasn't feeling well."

She stepped around the desk, coming closer. "Such a gentleman."

Okay, she wasn't getting what he was saying.

He dipped his chin, staring her straight in the eyes. "I didn't leave that night."

"Oh." Her mouth dropped open a little. She snapped it shut and put on a professional smile. "Oh. Well, please fax the information to my office when you have it."

"Will do. I'll leave a note for my partner before I head out." He returned to his seat to write a quick message for Ben, asking if he'd learned anything new.

Before exiting, Victoria turned, her brazen grin back in full force. He understood where Harper inherited her fire.

"I'll have to stop by my daughter's gallery before leaving. I'll tell her you said hi."

He grinned. "Please, do."

· · · · ● · ● · · ·

Harper was flipping the closed sign as her mother strolled through the door. Something in her smile said, 'You've been misbehaving, and we will be discussing it.'

"Harper Lee Marquette."

Uh-oh, my full name. What did I do? I hope it was fun and worth my mother's needling.

"Yes..."

"Why didn't you tell me you're *friendly*," her mother winked, "with the landlord."

Harper cheeks flamed, the blush damn near reaching her toes.

She walked to her office, avoiding her mother's question by asking one of her own. "How do you know Lucas?"

"I stopped at G&D to discuss the next-door rental."

Harper twisted around, anger burning away her embarrassment. "Damn it, Mom. I told you I'd look into it. Why do you have to treat me like a child who can't handle her business?"

Her mother stepped closer, patting Harper's shoulder. It managed to be comforting, placating, and condescending all at the same time. "I'm aware you can take care of yourself. I figured the two of us inquiring would add more pressure. But..." An impish smile matched the tone slinking into her voice. "Apparently, you're giving the matter your full attention and dedication."

She couldn't help laughing at her mom's bluntness. "Again, how did it even come up in conversation that he and I are dating?"

"Dating? There was more than the one time? Why, daughter, haven't I heard of him until now?" Her mother rested her hands on her slim hips, her curiosity was so strong Harper could almost smell it.

"Okay, fine, 'dating' might be a bit of an overstatement. How do you know he and I slept together?"

"From him."

Okay. She had to hear how and why Lucas discussed such a thing with *her mother*.

However, she didn't get the chance because Patricia walked into the office, adding, "Don't forget your hot date at the senior citizen center last week."

"Where did you come from?" Her mother's brows pulled together. "Also, what are you talking about?"

"I was in the back," Patricia pointed with her thumb over her shoulder, "checking through stuff the UPS guy dropped off."

"All of it good?" Harper asked.

Patricia nodded as Mother cut in. "Will one of you please explain to me this senior thing?"

"I'm teaching a pottery class around the corner from here. Lucas went with me last week." She made a give-me gesture. "Now spill, Mom. He doesn't strike me as the kiss-and-tell sort of man. Especially if the person he was talking to was my mom."

"I asked him to dinner." Her voice held no apology, and her eyes sparked with mirth. "He said he met you at the wedding. I was a bit dense and didn't catch his hint. He, um, had to make himself crystal clear."

Harper groaned, flopping into a nearby chair, covering her face with her hands as Patricia's laughter filled the room.

"Don't worry, he was a total gentleman," Mom said, humor playing with each word.

Harper peeked between her fingers. "Unlike my indecent mother," she muttered.

"Hey, he looks like Gregory Peck. Hell, Peck's hotter brother. How do you expect me to resist? You know I have a thing for him." She wiggled her brows. "He told me to tell you hi."

"It's so nice when mothers and daughters have things in common," Patricia joked, clearly loving the show. She held up a finger as if struck by a great idea. "You both are so busy. Maybe he could date you both. Take out whoever is free."

Harper tossed a paperclip at her friend, groaning as her mom said, "I don't date."

"Ugh, Mom. That's your biggest issue with her suggestion, not the sharing part?"

Her mother shrugged, then, catching whatever horrified expression was on Harper's face, she burst into loud laughter. "I'm kidding. You are too easy to get a rise from."

Patricia wiped her bottom lashes, shaking her head. "I adore you two and would love to hang around, but I'm meeting Alex at the Fisher."

"Oh," Mother rested a hip against the tall, metal desk, "lucky lady, you got tickets to Hamilton. Even as a season ticket holder, I had a hell of a time getting mine."

"Things are going good with Alex?" Harper asked. "This is what, your third date?"

"Well, he's taking me to see Broadway's top show, so I'm happy."

Harper folded her arms across her chest. "Glad you have your priorities straight."

"I think she does," Mother declared. "He likes the theater and has excellent taste in shows. Is he handsome?"

"Of course," Patricia said.

"Why? You going to ask him out?" Harper teased.

"I might."

Patricia laughed, waving goodbye.

As the clicking of her friend's heels grew quieter, Harper pushed aside her amusement and mild embarrassment, smiling at her mother.

Yes, having her hit on the guy Harper was dating was kind of strange. Yet another part of her admired that her mom did as she pleased, not bothering to play by society's rules.

She was a powerhouse in a male-dominated business world. A temptress to men, seducing from thirty to whatever age pleased her.

She wished she had half her mother's confidence.

"Did you come here to harass people at G&D and hit on my," she paused, stumbling, not sure what to call Lucas and finished lamely with, "the guy I'm dating?"

"Nope. I had business reasons for being here. Visiting with you and the other stuff was an added bonus." Her lips pressed together with amusement. "Your man turned me down for dinner, want to take his place?"

Harper snorted. "Sure, but not that Cajun restaurant you love. It has the slowest waitstaff in existence. I need to do a few more things this evening to prepare for the gallery opening. I don't want to be up half the night."

"Works for me. Let's go. I'm starving."

Chapter Ten

In the last couple of weeks, Lucas had fallen into a routine. On Wednesday evenings, he helped Harper at her pottery class, and afterward, they'd have a quick dinner. Most days, he'd stop at the Roasting Bean and order three coffees, drinking his with her, and sometimes, Patricia.

Afterward, he'd visit the sixth floor. He decided to move Energy Solutions to the Salvador building, so he'd check on the progress before either heading to his old office or stopping in at G&D.

His favorite part of these days were those stolen moments with Harper. He craved his time with her way more than the coffee. Especially since it was all they had together.

The opening of her gallery was on Friday. When she wasn't meeting with event planners for the grand opening or putting on the final touches to make everything perfect, she was at her mom's working on her showcase piece—a sculpture that paid homage to her favorite childhood stories.

She told him finishing it on time was a huge stress, yet she was determined to do it, positive it would 'wow' people and set the tone of her gallery.

The way she described it to him, he was eager to see it. The statue was carved from stone, life-sized, and magical. She said the small, detailed chiseling was exhausting but worth it.

For selfish reasons, he also couldn't wait for the opening. It'd mean she'd have free time, giving him a better understanding of where they stood.

He'd made his intentions clear after the pottery class. He wanted all of her. What he wasn't sure about was what she wanted. Sure, she'd admitted her fear of falling and getting hurt, but it didn't mean she *was* falling.

He shook his head. Harper had him in knots. He was like a damn high school kid fretting if his crush was into him.

The door to the gallery chimed when he opened it, causing Harper and a man behind the sales counter to glance up at the sound.

She smiled and waved. The guy frowned before returning his attention to the computer.

The man was around her age, maybe two inches taller with curly, perfect blond hair and a face most women would admire.

What Lucas didn't like was how close he was standing to Harper. When he came closer, he noticed neither appeared happy.

"Everything okay?" Lucas asked.

"Who are you?" the guy demanded.

"Lucas. And you?" He left it to Harper to answer who he was to her. Lover, friend, landlord. He'd like to be the first two.

"Warren," the blond answered, inching closer to Harper.

An unfamiliar possessiveness reared in Lucas. He wanted to ditch the idea of waiting, letting her take the lead. The desire to come around the counter and show their connection by bringing her against him and tasting her kiss was powerful. Staying where he stood and keeping an impassive expression was difficult.

However, she wanted to keep everything professional at her work. She loathed the idea of other tenants gossiping, and he wanted to respect her wishes.

"Is that Lucas with our coffees?" Patricia came from the backroom and sighed happily, taking her java and nodding a thanks. The woman had the nose of a bloodhound when it came to what she called her liquid gold.

"What are you, their personal barista?" Warren's lip curled.

He looked and sounded like a snob. Lucas's dislike for the guy grew.

"Yes," Patricia wisecracked, further dissolving the tension by taking a loud slurp of her coffee.

Harper lost her tight expression, making some of Lucas's irritation fade.

"Glad you approve, ma'am." He bowed low.

"Lucas and I are dating," Harper told Warren as she came around the counter. "Although with the gallery opening looming, we haven't been going out much."

Warmth spread through his chest at Harper's words. He met her halfway, kissing her cheek. His lips lingered, taking in her lovely earthy scent of vanilla and wild creativity.

He forced himself to move away. "Oh, come on, your pottery classes count. They're entertaining."

Now she full-on belly laughed. He loved the sound.

"Very true," she agreed. "Hey, did I see Margie slip you her phone number?"

He snorted. "Yes. Told me she's always had a crush on Gregory Peck, putting me squarely on her bucket list." The women's giggles filled the room.

"Your class? What class?" Warren asked, clearly confused.

Lucas liked that the other man didn't seem to know what Harper did with her free time. Lucas's caveman reaction surprised him. He wasn't normally the possessive type, but something about the other man bothered him.

"A pottery course at the senior center nearby," she explained.

"You're teaching old people? Why?"

"Because it's fun." Harper sounded a touch defensive and annoyed, as if this wasn't the first time she had to justify her reasons. "Also, I want to be part of this community."

"Why? I don't get why you were hell-bent on Detroit. The clientele in Petite Bois would have been better. They have the money to spend on high end art. Plus, you wouldn't have the long drive to your mom's place to work on the stone and marble pieces."

Okay, on second thought, Warren did seem to know her. Way more than some random guy hired for whatever they were arguing about when he arrived at the gallery.

"Are you a friend?" He asked Warren.

"Yes. We've been together since high school."

Odd wording.

He was willing to bet both his businesses Warren had a thing for Harper.

"He, Patricia, and I were in the same graduating class in high school. I met them my freshman year. After graduation, we ended up going to the same college." She squinted playfully at them. "I'm hoping they like me as a person and not because they can't get rid of me."

"Define 'like'," Patricia teased.

At the same time, Warren said, "It's hard to say."

The two looked at each other and high-fived. Lucas couldn't help smiling.

Although his friendship with Jacob and Will didn't go back to high school, he was sure the sentiment was the same. They were his second family, and he cherished them.

"Thanks, *friends*." Harper laughed, shaking her head. "The question is, why do I keep you two around? Especially when you do this to me, Warren." She tapped her laptop screen, stress leaking into her voice.

Warren groaned, pinching the bridge of his nose. "I'm sorry. I thought she was an accountant. I didn't know she was only in her first semester. Or that she changed her major six times."

"One." Harper held up a finger. "You're getting too old to date college girls—"

"Nope," he cut in, "When I'm sixty, I'll still be dating college ladies."

Harper and Patricia sniggered. Lucas suspected the guy wasn't joking. He was totally *that* asshole.

"Two, did you even ask if she was an accountant before handing her my information?" The tension visibly climbed as Harper hunched her shoulders.

"I did, but I had a few drinks the night we met. I can't remember *everything* we talked about. At the time, she sounded knowledgeable..."

Wow. Nice. He'd risked screwing with the gallery's future to get laid.

"Send me the files," Lucas interrupted their conversation. "I have a friend who's a CPA. The accounting firm he works for part-time handles all my business." He glanced at Warren. "For years. I know for a fact they're good."

"I can't ask you to do that. This is a mess." Harper sounded torn. The woman seemed to hate asking for help.

"You didn't. I offered, and it's no big deal. If Tanner can't take new clients, he'll give it to someone else in the accounting firm. I use them. They're first-rate."

Harper brightened. "Oh, I met him at Greta's wedding. His girlfriend is Maggie, right? I love her." She cocked her head to the side. "Isn't Tanner in Maggie's band? How is he also an accountant?"

It didn't surprise Lucas the two women hit it off. They were both artists with similar, strong personalities.

"Yeah, he is, but the guy's a numbers nerd. A CPA. He wants to maintain his license, so he takes on a few, select clients." Grabbing a scrap of paper, he wrote his email. "Send me everything, okay?"

Harper sighed, finally giving in. "Fine. Please forward the bill to this address. Plus, let him know I want to invite him and his girlfriend to dinner as a thank you." She smirked at Patricia and Warren. "It's my ploy to see Maggie again. It might be time to find new friends."

Both pretended different measures of horror and begged for Harper's forgiveness. Lucas sipped on his coffee, finishing it and trying not to laugh.

By the time she agreed to keep them around, he'd tossed his empty cup in the recycling bin. "I'll contact Tanner about your account and dinner before heading to the other building. Are you going to your mom's this evening?"

Her apologetic smile told him the answer before she spoke. "Yes. I have two days until the opening. I have to get this last piece finished."

Disappointment flooded him, even if he wasn't shocked. He understood her drive. He was the same when it came to his consulting business. He might not be creating stunning art, however, doing his part to protect the environment for future generations was extremely important to him.

He came closer, lowering his voice. "Fine, but after the opening, we're going to celebrate. In any way you want."

"I'm looking forward to it." The flicker of anticipation in her eyes told him she meant it, while also making him wonder how she wanted to celebrate. "Oh, wait. This'll go until eleven. I probably won't get out of here until midnight or later. Would you rather celebrate the day after?"

"No way. I'll wait. You're worth it." He stuffed his hands into his pockets so he wouldn't reach for her. The no PDA at her work rule sucked.

To his surprise and immense pleasure, she bounced forward, kissing him light and quick on the lips. "Thanks."

The alarm on his phone went off, startling them. He pulled it from his pocket and silenced the noise.

"Shit. I have to go. I need to be on the other side of the city in half an hour." He nodded to Patricia and a sullen-looking Warren before facing Harper. "Don't forget to forward me the accounting stuff."

Even though they were doing nothing more than drinking coffee and chatting, he didn't want to leave. The intense need to be around her was a little scary.

Not because she wasn't worth it, no, his terror was in if something happened to her. He worried his heart wouldn't handle the fallout.

It damn near died with Elizabeth. Could he survive that sort of pain again?

• • • • • • • • • •

"'Forward me the accounting stuff. My guy handles all my business,'" Warren mimicked, mocking Lucas. "I'm sure a barista delivery boy keeps his accountant busy."

Annoyance skittered through Harper. *Why does Warren have to hate every man I date?*

"Not that it matters, but he isn't a barista," she snipped.

"Well, he can't be very important if he has time to deliver coffee every morning and hang around with you two ladies." He paused, tapping his chin. "He was wearing a nice suit. Let me guess. He manages the shop next door."

"No," Patricia said. "He doesn't work there. He owns the freaking building."

Warren blanched. "That guy?" He pointed to the hallway, where Lucas had exited.

"Well, he's partners with another man," Harper clarified.

"He also has a consulting company." A provoking twitch played at the corner of Patricia's smile. "He might make more money than you, Warren."

"Who cares," he scoffed. The increased pitch in his voice said differently. "I still don't like him."

"Careful, Warren, your jealousy is showing," Patricia drawled.

His cheeks flush red. "Why would I be jealous of him?"

Patricia opened her mouth to answer, but Harper hushed them. She didn't want to hear what either had to say.

Too bad Warren wasn't willing to let the topic go. "I don't care for him because he's pompous and bossy. Demanding Harper send him the accounting stuff, pushing dates on her."

Seriously? Warren handed over her account to get laid and now had the nerve to insinuate Lucas was the asshole. Irritation raced through her.

"That's not how I see it. At all." She narrowed her eyes at Warren. "He's trying to help me fix *your* mistake."

"He's a dick," he retorted. "He reminds me of Edward."

"How?" She rubbed her forehead, worry tugging low in her subconscious. "Also, I thought you liked Edward? He was the only boyfriend of mine you didn't despise."

"Well, he's a cool friend, but definitely a shitty guy to date."

Harper smacked Warren's shoulder. "Thanks. Why didn't you mention this when I told you he asked me out?"

"I knew he was arrogant and shallow. It wasn't until you two began dating I realized he was an awful boyfriend."

At least he had the decency to sound contrite. However, she couldn't let it go completely. "Those first two traits weren't enough to warn me?"

He shrugged. "I figured if you didn't care or notice, why should I?"

Why hadn't I seen it? Am I a terrible judge of character?

"Of course, it would have mattered to me." Her defensiveness kicked in. "He kept his worst deeds hidden from me. And, well, for the rest, I'd hoped he'd changed."

He snorted. "Okay, fine, I didn't warn you about Edward. I won't make the same mistake now. This Lucas has the same self-important bearing. Like he knows everything, and everyone must fall in line with him. Do as he commands. He'll try to step in and solve all your problems. Make you need him. Depend on him. And when that happens, he'll take you for granted. Use you."

Doubts trickled into her cheery mood and confidence. She refused to show it, unwilling to give Warren more fuel for his unreasonable argument.

"No. As he said, it isn't a big deal. He's merely passing along my account. It's a simple reference. I'm hiring them, not him." Agitated, she tapped her nails on the counter's glass top. "As for Edward, he was wrong. I wasn't always around. I left."

Warren jutted his stubborn, haughty chin. "Yeah, not because he treated you like shit. No, it took you going through his texts and finding all the women he had on the side to leave."

Tears of humiliation gathered behind her lashes. She'd been so stupid.

"Enough, Warren," Patricia said sharply.

"Fine." He made a dismissive gesture with a flick of his wrist, turning to Harper. "I'm merely trying to protect you. I'll wager a year's paycheck you'll never get a bill for the accounting shit. He'll pay it, handling whatever you allow him to, slowly and methodically taking control of you."

"No," she said firmly. "He isn't like that."

Warren's pitying look made her question her resolve. Was she ignoring signs because she was so drawn to Lucas?

As if sensing her doubts, Warren dug in, his voice oozing sympathy, as he said, "I love you, but let's face it, you aren't the best at deciding who gets your heart."

True. Her relationship record was dismal. However, Lucas was different. Right?

She faced Patricia, who'd become unexpectedly quiet. The woman always had something to say.

"Well, you know Lucas a little," Harper said, hating how pathetic she sounded. She loathed that she was begging for reassurance, but it didn't stop her. "You've been here during most of his visits. What's your opinion?"

Patricia glanced to the right, tapping her lip. After a long minute, she said, "There's no doubt the man is into you, and I highly doubt he's the deviant Warren is trying to paint, yet something is off. He runs into you after eight months have gone by and immediately begins pursuing you, yet he's completely fine with not being exclusive. Why? It's like he wants you, but not an actual relationship."

"Wait. What happened eight months ago?" Warren asked.

No way in hell was she going to share her hot night with Lucas. Or that he'd taken off before she woke. Or his reasons for doing it. Both would give Warren the fuel and match for his argument. She didn't need her doubts catching fire.

She waved him off, telling Patricia to continue.

"Okay. All I was going to say is I get the vibe he might be a commitment-phobia guy." She tilted her head toward Warren. "Like him, but instead of sleeping with everything that has breasts, your guy is good with one woman, happy not taking it deeper than pleasant dinners and fantastic sex."

Harper recalled her and Lucas's make-out session after their first pottery class. He been the one to put on the brakes. Telling her he wanted to prove he was after more than her body.

Those weren't the words of a man wanting only a shallow relationship.

Then again, their goodbye after yesterday's pottery class took nearly an hour and fogged all the car windows. He'd also asked her to come home with him.

He hadn't push when she refused. Now she wondered, was it because he was a gentleman, or merely not interested enough to pursue her with any real conviction?

No. He wouldn't keep stopping by with morning coffee and inviting her to dinner, if his interest was minimal. He wasn't after merely sex, or a friend. He wanted both. She was positive.

Her conviction returned, blossoming.

Patricia crushed it in a few short sentences. "Hell, maybe it's like you said," she shrugged, "he's got issues. I mean, he lost his wife. That has to mess with a person."

Warren's brows nearly reached his hairline. "The guy is a freaking widower? Oh man, that's some heavy baggage. You sure you want to carry it?"

"Enough." Harper knocked a palm onto the glass counter. "I'm going in the back to work on the painting I started yesterday." She needed space from her friends and doubts.

Patricia held up a hand. "Wait—"

Harper shook her head. "No more talk of Lucas. He and I are both very busy, barely having a spare minute to see each other. I don't need to worry about this crap you two are filling my head with. Anyway, we're keeping it light and fun. I'm not going to fall in love with the guy."

The last part tasted like a lie on her tongue, leaving bitter concerns to linger and stew in her once light heart.

Chapter Eleven

A light headache twisted, building along Harper's shoulders and neck. It wasn't the kind that threatened to bloom into a migraine. Those were brought on by loud noises and bright lights. This one was all anxious butterflies.

She made sure none of her triggers were present tonight. The lighting in the gallery was dim and inviting. Soft, soothing music floated from a purple baby grand tucked into a nook she had specially made for it. The talented pianist was doing a spectacular job of projecting a calm and enticing ambiance.

Not that she was serene. Her heart was pounding, her mind racing.

In the beginning, she feared no one would attend. When that didn't happen, anxiety bubbled, nibbling away at her confidence. It whispered people were going to hate the art, her gallery.

She pictured the society papers crucifying her, artists pulling their work, and her walls and bank account stripped bare.

The worst image she conjured: her mom trying to pretend she wasn't disappointed.

Harper ran her palms along the side of her silk dress, hoping she wasn't leaving a trail of nervous perspiration behind. She wished her mother hadn't been called out of town for work at the last minute. Her confidence and easy way with people would have helped to calm Harper's run-away doubts.

At least she had Patricia. The poor woman was almost as tense as Harper, and for some reason, she found comfort in it. Glancing at her, she gave a tight-lipped smile.

Maybe because it meant her friend took the success of the gallery seriously. It wasn't just something to do until her prince, dripping in diamonds, arrived to whisk her down the aisle.

Warren had also come and was his usual unflappable self. Nevertheless, it didn't transfer to Harper.

Nope. Her go-to for inner peace was her mom and Cindy.

Tonight, neither would be of help. Mother wouldn't return until tomorrow, and her cousin was having a mini freak-out.

She'd decided to take the leap with her writing and photography, making her a jittery mess. She was asking a million questions and quoting statistics about how many artists failed or barely made a living wage and were always hustling to sell their talent.

Harper understood her cousin's high level agitation. She was considering breaking away from her successful modeling career to pursue her art. That was scary enough, but unlike Harper's mother, Cindy's didn't even pretend to be supportive. She ridiculed her daughter whenever she stepped outside of what was deemed proper and respectable for their social circle.

Harper said a silent thank you to her mother.

She took a deep breath. Thanks to Mom, she'd never be a starving artist. However, money wouldn't protect Harper from failure.

Which meant she needed to do everything to make sure that didn't happen. She needed to ignore her fears, maybe avoid her cousin as well, and socialize.

She mingled with patrons, answering questions, chatting, and pretending she oozed confidence, all the while craving someone to lean on.

Lucas stepped behind her. She didn't have to turn to know it was him. His warmth and intoxicating scent wrapped around her, offering the comfort she needed this evening.

Twisting around, she fell into deep green eyes.

"Sorry, I'm late," he murmured near her ear. "I was working at a job site. It took longer than expected. Then I rushed home to shower and change. I didn't want to arrive here in dirty jeans and a sweaty T-shirt."

Worn cotton clinging to his broad chest, and warm, masculine sweat rolling off him was something she definitely wouldn't mind seeing. She took in his mouthwatering navy slacks and jacket with black lapels and matching tie. The crisp white shirt was the perfect finishing touch.

On second thought, she'd take both versions.

"No worries. I didn't expect you to be here from beginning to end." Although it did touch her heart it had been his plan. "Plus, I've spent most of the evening circulating the room without a moment's rest. You'd have been bored of staring at the same art you've seen for weeks now."

"Not at all. Your pieces and the others chosen for tonight are stunning and intricate. I always find something new when studying them." He squeezed her hand briefly. "Also, tonight is your night. I'm here to support you, not to be entertained."

Hell, had the man dipped into her mind, finding the perfect things to say?

He came around to stand in front of her, keeping a polite distance. Less civil was his gaze. It reflected lust and temptation. "I should tell you. I've been here for around fifteen minutes, watching you. The way you move in your dress could keep me distracted for hours. It's like midnight water flowing and caressing your curves."

Her cheeks warmed, and heat pulsed between her legs.

Wow, desire was fantastic at melting stress.

"Harper," Patricia said, breaking the sensual spell. She greeted Lucas before returning her attention to work. "We made another sale, but I need your help with this one."

"Okay." Harper rested a hand briefly on Lucas's arm. "Let me see what she needs. Then I have to make a quick circuit around the room, before coming back to you, okay?"

"Take your time. I'll be here." He smiled, appearing relaxed and happy.

He really was the perfect man. If she could have all of his heart, she'd never want for more.

Tonight wasn't the time to dwell on such things, and she shook away those thoughts.

Right now, her gallery needed her attention. It was her moment to prove her art wasn't merely a fanciful hobby.

Perhaps tomorrow was for deciding if this wonderful man was for her.

She followed Patricia, a touch of her stress prickling her nerves. Looking over her shoulder, she found Lucas again. He smiled, his calming presence reassuring her.

Hours later, she straightened a pile of receipts at the counter. The glow of success wrapped around her.

"The opening went well," she told Patricia. "The turn-out was great and we made some good sales. If we get lucky, it'll lead to media attention. If not, I've taken photos of everything that sold tonight, along with the pieces still for sale. All of it will be great for posting on social media to create a buzz."

"If you want to keep this momentum, you should do another party in a month or two," Patricia said, a big smile lighting her pretty face.

Harper clapped, unable to hold in her glee. "This might actually work," she practically squealed.

They embraced. "You're going to do it. You will be a success." Patricia patted Harper's back before stepping away. "I'm leaving. Go celebrate with your man."

"Lucas isn't my man." She watched him at the front of the gallery, locking the door, and wished her words were false.

"He wants to be. Don't listen to my earlier doubts. I was wrong. So is Warren. He's filling your head with them for his own reasons." As if sensing she was going to argue, Patricia shushed her. "I'm right."

"Okay. Fine, whatever. Forget Warren. I have my own reservations with Lucas."

Harper slumped onto the counter, resting her elbows on the glass. Suddenly, her worries made it difficult to stand straight.

"I get it. He has a history, but you do too. Edward and your father broke your faith in men. You expect the worst from them. I don't believe Lucas is like them."

Maybe. Trust wasn't her only issue.

What was her mom's mantra when it came to relationships? 'The key isn't falling for what's easy to like and admire in a person, it's learning their bad side and deciding if you're willing to love those parts too.'

His worst might be that he didn't have room in his heart for Harper. Would she have to settle for second place to the memories of his wife? Was she willing?

"What are you beautiful ladies whispering about?" Lucas strode toward them, holding two champagne flutes.

She jerked upright, guilt infusing her as she took in his tender smile. "You."

"Me? All good, I hope." He tried to hand a flute to Patricia.

She shook her head. "You have it. I'm going home."

He set his champagne on the counter. "It's late. I'll walk you to your car."

Patricia mouthed to Harper, "He's a keeper." Facing him, she said, "No, thanks. I valet parked."

"Okay. Drive carefully," he replied.

"You two have fun celebrating." She kissed his cheek, then Harper's before leaving in a flurry of expensive perfume and clicking stilettos.

"We do have to celebrate. I've been to a few of these parties. This one was by far the smoothest. Not to mention, has the best art. I'm proud of you." He handed her one of the champagne flutes.

His words were balm to her soul, though she acted like it wasn't a big deal and teased him. "I hope you mean *my* art was the best."

"Of course. That goes without saying." He kissed her, quick and light before lifting the other flute. He clicked it against hers. "To your success."

She sipped the bubbly drink. The crisp, tart taste was perfect.

"How long were you married?" she blurted, shocking herself.

Judging by his quiet gasp, she surprised him as well.

I guess a successful night and a few sips of champagne made me brave.

She backtracked. "I'm sorry. It's none of my business."

He took another swallow of his drink, like he needed the alcohol. "No. It was just unexpected. You never ask about my marriage."

"I've been afraid. I don't want to cause you pain."

She also feared his answers. Sure, almost three years had passed since he'd lost her, but if they'd been together since high school...

He set his glass on the table, running a finger along the rim. "We were married for almost two years."

She needed to ask her questions now, before her tiny bit of liquid courage dissipated. "Were you high school sweethearts?"

"No. We were together for less than a year before getting married." His gaze became far away as if he'd fallen into his memories. "I met her toward the end of my second year in college. I liked her immediately but didn't ask her out until our final semester."

"Why?"

"I didn't want to be distracted from my college shit. I had a feeling if we started dating, I'd want to give her all my time. Instead, when we ran into each other on campus and parties, we'd spend hours talking and such. During our final semester, she got tired of waiting and asked me to one of her sorority parties."

Harper chuckled. She'd have liked his wife.

Her heart hurt, ached for them, and for the woman she'd never meet. Her life was cut short, stolen from her. It made Harper feel like a thief for wanting her man.

"After we began dating things moved fast. It surprised the hell out of our family, but not us. We knew from the start." His smile turned sad. "Or maybe the fates understood the clock was ticking and didn't want us wasting any more time."

Damn it. She was wounding him.

She needed to do something to fix things but wasn't sure how.

"Fuck. I'm such a Debbie Downer," she muttered.

His loud bark of laughter lightened her.

"What?" She grinned shyly. "I love *Saturday Night Live*."

"While I'm not surprised you know the SNL skit, I can't believe you said 'fuck.' You rarely curse, let alone drop an F-bomb."

Hearing the deep rumble of his laughter at her teasing comment, knowing she chased away his sadness, made her feel like a queen.

She clutched his tie, bringing him to her lips. After kissing him deeply, she winked. "Hang around for a bit. You'll learn I'm full of surprises."

"I have no doubt." He rested his hands on her hips. "Now, how do you want to celebrate your successful evening?"

She shifted closer, leaving no space between them. Standing on tiptoes, she nipped his chin. "Didn't you promise me a drink at some fancy bar?"

Honestly, she didn't want a damn cocktail. She thirsted for the heat his eyes promised.

His hands tightened on her. With his body so close, the effect she was having on him was apparent. Yet, he stepped away and took her hand.

"I sure did." He started for the door. "Come on. I know a place close by."

She was tempted to tell him she was kidding, bringing him back into her arms, but that wasn't smart. She tended to lose all reasoning and caution around him, and they were in the middle of her gallery. One with large glass windows, and even at this late hour there was a chance someone might wander by. Best to keep things chaste.

At least for now.

Remembering her shawl, she stopped. "Wait, I need to get something from my office."

His heavy footsteps followed behind her. When they cleared the arch into her workspace, his soothing hands rested on her shoulders, thumbs kneading the knots that formed during the stressful evening.

Moaning in relief, she let her head fall forward. "That feels incredible. How do you know the exact spot?"

"I noticed your posture was stiff tonight. I tend to do the same. I'm familiar with where it hurts."

Her black silk dress had only two thin straps crisscrossing her back, tying at the arch of her spine and allowing plenty of skin to skin contact. His touch was heaven.

He traced her spine with his fingers as his lips skimmed lightly along her shoulder. The combination heated her blood while relaxing her muscles.

"This is my kryptonite," she breathed, reaching behind to grip his powerful thighs.

Chuckling, he asked, "My kisses or massages?"

He bit lightly on her bare shoulder. The slight sting of pain with pleasure made it impossible to answer. She dug her nails in deeper, reveling in his euphoric strength.

His hands dropped to her side, fisting her gown, lifting it slowly and seductively. "It's only fair. You and this dress have been driving me insane all evening. The way the silk slides over your legs, clutching your breasts, caressing your ass." He rubbed his erection against her backside. "I'm damn near drowning with the need to touch you. To taste you."

She twisted around, gripping his neck, kissing him with all the passion she'd kept in check during the party. He walked her backward, his tongue making love to her mouth as his hands continued to hitch her dress to her thighs. By the time the back of her legs bumped into the desk, the hem was nearly to her bottom.

The dress's fitted silk showed every line, so she'd skipped panties. She was precariously close to exposing herself.

She didn't care. Modesty had no place in his arms. When the dress was right below her ass, he asked if he should keep going. She nodded, anticipation coiling tight around her.

One of his hands clutched her gown, the other skated under it, to her hip. Finding bare skin, he groaned, breaking the kiss.

"No panties?" His voice dripped with desire.

She shook her head, biting her lip.

He slid a hand between her legs while trailing kisses from her collar to her chest. Her head fell back as pleasure zinged through her.

She was dimly aware of something clanking and rattling closer, but curiosity was impossible when Lucas was creating sinful magic with his hands and fingers.

Without warning, he moved away. Her eyes flew open, her gaze seeking him.

He hadn't gone far.

The earlier clatter had been him rolling the chair closer. He was sitting.

Between her legs.

She'd be self-conscious if he weren't wearing a predatory look of absolute hunger.

He slid his hands to her thighs, scooting closer. His fingers dug into her skin, and she involuntarily clenched in anticipation.

Seeming to take it as a wince, he blinked rapidly and loosened his hold. "Sorry. I'm hanging on by a thread here. Do you want me to stop?"

Hell. No.

Her crushing desire made her bold. She rested the arch of her foot on his shoulder and shook her head.

His expression was nearly feral. It spoke to her wild side.

He grasped her ankle dangling from the desk. Kissing it, he worked a sensual trail up her leg. By the time he reached the apex of her thighs, she was near mad with wanting.

Her fingers inched to grab his head and take him where she needed him.

It wasn't necessary. He gripped her waist, pulling her to the edge of the desk, and taking what they both wanted.

His mouth and tongue were enchanting and had her climaxing in minutes. She cried his name as her hands slid through his hair, clutching him tightly, needing to hold on to him as she fell apart.

The pleasure was exquisite, almost more than she could handle. She pushed him away, pleading for mercy.

His low chuckle vibrated, melting into her raw bliss. He ran his tongue along the inside of her thigh. When he was near her knees, he kissed both before standing, bringing her into his arms.

First, a mind-blowing orgasm, now the comfort of his embrace. Was he trying to meld her heart to his?

There wasn't a millimeter of space between them, his arousal insistent and enticing against her stomach.

However, when she went for his belt, he stepped away, taking her hand in his.

"I don't expect you to reciprocate," he said, nipping her ear.

"This isn't about returning a favor. It's taking what I want." She purred before licking his Adam's apple.

A shudder ran through him at her play, showing her he wanted what she desired to give. Yet, when she tried again, he held tighter.

She cocked a brow, bumping her hips to his groin. "You honestly want to deny what we both want?"

"Temporarily. If you touch me, my restraint is going to snap. I'll bend you over this desk, taking you, rough and reckless. I want to give you more than that."

The image played in her kinky mind. Her greedy body flushed with wet heat. She needed him on her tongue, or giving her another toe-curling orgasm.

She tried for his belt.

He held tight.

"You have a thing for restraints?" She rubbed against him.

His hardness against the silk of her dress hit all the right spots. She moaned, her eyes fluttering shut.

He brought her hands around her back, pinning them together. Her breasts were thrust forward, pressing against his chest.

"I have a thing for you," he murmured, his voice lava seduction.

Ducking, he used his mouth to play with her nipples, teasing them through her dress. The soft material stroked her needy buds.

She arched against him. He groaned, grinding into her. The contact made her whole body beg for more.

"Lucas, please."

"Come home with me," he said, against her heated skin. "Stay the night. I've had a taste of you. Now I want to worship your body for hours."

She'd never wanted anything so much, but worry whispered under her desire. If he had midnight regrets again, her heart would break.

She searched his face. "Are you sure?"

He cupped her cheek, a little of his heat dimming. "Yes. Listen, I know, I fucked up our first night together. I won't this time. I swear. I'm ready."

"Sure, your body yearns for mine, but does your heart?" Placing a hand on his chest, she smiled, feeling it frantic beat. His body was stiff with what she assumed was alarm. "Don't worry, I'm not asking if you love me, it's too soon. I'm wondering if it is a possibility. Someday. Is there room in your heart for me as well?"

The courage to ask such a bold question surprised her to the core, even if it shouldn't. She was falling for him and couldn't bear to be a consolation prize.

She needed to know. Was he able to love only one woman? His wife.

He sucked in a slow breath, exhaling through his nose. Dropping his hand from her cheek, he shook his head. "You're asking me to predict the future, my feelings. That's impossible."

She swallowed her soul-crushing disappointment as bile from her fading happiness churned in her stomach.

Well, she did ask for honesty. She couldn't blame him because she didn't like the answers.

Pulling herself together, she was going to suggest they stick to a celebratory drink, taking separate cars, when he grasped her chin.

"All I can tell you about is right now. The present. I want to be around you every damn second. I want you in my bed at night and to wake with a smile each morning because you're next to me. You make me laugh, smile, feel alive." He kissed the corner of her mouth. "Is that enough, for now?"

She hugged him tight. "Yes. Now, let's go home. To your place."

Chapter Twelve

"Do you mind if we drive together? We can take your car. Wait," Lucas paused. "Did you drink?"

She glanced at the ceiling as if trying to recall how much she drank. "Not much. I made a toast at the start of the evening. Maybe took a sip or two of champagne throughout the night. Oh, yes, there was the glass you gave me at closing. However," she smiled shyly, "I'm sure our backroom fun burned off all the alcohol in my system."

Craving another taste of her, he kissed her neck, running his lips along her collarbone. He leaned back to check in with her. "Ready?"

She nodded. "Oh, yes."

They shut off the lights, and after locking the door to her gallery, she asked. "But why do you want to leave your car here? We could drive separately."

"No way. I'm not letting you out of my sight," he teased, bringing her against him.

She laughed. "What? You afraid I'm going to change my mind and head home?"

He squeezed her hip playfully. "I'm not willing to risk it."

"Oh, please. After what you started in my office, I'm *so* not ready to call it a night."

Jesus, her candor and confidence is such a turn-on.

Opening the main gold and glass door of the building, he stepped aside, letting her pass. "Aren't you an insatiable woman?"

"Yes, I am." She shifted, her hand subtly caressing him as she passed. "Are you *up* for the challenge?"

Shit. Up and hard as freaking steel.

"Come here," he growled, kissing her until they were both breathless, and he was aching. He needed to get her in bed and under him. Now. "Where's your car?"

"This way." She took his hand. "Aren't you worried, leaving yours here? I'm almost positive the parking attendant doesn't stay all night."

"They don't, but it doesn't matter. I drove my truck in because Ben wanted to use it tomorrow. He took it home."

"You have a truck?"

"Yes, an F-150. I need it for both businesses. Ben and I started with house rentals. We've kept the highly profitable ones. The truck is necessary for maintenance before or after tenants leave. I also use it for my business. I'm hired not only to tell them what they need to do for the LEED certification, but I also help with the physical converting." He shrugged. "Anyway, Ben needed it tomorrow for one of the rentals. I drove it in. He took it home."

"What if I wasn't able to go out after? You would've been stranded here." She smiled, amusement dripping from her words.

He laughed. "Ben doesn't live far from me. He'd have come if I called. Or I'd have called an Uber."

She shook her head. "No. No. I like the fantasy playing in my mind. The one where you're at my mercy."

Desire thrummed through him, his wicked fantasies playing with hers. "Is that so? Do tell..."

Arriving at her car, she clicked the unlock button, her gaze never leaving his. The smirk she wore was pure sin.

"I'd rather show you," she purred.

"Woman, you're killing me." He groaned, opened his door, and slid into the passenger seat.

He adjusted himself, trying and failing to get comfortable. The anticipation was sweet torture.

She asked for his address. After pulling into the street, she skated a warm palm up his inner thigh.

He closed his eyes, his head falling back, letting her do as she pleased. He was too turned on to care if she exposed him to vehicles riding much higher than her sleek Mercedes. All that mattered were her magic, teasing hands.

Reaching the zipper of his slacks, she gripped him through the material. He dug his fingers into the supple leather of the seat as his blood and lust shot toward her tantalizing touch.

"Harper," he begged. Not sure if he was pleading for her to keep going or to stop. He was close to losing control.

"Yes?" Her voice dripped with debauchery.

Nope. He most definitely *didn't* want her to stop.

She popped the first button of his slacks. "Which one?"

"Huh?" he grunted.

Confusion dragged him from her touch, and he took in his surroundings. They were on his street. He wanted to shout in relief.

"The one on the left." His words were thick and heavy with desire. "The Tudor with the green slate roof and trim."

As soon as the car was in park, he yanked open his door and came around to her side, helping her out. She gave him the keys. Sliding them in his pocket, he lifted her in a bridal-style hold and nearly sprinted to the front door.

Laughing, she wrapped her arms around his neck. "What has you so impatient?"

"You and your busy hands."

In record time, he was stepping onto the porch. He hunched to get the key in the door without having to let go of Harper.

"What about my eager lips?" She trailed hot kisses on his jaw. He felt them all the way to his dick.

"Yeah, I like those too. I want these lips," he kissed her once, hard and quick, "on my mouth and the other ones gripping me tight as I bury myself deep inside you."

She smacked his shoulder. "Lucas! You dirty man."

He heard the wicked tone in her voice and met her gaze. Yup, she was hedonistic seduction.

"Are you sure that's how you want to play? I do believe your cock would look lovely with my lipstick on it," she purred.

Pushing through the door, he stumbled a step. This woman was full of sexy surprises.

"I can't believe you just said that," he choked.

She raised a brow. "Why? Does it bother you? Do you prefer your woman prim and proper?"

"Hell, no. I love your filthy mouth. It matches my dirty mind. The only problem we'll have is you're going to have me going off like a fucking bomb well before either of us are ready."

He tossed the keys on the rough foyer table, where they slid across the wooden surface before hitting the floor. Fuck it. He wasn't searching for them now.

Toeing off his shoes, he started for the bedroom while she worked on the buttons of his shirt. Something thudded to the ground as they passed through the living room.

He stopped. "What was that?"

"My heels. I'll get them later." She kissed his throat, moving to his jaw. "Keep going, and get in the bedroom. Now."

"What? You don't want a tour of the house?" He smiled.

"The only thing that interests me," she hummed, "is seeing you naked and pleasuring me."

"Woman, your mouth is as hot as your curves."

Once in his room, he laid her on his king-size bed, prowling over her body. He conquered her mouth with his lips, while cupping her breasts, caressing and teasing her into a frenzy. He didn't stop his play until her breaths became pants, and her words unintelligible.

He might have taken away her ability to talk, but her nimble fingers were perfection. She deftly unbuttoned his shirt before moving to the zipper of his slacks.

Shifting to his side, he shrugged out of his button-up before removing his T-shirt. She slid a hand inside his pants, and he groaned in ecstasy as her soft, skilled hand wrapped around his hard length. He rocked with her firm strokes.

Letting go, she tugged on his pants. "Take these off. I need to feel more of you."

Happy to comply, he did as she demanded. Then he reached for the lamp on his nightstand, flicking on its lowest setting.

She blinked. "Why?"

"Because I need to see you." He fisted a handful of her dress, pausing when he noticed the slight tense set of her spine. "Does the light bother you? I don't want you to be uncomfortable, but you are gorgeous. You have curves begging to be savored with the eyes and by touch."

A shy smile played on her lovely mouth. "Well, when you put it like that..."

She scooted to the center of the bed, raising her arms over her head. Whoever had made her doubt her beauty was an asshole of the first degree. He'd love to break who'd done it to her.

Instead, he focused on the fact that she trusted him enough to set aside her insecurities.

Determined to make sure she didn't regret her decision, he took his time telling her how much he loved her body, from her smooth, creamy skin to her sensual curves and so much more.

When he dragged the fabric up past her hips, then her breasts, he lost his words. Desire choked him.

She'd skipped all her undergarments. He took in smooth flesh, pert nipples, and wet thighs, begging for him to please her.

"Damn. I'm so fucking glad you let me leave on the light," he rumbled, lust thick in his voice.

"Me too," she whispered. "The way you look at me makes me feel beautiful."

"It should. You're stunning."

Tracing her collarbone with his finger, he trailed it between her breasts, to the underside of each. He bent, flicking a nipple with the tip of his tongue.

She gasped and gripped his head, keeping him there. He was more than happy to stay. His hands continued to explore her sweet body, taking his fill of warm, velvet skin.

When that wasn't enough, he made his way to her lips, capturing her mouth with his. He thrust along her, aching to be in her.

As if reading his mind, she wrapped her legs around his waist, rubbing against him.

In a needy whisper, she pleaded, "Please."

He was right there. All he had to do was move forward, and he'd be sinking into her hot, blissful euphoria. Before his willpower snapped, he shifted, opening his nightstand drawer for a condom.

She tightened her hold, stopping him. "Could we skip using a condom?"

He froze. Being closer to her definitely worked for him, but the request was a surprise, given her hesitation to even date him.

"I don't want anything to separate us," she whispered. "I've been on birth control for years. Also, I saw my doctor after we slept together at the wedding. I got tested, and everything is fine. haven't been with anyone since then."

He let go of the handle, bringing his hand to her forehead, smoothing her hair. "Same. I've only been with you."

There was one time he'd come close. Yet, when he kept picturing Harper, he'd stopped before things went further.

"Are you okay going without?" she asked.

With you. Yes.

He nodded.

"Then, please, Lucas. Now."

He took his time, going slow, watching for signs of discomfort. The heels of her feet hooked under his ass, urging him on, and he sank into her warm, tight heat.

Pleasure shot through him, ripping a guttural groan from his throat.

"Fuck. Harper." He growled against her neck, finding a rhythm made her clench tight around him.

She rocked, urging him with her hips and breathless moans. When her legs fell to his sides, he shifted her on top of him.

Without hesitation, she took control. Sliding her legs under her, she rose, her hands clutching his shoulder, riding him as if she owned him.

Hell, maybe she does.

His orgasm coiled tight, but he wanted her to go first.

He slid a hand to where they were connected, searching with his fingers to find the sweet spot that would have her tumbling into bliss. When she began to pant and urge him on, he kept working her with one hand, gripping her waist with his other, demanding her climax.

Right before she detonated, she pressed every inch of herself against him. Kissing him, whispering against his lips that she was almost there, and she wanted him to come with her.

He rolled her onto her back and thrust into her fast and deep. She cried out his name as her body shuddered and stiffened. Her pleasure took him over the edge. Together, they plummeted into orgasmic ecstasy.

Chapter Thirteen

Waking, Harper reached for Lucas. His side of the bed was empty. The sheets cold. Déjà vu crashed into her.

She opened her eyes, muttering, "Are you flipping kidding me?"

Tented on his pillow was a bright pink piece of paper. Written in huge bold, black letters was one word: *Coffee.*

What the hell?

Picking it up, she saw there was a note scribbled on the other side.

I really hope you don't wake until I'm back because I know what you're going to think. I slept soundly and woke a happy man. I'm out of coffee and milk, and I'm dying a slow death without them. I went to get some.

On the dresser is a pair of my boxers and a T-shirt for you.

Now is your chance to snoop and find out all my dirty secrets. Have fun!

Laughing, she set the letter on his pillow. Spying the clothes, she kicked off the covers and padded across the bedroom.

She scooped up the clothes and set off to find a bathroom. His house was older, probably on the historical registry. Meaning, it was beautiful and unique but didn't have all of the modern luxuries. Such as a master bath.

After a stressful night at the gallery's opening and three rounds of vigorous sex, this girl needed a shower.

She found the bathroom at the end of a narrow hallway, in the center between two bedrooms. The style, location, and layout shouted 1920's, but the bathroom was a modern dream. Her favorite feature was the large rain shower head.

That, and using Lucas's bath products. They smelled like him.

The combination of his heady scent and the warm water soothed her tender areas. Soon her body tingled. The slight throbbing between her legs switched to a different sort of ache. She toyed with the idea of waiting in the shower until he came home, luring him in with her.

Her stomach growled, changing her mind. Food first, then sex.

Giddy with her plans, she whistled an off-key tune while drying herself and getting dressed. She had to roll the boxers several times to keep them on her hips. The shirt hit mid-thigh, and the sleeves ended at her elbows.

Oh well, better than scoping out his place in the nude.

After brushing her teeth, and hoping he didn't mind her using his toothbrush, she snooped, or rather, took a quick tour of the house.

The first room she ducked into appeared to be his home office. There was a large, black metal desk piled high with papers. In the center was a closed laptop, and behind it was a plush office chair. Besides the dark, braided rug covering most of the oak floors, there were no personal touches, not a framed picture or a single piece of art on the walls.

The other room across the hall had even less personality. The walls were white with gray blinds on the two windows. Opened and unopened boxes were scattered everywhere.

His bedroom was the same. There was nothing on the dressers or the walls.

This was a house, not a home. Perhaps he moved in recently. Or maybe, he bought it with his wife right before she died.

A terrible thought struck her. What if her presence was intruding on the few happy memories he made here?

Some of her buoyant mood drained as Harper closed the spare bedroom's door.

She wandered toward the living room. From there, she spotted a piece of paper taped to the front door. Smiling, she removed it.

In case you missed the note on my pillow. I went to get coffee and breakfast. Make yourself comfortable. I'll be back soon. There are clothes for you on the dresser.

On second thought, if you're at the front door naked, please stay that way.

On third thought, move to the couch. I have a nosy neighbor across the street whose hobby is spying on everyone from his front window. He'd LOVE to see you naked, but too bad for him, only I get such a morning delight.

She snorted. Lucas was cute *and* funny.

As she re-read the note, the lock clicked, and the door swung open. She squeaked and jumped back.

"Shit! Sorry." A paper bag slipped from his hand as he reached for her.

Clutching his arm to steady herself, she grinned. Scruffy Lucas was new. And hot.

He wore faded jeans, a threadbare T-shirt, and a baseball cap. There was even the shadow of a beard.

Casual on him was as deadly sexy as his tailored suits.

"Nice boyfriend." She stuttered over the title, but when his smile brightened, she savored the taste of claiming him. "He deprives me of wake-up sex, then tries to knock me out with his front door."

"But I brought coffee and bagels." He showed her a cardboard tray with two travel mugs before grabbing the bag he'd dropped. It smelled of carby goodness.

She grabbed one of the coffees and took a small sip. Then a bigger one. "Okay. You're forgiven for trying to kill me with your door."

He chuckled. "What about missing wake-up sex?"

"I'll have to get back with you. Let me see how good those bagels are."

"They are excellent. Nonetheless, I can guarantee they aren't as tasty as sex with you." He kissed her, two playful pecks before taking the post-it note from her. He ran a finger across the neck of her borrowed T-shirt. "You found the note on the pillow, huh?"

She laughed. "Yup."

"Damn..." He playfully pouted.

"Feed me." She pointed with her chin at the gray leather couch. "Afterward, we can test out the back of that. Discover if it really is perfect for bending me over it."

She started toward the kitchen, but his quick steps caught her. He wrapped a hand around her waist, pressing into her. The bag crinkled, warm against her bare legs.

"You know, suddenly I'm not hungry for food," he murmured against her neck, teasing her with his lips and teeth.

She kept walking, closing her eyes and focusing on the all-consuming sensation that was Lucas. Her bare feet hit something, and it clattered against the wood floor.

Glancing at the floor, she saw one of the high heels she'd dropped last night. The other was closer to the wall.

Taking in the rest of the space, she spotted Lucas's button-up, crumbled on the ground half inside his bedroom. Recalling the heat and need as they made their way to his bed had desire blooming low and heavy in her stomach.

They had sex three times during the night, and while both deeply satisfying, she wanted him again. This near constant fevered need was new and unsettling. What if she began to need him like a drug and couldn't break the addiction?

Somehow, he managed to steer her into the kitchen. After emptying his hands, he turned her, his lips teasing hers. She set her mug on the table, no longer craving caffeine. She clutched his waist, bringing him closer and deepening the kiss.

He wrapped a fist around her damp hair and tugged gently, halting her exploration. "Eat. Drink your coffee."

She blinked, puzzled at the abrupt shift. "That's not what I want anymore."

"Me neither." He stepped from her, opening the bag of bagels. "But I don't remember you eating any of the snacks during your gallery's opening. I bet you skipped lunch too."

"I ate some almonds before everyone arrived," she muttered, sliding into a chair, accepting the sesame bagel he offered.

• • • • ● • ● • • •

Lucas gathered their dishes, dumping them into the sink. Turning, he caught Harper dipping, then licking the knife from the cream cheese. "Taste good?"

Smiling, she nodded. She was freaking adorable.

He took the knife from her and tossed it on to the counter. She hooked her fingers through his belt loops, yanking him against her.

"I ate two bagels heaped with cream cheese. Will you be a gentleman and help me burn off some of those calories?"

Slipping a hand under her T-shirt, he cupped her breast. "I'm happy to be your man, but do I have to be gentle?"

He pinched her nipple and drank in the way her breath caught. She matched him perfectly when it came to sex. They both liked a mix of rough and tender.

They were compatible out of the bedroom as well, and with her pulling on the zipper of his jeans, his mind was absorbed with the carnal side of things.

He laid her on the kitchen table and gripped the waist of her borrowed boxers. Right before he yanked them off, Ben's voice boomed from the front of the house.

"Lucas, you asshole, half the tools I need aren't in the truck."

Shit. Giving him a key was the worst idea ever.

"Ben, give me a minute," Lucas hollered. He faced a wide-eyed Harper. "Sorry," he whispered. "I'll get rid of him."

Lust turned to lead as he left the kitchen. Ben was a good man, but he probably wasn't going to welcome her with open arms. When Lucas mentioned he was talking to the gallery owner in their building. Ben hadn't been happy.

He tried to pretend it bothered him from a business standpoint, but that was bullshit. They both knew it.

Harper and Ben in the same room would be a disaster. She wanted to forget he had a past, and his brother-in-law wanted him to remain there, forever in love with Elizabeth's ghost.

A man could only hold on to yesterday for so long. Lucas treasured every minute he spent with his wife and held tight to those memories. However, he'd relegated them to his past, in order to have a future.

He hoped Harper would realize this eventually. He figured the more time passed, the easier it'd become for her to understand and accept.

This morning was too soon.

Rounding the corner from the kitchen, he stopped short. Ben stood in the hallway, staring at Harper's high heels.

"Is someone here?" he asked.

Before Lucas could answer he heard Harper's bare feet close by. Ben's expression hardened.

She didn't seem to notice. When she moved around Lucas and offered her hand to Ben, her smile was warm. Thankfully, he didn't refuse the greeting.

"Are you Ben? The other owner of the Salvador building?" she asked. "It's nice to meet you."

He nodded stiffly, taking in her oversized T-shirt and boxers. "I take it you're the gallery owner Lucas is *seeing*."

She let go of Ben's hand as if he injured her. In a way, he had, with his attitude.

"Ben," Lucas warned. He wrapped an arm around Harper's waist.

"Whatever." His brother-in-law swung open the front door. "I need the red box of tools you forgot to put into the truck. Is it in the garage or the spare room?"

Lucas pulled his lips into a tight line, trying to decide if he should call Ben out for being a jerk. In the end, he figured it best for him to get his shit and leave.

He pointed with his chin. "The garage."

Ben backtracked to the porch, retreating down the steps toward the detached two-car garage. Lucas followed.

When Ben dropped from the top step, he asked, "Are you going to meet me there later to help."

Lucas shrugged. "I want to see what Harper has planned today. Plus, it's Saturday. Take a break, man."

"I'd love to, but there's work to be done." Ben kicked the cement with his steel-toed boot. "What happened to your promise of being more involved with our business? First, you bailed on me when Liz died. Now that you're moving on with your life, promises are forgotten, right?"

"I've been busting my ass to make up for the mess I created. How many times do I have to apologize?" Guilt mixed with his growing anger. Lucas gripped the porch railing. "You aren't being fair. Yesterday you never mentioned needing my help."

"Well, I'm saying it now."

"And I'm telling you, I'll let you know."

"Fine. Do whatever you want." Ben headed to the garage.

Lucas stepped backward into the house, closing the door slowly. The click of the latch somehow sounded ominous. He didn't have to look at Harper to know their perfect morning was ruined.

No sense avoiding it.

He faced her. "I'm sorry. He's being an asshole."

She pinned him with her gaze, crossing her arms over her chest. "No doubt. Why does he hate me?"

"He doesn't."

"It's too early in the morning for his shit and your lies." Pivoting on her heel, she stomped to the kitchen.

He went after her and found her sitting at the table, sipping her coffee. She was obviously pissed. He wasn't sure what to say without upsetting her more.

She spoke first. "Is it a big deal to him that I'm renting one of your shops and dating you?"

Rubbing the back of his neck, Lucas took the seat next to her. He considered playing dumb, positive the real reason would bother her.

Ben and Harper both seemed to believe he was incapable of caring for two women. That it was impossible for him to love Elizabeth's memory while falling for another woman.

Unease spilled through him. Was he falling in love? Maybe.

Was he ready for it? Probably not.

It terrified him, but she was worth the fear, the possible loss, and devastation.

However, first, he needed to find out if she could handle the fact he had a life before her. "Ben is Elizabeth's brother."

"Your partner at G&D is your brother-in-law?" she asked, her voice rising in pitch.

Lucas sat, propping his elbows on the table, linking his fingers together. "Yup. The idea was Ben and Elizabeth's, and they handled most of it since I had my consulting company."

He took her hand resting next to his coffee mug. She didn't flip and link their fingers, as she had earlier, but at least she didn't pull away.

"After Elizabeth's death, her shares went to me. I didn't want hers or mine. I tried to give them to Ben. He wouldn't take them. I didn't argue. I didn't do shit. I gave up on everything for nearly a year." He shrugged as a chill ran down his spine. Those dark days of depression still scared the hell out of him. "Anyway, I got better. I'm trying to make amends for bailing on him when he needed me as a friend and business partner, but it hasn't been easy. Things aren't the same between us. I offered him my shares again. The stubborn ass, once again, refused. Anyway, he and Elizabeth were super close, and he sees me as some sort of link to her. I believe you and I dating bothers him."

Harper drummed the side of her mug. The light sound clinked around the otherwise silent kitchen.

Lucas waited.

She stood. "I need to go."

Anger washed through him. He'd shared a slice of his pain, and her reaction was to run. "That's it? Every time you're reminded I was married, that I loved someone else, you take off?"

"I'm not running. My—"

"Don't tell me it's work again," he folded his arms across his chest. "Or you're busy and don't have time for a relationship. If I'm important enough, you'll make time. So, which is it? Am I nothing special to you, or are you punishing me because I had a life before you?"

"Don't be ridiculous. We aren't teenagers. We've both lived lives before meeting each other."

"Then why when a piece of mine arrives at my front door, you suddenly *have* to leave?"

"Ben has nothing to do with it. My mom's arriving home from her business trip this afternoon. We're supposed to meet to discuss the opening."

She left the kitchen, her half-truths following close behind her.

He heard her grab her shoes. Next would be her dress. Last, the click of the front door closing.

Her dismissal of him, of them, hurt. It pissed him off too.

Maybe she didn't want to date anyone, or more specifically, him. But there was no doubt Ben's connection to Lucas freaked her out. She was acting the same as when she learned he was a widower.

He understood her hesitation that time. The way he left in the middle of the night screamed a man with major issues. However, this time, this hang-up wasn't his. This one was Harper's.

He went to find her. His new place was much smaller so it would be easy.

He sold his old house last year. It was more space than he needed. Plus, it had him drowning in memories and what-ifs.

Glancing in the living room, it hit him: this place was no more a home than his last one. There was no real life, devoid of things that make it a home. No pictures, no mementos. Almost everything was still in boxes.

Same with the hallway. Nothing. Not even a poster or print.

He learned to survive after Elizabeth's death, but had he really begun to live?

Noise from the bedroom snagged his attention, making him forget his boring-ass, empty house. Harper had laid her dress on the bed and was staring at it. The silk was a crumbled mess.

A floorboard creaked under him, and she turned. Her eyes were so damn sad.

His anger drained away. Whatever her issues, she did care about him. At least a little bit.

He came inside the room. "Will you tell me what's wrong? Please."

She sighed, misery on her exhale. "It's nothing. I'm tired. Drained from yesterday. From last night." That earned him a ghost of a smile. "I want to sleep all day. Instead, I have to go home to change, pack a bag, then meet my mom for dinner."

"It isn't Ben? The way he acted?" He replayed what she said in his mind. "Wait. Pack a bag. Where are you going?"

"My mom's. I asked Patricia to manage the gallery for a few days. After the stress of organizing the opening, I need a few days with my art."

"Time away from me, as well?"

She broke eye contact. *Damn it.*

"Maybe. I should be concentrating on my art, my gallery. And you're very distracting." She offered her favorite excuse and another weak smile. He didn't return it.

"Anyway," she continued, "I want the gallery out of my mom's name by the end of the year. Which means I need to create more pieces and find more artists. I don't have time for a boyfriend."

Well, there was the answer to his question if she wanted more. The answer was loud and clear. No.

"Fine. Do what you need to do." He turned to leave the bedroom, planning on giving her the space she desired.

She stopped him with a hand on his bicep. "I like you, Lucas."

He shoved his fists into his pockets, letting her hand fall away. "Great. Let me know when you like me enough for more than a coffee break and a fuck."

She jerked as if slapped. "You're not being fair."

Is she kidding?

"I'll get a bag for your dress. You can wear my stuff home."

"Thanks," she whispered.

He offered a quick jerk of his head. "Guess I'm helping Ben today. I'm going to get in the shower."

Walking from the bedroom, he nodded a goodbye, unable to say the words.

Chapter Fourteen

When the pipes to the shower rattled and hissed, Harper gathered her regrets and ruined dress to leave. She wanted to be gone before Lucas was done.

It hurt too much, this pretending like she didn't care.

Yet, the truth was worse.

His anger was devastating, but she'd take it over disgust. He'd hate her. Hell, she hated herself for her stupid, jealous thoughts.

He was wrong. She did want more than his body. She wanted all of him, his present and future.

But his past was in the way.

Quietly closing the front door, she hurried to her car. Getting in, she blinked back warm tears.

They were for her and Lucas. For a situation she made impossible because of her fragile, weak confidence and her damn, envious heart. If it were ripped from her chest, she'd find it beating green instead of red.

That was what made her drive away, acting as if she didn't care. She couldn't admit to him it wasn't because he had a life before her. No, what killed her was he loved his old life. He'd take it and his wife back in a heartbeat.

Elizabeth was his first choice. Harper was forever his consolation prize.

Ben's attitude drove home the point. Lucas's past would always be part of his present. It, and his wife's ghost, would follow them everywhere, reminding Harper who he'd rather love.

Part of her understood she was acting stupid and selfish. She was nearly thirty, and he was older. Most people their age had baggage from previous entanglements.

Maybe her problem was a lack of relationships and impossible expectations. Just because she never loved someone with all her heart, didn't mean she should expect the same from him.

Logic and reasoning didn't matter. She wanted it so bad with him it ate at her soul.

"I'm an idiot," she muttered, wiping away a stray tear.

At a red light, she scrolled through her many playlists until she found her workout music. After hitting play, the loud beat and heavy bass boomed through her car's speakers. It didn't completely obliterate her sadness, but it did help.

The rest of the drive, she used every trick she knew to clear her mind of Lucas. She thought of the slab of marble waiting for her at Mom's, blasted her favorite songs, even came up with a few lines of bleak poetry.

Harper decided to skip stopping at her place, and by the time she parked in her mother's driveway, the lump of tears lodged in her throat had shrunken from a boulder to a fist of marbles.

Clicking the button attached to her car's visor, she waited, then parked in her bay of the five-car garage. She was surprised to see her mother's Audi parked in its spot.

What was she doing home? Her flight wasn't due for another three hours.

Stepping into the hallway from the garage, Harper called to her mom. She was met with silence. No big surprise; the house was huge.

She came around to the stairs and shouted for her mom. This time she answered. "I'm in my bedroom, honey. Unpacking. Come tell me how the opening went."

Even in her morose mood, the reminder of her successful opening put a bounce in her step as she made her way to the second floor.

Her mother's suitcase lay open on her bed, and she was striding toward the master bathroom, cradling a pile of clothes in one arm. Even after a five-hour early morning flight, her mother was the epitome of graceful beauty.

She stopped and scanned Harper. One elegant brow arched as she took in Lucas's oversized T-shirt and boxers.

Dropping the clothes in a hamper, she said, "Fun evening? Did you celebrate your successful night with a handsome stranger or Lucas?"

There was no censure in her tone. Her mother wasn't the type to judge.

Plus, she didn't do relationships. The last one was with Harper's father. He'd left to marry his high school sweetheart, giving them a lame apology, saying he never stopped loving her.

Now, Mother's men were young, gorgeous, and didn't want anything serious. If they did, she left them in a heartbeat.

She'd never be harping for grandchildren. It was a relief and a little depressing.

"I was with Lucas. We're seeing each other," Harper said. A jolt of sadness shot through her. "Well, we *were* seeing each other. I told him I didn't have time for a boyfriend right now."

"Oh." Her mother cringed. "Was the sex that bad?"

Harper laughed. "No, the sex was fantastic. His personality is great too, Mom."

She waved this off, gathering more clothes from her suitcase. "They're all terrific gentlemen. In the beginning."

Harper shook her head, resting against the doorframe. "You might be a tad jaded."

Her mom raised a hand, index and thumb an inch apart. "Maybe a smidgen, but who cares? The ones I date don't mind my attitude, and I'm fond of them. I even enjoy them." Her smile turned impish. "Just not for their personalities."

Harper rolled her eyes. "Well, I like all of Lucas."

"Then why did you tell him you didn't want to be his girlfriend?"

"Because I'm busy. I need to focus on the gallery, my art," she repeated her mantra.

Maybe if she said it enough, she'd believe it. Coming inside, she sat on the edge of her mother's bed. She needed to unload. "He's a widower. I feel like his wife's ghost goes everywhere with us."

Her mother froze in the middle of zipping her now empty suitcase. "Lucas from the gallery, the one who owns the building?"

"Yes, him."

"Wow." Mother slid the Louis Vuitton luggage from the bed. It hit the hardwood floor with a muffled clunk. "He's so young. Was it recent?"

"His wife passed away somewhere around three years ago. Why?"

"I wondered if you were a rebound. Was he married for years?" She waved a hand. "Never mind. Time doesn't matter with love. It's different for each person. What matters is, do *you* think you're a rebound? And do you care?"

"I wish I didn't. After learning of Edward's million betrayals, I vowed to take a break. Keep things simple and fun. I'm finding it difficult with Lucas."

"What does he want?"

"I believe he wants more. He was pissed at my brush off this morning, but I'm not sure he's ready."

"Why?"

She told the whole story. About the night at Greta's wedding, his explanation, and finished with Ben and her fight with Lucas.

Admitting all of this was slightly embarrassing, but also a relief. She loved talking with her mother. She was a busy woman, and Harper spent most of her childhood alone or with nannies, but whenever there was a problem, her mom always listened, offering comfort and advice without judgment.

"Wow. You two were off to a rocky start," she said. "I'm not sure what to tell you. His reaction your first night together, coupled with the fact you're the only woman he's been with since his wife is worrisome."

"Well, there was eight months between the wedding and when we ran into each other again at the gallery."

Although she doubted he slept with anyone between then and now, either. He basically admitted it when she asked him to skip the condom.

"True," her mom said. " That's what makes me believe he *thinks* he wants more with you."

"Thinks?" She heard the hesitation in her mother's voice.

She patted Harper's knee. "As I said, love is complicated. Messy. Unfinished love is a freaking disaster. You saw it with your father and me. When we break up with someone, bad memories outweigh the good, making it easier to get over the person. If it's unfinished, the what-ifs and happy times tend to erase the ugly memories. That's a lot of competition for you."

She rested her head on her mom's shoulder, running her words through her mind, trying to separate the truths from fallacies. An antique clock ticked on a mahogany dresser, counting off her indecisions.

"Did I ever tell you, your father's wife—"

"The one he cheated on you with and abandoned me for?" Harper spit with enough venom to kill.

Her mother's quiet, breathy laughter brushed against Harper's forehead, ruffling a few rogue hairs. "Yes. Her. She was your father's high school sweetheart—"

"I know all this."

"Hush, daughter. Let me tell the whole story."

"Sorry." She made a zipping motion across her lips.

"The reason they split," her mother continued, "was because she and her family moved overseas her senior year. The way he'd reminisce about his time with her, I knew he hadn't let her go. I hoped one day I'd be enough. I wasn't." She pointed at herself. "That was my fault. I shouldn't have settled for someone who was in love with another person."

Harper took in what her mom told her. She was aware of the 'old-flame' part, but not that her father was in love with another woman when he married her mother. Or how he made her feel like she wasn't enough. Her loathing for her dad grew.

It also filled her with doubts about Lucas.

"Well, shit, Mom, that's depressing. For you and me. I meet a great guy, and you're basically saying we're doomed."

"One. Don't be sad for me. I got you out of the deal. I'd have been miserable as a married woman. Happily-Ever-After isn't for me. Make-Me-Happy-Now works much better. Two. I'm not saying you two are doomed. Some are able to leave the past in the past. Maybe Lucas is one of those men. My advice, if you like him, enjoy him. Just pay attention before handing him your heart."

Too late.

Her mom shifted, lifting and shaking her wrist until her delicate gold watch was face up. The woman never seemed to rest.

"I have to stop at the office for a couple of hours. Are we still on for dinner? I want to celebrate, and hear the details about the opening."

Harper stood. "Yes. We'll talk this evening. Go. Do whatever it is you need to do. I'll head downstairs. A few new ideas are floating around in my mind, I need to get the sketches of them on paper. I also want to check out those new pieces of marble I ordered before we leave." She paused at the door, remembering something from their earlier conversation. "Why did you ask if the man was Lucas Genezen? Do we know another one?"

Her mother laughed. "No, I don't, but when you said he was a widower, I pictured someone way older than thirty."

Harper snorted. "Wouldn't that be something? You date men twenty years younger. I date them twenty years older. We'd be the talk of this little town."

"Aren't we already?"

"True." Harper laughed.

They didn't quite fit in with their conservative neighbors. Good thing neither of them cared.

"Thanks for listening, Mom."
"Always, daughter."

Chapter Fifteen

Lucas stared at the text he'd typed, debating if he should hit send. In the message he asked if Harper wanted to meet for drinks before going to Sweet Surrender, Will's restaurant.

That evening his friend was having a pre-party before the grand opening next month. It would be small and intimate, only friends, family, and important people from the food industry.

Meaning, it would probably be awkward for Lucas and Harper.

After their disastrous goodbye a month ago, they'd barely spoken. She called the next day, apologizing for her abruptness. Said she was confused and needed some time to think.

He'd given her the space she desired. He didn't call her. Nor did he visit, even though he was in the process of packing his old office and moving it to the Salvador building.

The only time he texted was over a week ago. He'd spotted a new, phenomenal statue in her gallery and told her it was beautiful. She'd asked why he hadn't come inside.

He never responded. She knew why.

Fuck it. He hit send on his phone, then set it on his desk.

Her response was immediate: Yes.

He exhaled, not realizing he'd been holding his breath. Smiling, he typed he was in her building, suggesting they drive together, finding a place between here and Will's restaurant.

Again, she agreed.

The rest of the day passed agonizingly slow. Lucas was busy, but somehow each tick of the clock felt like a freaking hour. He was worse than a damn teenager with his first girlfriend.

Which reminded him, Harper didn't want a boyfriend or didn't want him as one. She believed he was too broken.

He groaned, closing his email. He needed to switch to a project that actually interested him, in hopes it'd banish her from his thoughts.

It helped. Sort of. She hung out in the outer corners of his mind, but most of his attention was on the work before him.

Sometime later, he was startled by a light knock on his office door. Harper stepped inside, and his heart skipped a beat. The woman was stunning.

She wore a light blue dress reminiscent of another era. High collared, fitted around her upper body, flaring at her waist, stopping a few inches above her knees. It showed off her shapely legs and sexy heels. She wore her hair loose, styled with big, bouncy curls.

He recalled how soft those locks felt when he wrapped them around his fist, pulling her in and painting her neck with kisses. The way she moaned and begged for more was seared into his memories.

He shook his head, needing to clear his mind of those images. "Sorry, I lost track of time. Are we late?"

He hadn't unpacked his wall clock, and his cellphone was...somewhere. He was constantly losing it.

"No," she said. "I was impatient to see you, so I closed early."

A flush of happiness infused his veins, giving him a pleasant high. It also muddled his mind.

For weeks she ignored him. Now she says this stuff.

Being around her was like stepping onto merry-go-round. He never knew which way she'd turn. Would she be bold and confident, or insecure and distrustful? At times, like now, he was left feeling dizzy and confused.

Unsure how to address her, he mumbled, "Um, okay. Give me a minute to shut off everything. Do you want to try the new bar that opened here in the building?"

She tipped on one heel, swinging it from side to side. He didn't know if the gesture was nerves or if she was debating her options.

"Let's go somewhere else. I'd rather not fuel the gossip."

He shrugged. "Okay, but do you honestly think in a building this big people will even notice, let alone care enough to gossip?"

She laughed lightly. The sound warmed his heart, and other, less pure, places.

"Gossip is a favorite pastime for many people. Location and size don't matter." Amusement lit her eyes as her cheeks flushed pink. "Do you remember the clothing store next to my gallery? The one that closed last month?"

He nodded.

"Well, he once asked if my rent went down when I went down on you."

His skin heated with anger. "Good thing the fucker's shitty store went under within the first month." He came around the desk. "Why didn't you tell me?"

"It's not a big deal. He was lashing out. It has to hurt to put all your money and dreams into something only to watch it crumble and die within a few months. Anyway, he'd run his mouth right after, um, we'd stopped talking." She smiled, her gaze danced playfully over his face. "From the way steam is practically coming from your ears, I'm glad I didn't have the chance to tell you."

"Maybe. I'd have kicked his ass." He grinned. "Then raised his rent."

"Great. Give Ben another reason to hate me."

Lucas scowled, some of his good mood slipping. "I'm not worried. Why are you?"

His voice was sharp, and she flinched. He silently counted to five, trying to smooth the jagged edges of his irritation. "Have you tried Vivio's? They have great drinks."

She scoffed, her smile returning. "Those massive Bloody Mary's aren't drinks. They're dinner. Will would be heartbroken if we arrive full. And drunk. Want to try Bad Luck Bar?"

They started for the door. "Fine with me, but, um, you don't have to order the Bloody Mary." He rested a hand on the small of her back.

She leaned into his touch, a teasing lilt when she spoke. "It's *Vivio's*. It'd be like going to a Brazilian restaurant and ordering a vegetarian meal."

He chuckled. "Good point. Plus, I haven't tried Bad Luck Bar."

"Perfect. I'll drive."

"Works for me. I like it when you drive. It lets me—"

He was going to say, play with you. He held it in. They needed to talk, not flirt.

The problem was, it was easy to slip into their relaxed, teasing banter. That thought reminded him, they weren't together. And, if by chance they got back together, he was serious about wanting more than a few erotic nights.

"It'll let me check my phone messages," he finished lamely.

She snorted, somehow managing to make it sound cute and dainty. "You do that."

He didn't respond, just tickled her lower back, not wanting to let go.

$$\bullet \ \bullet \ \bullet \ \bullet \ \bullet \ \bullet \ \bullet \ \bullet \ \bullet \ \bullet$$

The hammering of Harper's heart was so loud she was surprised Lucas hadn't heard it when she lingered at the door of his office, watching him. Well, more like drinking him in as if dehydrated and thirsty for a taste of him.

Whatever he'd been reading had his complete attention, and she'd toyed with the idea of lurking in his doorway until he noticed. Not only because being near him fed her starved heart, but it bought borrowed time in the valley of the unknown.

She feared when he looked at her, there'd be no warmth, only bored indifference. That his reason for wanting to meet with her wasn't because he missed her, but wanted to smooth things out between them. To make sure it wouldn't be awkward during Will's party.

Before uncertainty stole her courage, she tapped the door's glass window. Lucas startled, his gaze snagged on her, then seemed to swallow her with its intensity and hunger.

When he'd spoken, the foreplay continued. The slight husky tenor kissed her famished heart, feeding her lust.

It also reminded her why she hadn't called him these last couple of weeks. She wanted to see if being away would lessen her need for him.

It hadn't. Nothing had diminished.

Instead, it quietly grew in the dark corners of her desire. Attacking her the first time she saw him and heard his deep baritone.

She should've known. When he left her in the middle of the night after their first time, he snuck into her thoughts, no matter how hard she tried to forget him. It was the same when she walked away after the barbeque.

She was delusional, believing this time would be any different.

Since moving on was impossible, all that was left was to come clean with her fears and insecurities. Either he'll end it, repulsed with her, or find some way to understand her selfish, small heart.

On the way to the bar, they slipped into their usual easy conversation. The coward in her wanted to stay there, ignoring the fissure between them.

Until she recalled the way he'd shut down when she opened her big mouth about Ben. It was a reminder of why they must talk. The way she left him the last morning they were together was wrong and had hurt him. He deserved an explanation.

"You're quiet," he said, as they slid into a black leather booth at Bad Luck.

Gathering her concerns and shame, she studied the bar off to their right. The shelves of drinks were backlit by warm, inviting light. She eyed the bottles. Something strong, to numb her nerves, would be nice.

"I want to say so much and, at the same time, nothing at all," she admitted.

He frowned. "I'm not sure how to take that."

Before she could respond, a waitress stopped at their table. They gave their drink orders, and when she left, Harper dove into her sins.

"I'm incredibly jealous of your wife," she confessed. "She makes me feel small, insignificant, and petty."

He gaped at her for a few heart-stopping seconds, then asked, "Why?"

He didn't sound angry, merely confused. The urge to leave him puzzled as she back-peddled was fierce. Almost every part of her wanted to stick to the ruse that she was too busy for a relationship.

It was better than the ugly truth.

She played with a napkin, shredding the edges. "Your wife, she loved you, treated you good, right?"

He nodded.

"I bet she was a nice person. A fantastic friend, wonderful daughter, and a great sister."

"She wasn't perfect, no one is, but yes, she was kind and adored those she loved," he replied, confusion evident in his tone.

"A good person, deservedly missed, yet a small part of me wishes she was never born."

Lucas sucked in a breath. Harper held up a hand, recognizing she'd misspoken. Even she wasn't that cruel.

"That came out wrong," she amended. "I wish she'd never met you. That you'd never loved her."

"Why?" he said quietly, again without anger. However, she caught an undercurrent of hurt.

It cut her.

She crumpled the napkin she shredded to pieces, unable to meet his eyes. "Because she'll always have your heart. I never will, and I want it. There will never be room for both of us."

Quietness descended on their corner booth. When the silence became unbearable, she peeked at him. His expression was unreadable. Finally, he spoke.

"This is a lot to take in. I assumed you liked me as a mild distraction. Nothing more. Now you're telling me this…" He rested into their plush booth, clearly surprised.

Wow. She was a better actress than she realized and almost wished she kept the performance going, since the real her was damn appalling.

Her shoulders slumped. "You are definitely not a mild distraction. The problem is I like you too much. I want you all for myself. I'm so damn selfish I don't want to compete with the memories of your wife." She ran her hand through her hair, glancing away. "I'm a terrible person."

Glass clinked, and quiet conversation murmured around them as an awful silence covered them again. She stared at her torn napkin, tears gathering and clouding her vision.

His finger brushed her temples as he pushed a lock of her hair behind her ears. "You're a good person, Harper."

"Have you been listening to anything I've said?" she breathed, shame clinging to her.

"Yes, and I get where you're coming from. If we're together, you want all of me. You won't risk handing me your heart if I can't do the same."

He stretched his arm across the table, palm up. Waiting.

She laid a shaky hand on his. He slid his fingers through hers. "What you don't understand is Elizabeth is my past. I can't take her with me. My love for her is separate. It doesn't play a part in who I might love now."

"Would you trade us for her?" The question was unfair, yet it didn't stop her from asking. She couldn't be with a man who longed for his past.

"Harper—"

The waitress returned with their drinks, cutting off Lucas. Seeming to sense the tension, she set their glasses on the table without a word and left.

He stared at his bourbon. After a moment, took a sip then said, "Your question is a dark road, one I refuse to travel. I *can't* trade anything to have her back. What-ifs and wishes won't change a damn thing."

She was hurting him. Unnecessarily.

"I'm sorry," she said quietly. "I shouldn't have asked such a question. Especially now, when we've only begun dating."

He exhaled, and it somehow sounded sad. "I'm not going to lie. It surprised the hell out of me." Pausing, he took another swallow of his drink. "Shit, for this conversation I need something stronger."

A small laugh escaped her. "Isn't bourbon around forty proof or more?"

He smiled. "Yup."

"I'm sorry. You want to drop this conversation?" It was cruel of her to make him relive his pain to quell her insecurities.

He squeezed her hand. "No, let's get this all out. This is better. Clear the air. I need to know where I stand with you. This hot and cold is driving me crazy. I can't tell if you're afraid to date me or not very interested—"

"Really?" She bit her lip as disbelief bloomed in her chest. "I couldn't keep my hands off you."

"Well, I never doubted our chemistry." His smile was crooked and seductive. "I did wonder if you liked me for more than sex."

Damn, had she come off as that indifferent?

Trying to lighten the mood, she teased, "If that were all I wanted, most guys wouldn't bother questioning their good fortune."

His lips twitched, but his tone was serious when he said, "I'm not most men. Moreover, you're not most women."

Happiness filled her with bright sunshine. The direct way he spoke was new and refreshing. It also had her at a loss at what to say, which seemed fine, as he wasn't done.

"Anyway, given my colossal fuckup the night we met, then the way I so clumsily dumped my reasons on you for doing it when we met again at the barbeque, no wonder you're wary of dating me." With his free hand, he rubbed it against his cheek, clearly agitated. "I get it. Although, for my own sanity, I need to know if this is something you can't get past. You need to tell me. I can't keep doing this tug-of-war."

They were in a u-shaped bench. She scooted around until she was next to him. "I'm sorry, I wasn't playing games with you, I swear. I hate them too. Maybe even more than you." Recalling the awful ways Edward used and kicked around her heart, she said, "Anyway, I was ashamed of my insecurities and hid them while trying to figure out what to do with them."

"What have you done with them? What's changed?"

"Nothing. They're still there. All I've learned is I can't let you go. I tried these last couple of weeks. It didn't work. Plan B is throwing my issues onto your lap," she said with chagrin. "See what you do with them. I figured you'd tell me to leave. To take my pettiness with me."

His eyes searched her face as if hoping to find an answer he needed. "I'll be honest. I'm not sure what to do."

Her heart splintered. "Because you're appalled by my shallowness?"

"No. I get where you're coming from. You feel something for me and worry I can't reciprocate."

"Wow, it sounds way less crazy and not so cold-hearted, the way you say it."

He tapped his fingers on the solid wood table. "Listen, Harper. I love Elizabeth. I always will, but it's for what we had. Which is very different than falling for someone right in front of me. Still, my love for her won't go away. Is that something you can accept? If it isn't, we'll never last."

She nodded, finally understanding the difference.

"Are you sure? Because as much as I want to see where this goes, I can't keep chasing after you."

Shame dusted her, but relief brushed most of it away. She bared her insecurities and weakness, expecting disgust. Or for him to do as Edward had and use them against her. Instead, Lucas was his usual kind, sexy self, a sweet mixture of compassion and honesty.

"Okay," she whispered. "I swear, I'm done running."

"Good." He cupped her cheek before kissing her softly.

His lips tasted of bourbon, bliss, and new beginnings.

Chapter Sixteen

Greta waved across the bright, welcoming restaurant. Her gaze fell to Harper's hand entwined with Lucas's, her smile widened, but her eyes held no surprise. Their group of friends did love to gossip and speculate.

She wondered who told Greta. Cindy or Will?

Scanning the room, Harper was curious if her cousin would come tonight. With things strained between them, would Cindy support Will?

With the men of her past, she wouldn't have bothered. Although, Harper suspected things were different with Will, and she'd show up sooner or later.

She tugged Lucas's hand. "Come on. Let's sit with Greta and Jacob."

"Sounds good." He rested an arm around her, and she relaxed into him while checking out the restaurant. The combination of exposed brick, bleached cement floors, and a mix of thick, industrial oak tables gave the place a polished, welcoming feel.

"Will and his business partner out-did themselves. This place is gorgeous," she said.

"It is LEED certified too." Lucas shook his head, laughing. "That was a fun evening with the Grimm brothers."

"Something in your voice tells me you aren't telling the whole truth."

"Possibly." He kissed her forehead.

She loved his open affection. A woman with him would never wonder if she was cherished.

"What happened? Did the restaurant have a bunch of issues?" she asked.

He chuckled. "No. Thankfully. It was more me and Will were grumpy assholes who kept giving each other a hard time."

They'd reached the table, and he pointed at Jacob. "And this guy didn't like his eco-duties."

"That's right." Jacob snapped his fingers. "I have a threat to carry out with my big brother." Sitting straight, he smiled at his wife. "Do you have any tampons?"

Greta's lips twitched, but her voice was firm. "No, and I'm not even going to ask why you need them."

"Fine," he muttered. He focused on Lucas, eyeing his arm around Harper. "I see you're in a better mood than that night."

A light flush colored Lucas's neck while a sliver of guilt ran through her.

Okay, knowing she mattered to him had delight chasing alongside her remorse.

"Harper," Maggie called from the other end of the table. She patted the empty seat next to her.

Nodding, Harper walked with Lucas toward them. She was thrilled to have the chance to chat with her newest friend.

Tanner's arm was hung loosely around Maggie's shoulder, rubbing circles on her upper arm, and she rested a hand on his thigh. While both were extremely attractive, they made such an odd couple.

Maggie, with her multicolored purple and black hair, tattoos, and nose piercing, didn't match Tanner's short, neat hair, ink-free skin, and almost conservative clothes. However, the way love wrapped around their private smiles and quiet touches screamed devotion and passion.

It made Harper's heart hurt with longing. Would she ever have that with someone? With Lucas?

She could admit to herself, she wanted it with him.

"How's it going with the gallery?" Maggie asked as they sat. Catching Harper's surprise, she clarified, "Tanner mentioned it when he was working on your account. Anyway, I went online to check out your art. I have to say, I'm impressed. I wanted to go to the grand opening, but we were playing a show that night."

Gratitude and embarrassment heated Harper's cheeks. It warmed her Maggie would have taken the time to visit the gallery opening, making her wish she'd mentioned it.

Her little art venture seemed trivial next to the other woman's growing fame. Even more humiliating was that Maggie learned of the gallery because Harper couldn't even manage to keep the books in order and needed Tanner to help bail her out.

"No worries. I understand your music keeps you busy. Whenever you have some free time, you're welcome to stop by." Harper said shyly, "In fact, I'd love your opinion with a piece I'm working on, once it's finished. After meeting you at the wedding, I got ThreePence's album and was inspired. *Love Songs* begged to be on canvas. I wonder if you'll recognize the songs in the paint."

Maggie clapped her hands. "That is so fucking cool! Yes, I want to see it. Your stuff is stunning. If the tone is right, I might want to buy it, use it as the cover image on our next album. Would that be okay?"

Her excitement was infectious, and Harper's nervousness died. "If you like it, I'll give it to you."

Maggie shook her head. "No. I may not paint, but I know a shit-ton of work goes into creating art. I wouldn't take it for nothing."

"Having my art attached to ThreePence is worth something to me."

"I've seen your work. It's worth more than free publicity."

A flush of pride welled in Harper's heart. "Thank you. Anyway, come see it first, in case it isn't what you're looking for." She snapped her fingers as a fun idea sprang forth. "Hey, I got it. If you want it, I'll sell it to you for two tickets to your next local show, with backstage passes and a promise to meet your drummer."

"You want to meet Lincoln?" Maggie's brows pulled together, her gaze moving to Lucas. "Um, you don't mind sharing?"

Aw, crap. Her request did sound seedy.

Edward would have been furious at the accidental wording. It would have put Harper's ex in a pissy mood, and he'd have made sure to ruin hers, and everyone else's, evening.

"Oh. I didn't mean it like that..." She peeked at Lucas. To her relief, he appeared amused.

He brought her close, saying, "How about I settle the bill? What's it worth?"

Maggie tapped her chin with one short, fuchsia painted nail, then leaned toward Harper. "Tell him two rentals in upper Michigan," she said, in a stage whisper. "On the Lake. One for me, the other for you."

"Done and done," Lucas said.

Harper laughed, kissing his cheek. "Before you go giving away prime real estate, you should know, Lincoln isn't for me. He's for Patricia. ThreePence's album was playing one time at the gallery after we closed, she liked the music and asked their name. I guess she checked them out on YouTube or something. She's developed quite the crush on their drummer."

"Well, in that case, I retract my offer."

"Damn," Maggie muttered. She rested her head briefly on Tanner. "Sorry, babe. I almost got us a summer house."

"Don't give up yet." Tanner smirked. "We'll get her tickets, then tell Lincoln to work his charm. On Harper."

"What charm?" Maggie retorted at the same time Lucas shoved Tanner's shoulder playfully.

"Shit, I thought you were my friend."

"Hey, I've always wanted a place on Lake Michigan," Tanner said, turning to Maggie. "I know you consider Lincoln a brother, but the man's got game. He must if he was able to convince your sister to go out with him."

Maggie's throaty laugh filled the room. "That isn't game. He wore her down. Have you noticed they only went on *one* date?"

"It doesn't matter either way," Harper said above their banter. "When it comes to me, whether or not he has game is irrelevant. Lucas has all my attention."

He kissed the side of her head as Maggie rested a hand over her heart.

"Aww. You two are a love song waiting to be written." She smiled at Tanner. "Would you get started writing it? You're way better at them than me."

"This is true," he agreed.

"Hey." She laughed, smacking him lightly on the arm.

A waitress came between them, setting a large tray on the table, announcing there were serving samples of the entire menu. She encouraged the group to try some of everything. She'd keep bringing tasters until told they were full. Will and his business partner, Tim, wanted to know what was loved and what they didn't like.

The time passed with glorious food that teased and delighted the taste buds. With the added side of fantastic conversation and seeing Cindy and Will work out their differences, the evening was near perfect.

Well, her cousin's reunion happened behind closed doors. Literally.

After most of the guests left, Cindy stalked into the kitchen, her shoulders tense, but her head held high. Harper recognized the stance. Her cousin wasn't going to leave until she got what she wanted.

Which, of course, she did.

Sometime later, Will and Cindy exited the kitchen to a chorus of cheers and cat-calls. Her hair was slightly disheveled, and her lips were swollen. Her arm was around a very cheerful and content looking Will. After their reunion, the restaurant celebration concluded quickly.

Harper and Lucas were invited to Maggie and Tanner's house for a game of Texas Hold'em with their bandmates. At first, Harper begged off, admitting she didn't know how to play, and she wasn't friends with math. Once they convinced her the game was about bluffing and not arithmetic, she was all in.

On the way there, Lucas gave her a crash course in the game. It seemed easy enough.

When they arrived, Maggie and Tanner were already sitting at the kitchen table with another man, sipping Turkish coffee while the stranger shuffled the cards.

He stood, offering his hand to her and Lucas, telling them his name was Amel, and he was the bassist for ThreePence. The man would have been intimidating with his shaved head, thick brows, and massive mountains of muscles, but he had such kind brown eyes and the most welcoming smile.

"Tanner told me you've never played," he said to Harper in a slightly accented voice that sounded like broken gravel. "Do you want to do a few hands with our cards showing?"

She exhaled with relief. "Yes, please."

Amel walked to the basement entrance and shouted, "Lincoln, get your ass up here if you want to play ."

"Don't get your panties in a bunch," floated a voice from the bottom of the stairs. A few seconds later feet pounded up them.

The man who entered the kitchen looked so much like Kurt Cobain, she sucked in a breath. He even had the elongated, dimpled chin.

No wonder Patricia wanted to meet him. In middle school, she'd had the biggest crush on the singer.

"That's quite a reaction," Lucas whispered in her ear, making her jump. "Do I need to give Maggie two of my lake rentals?"

Harper peeked at him and was relieved to find him smiling. Resting against him, she said, "Nah, Gregory Peck is my celebrity crush."

"That's a relief." He kissed the top of her nose before introducing himself and her to Lincoln.

The drummer smiled at them in a way that could only be described as devilish, his impish gaze landing on her. "Maggie texted me before you got here. Told me we'd have a card virgin tonight. Let me thank you in advance for my new set of cymbals."

She pretended to be offended. "Lucas taught me the game on the way here. By the end of the night, I'll be the queen of Tennessee Hold'em," she quipped, purposely botching the name. Best to let him have low expectations of her.

Lincoln burst into hearty, loud laughter. "This is going to be fun. Maybe I'll get a snare drum too."

They played two hands with the cards face up, then she declared she was ready. An hour later, a decent pile of chips was in front of her, and Lincoln was losing some of his cockiness.

Continuing with her clueless act, she blinked, wide and innocent, proclaiming. "Wow, I have no idea what I'm doing. Talk about beginner's luck."

Lucas tipped his chin. "Funny. You've been 'lucky' the last four hands."

She smiled and winked at him, accepting two new cards from Tanner.

Peeking at them, her pulse raced, but she managed to school her features. She had two freaking Aces!

Leaning toward Lucas, she whispered loud enough for everyone to hear, "Out of curiosity, which is higher, puppy paws or hearts?"

He snorted. "Puppy paws?"

She drew the outline of the suit on the tabletop with her index finger. Holding her guileless, confused face was difficult, and she could tell he wasn't buying it.

That was fine. He wouldn't out her. Although he did mutter, he was going to fold.

Amel, sitting on her left, laughed. "You mean the club?"

Maggie's eyes flashed with humor. "Looks more like a clover to me."

Harper snapped her fingers. "Yes! That one."

"In most cases, they're equal," Lucas said, sounding as if he was having a difficult time not laughing. "Remember, pairs are what's important. Like two Aces or two Clubs."

At the mention of her hand of cards, her heart rate spiked, but she kept her outside cool and calm.

Adrenaline surged through her as she made her shoulders droop. "Oh. Okay. Well can I have two new cards?"

"Honey, no." Lucas choked, his laughter booming through the kitchen. Under the table, he tickled her knee.

The first chance he got, he folded. Yup, he knew exactly what she was doing.

When the fifth card was flipped, all that remained was her, Lincoln, and Amel. Lincoln grinned so wide even his molars were visible.

"I almost feel bad taking the pot," he cooed. "Why didn't you fold, Harper?"

He flipped his cards. Two Kings. Amel cursed in what sounded like Arabic, dropping his hand. A ten and Jack of Spades. Not bad. Considering there was a Queen of Spades in the community pile.

Lincoln's gaze landed on her. She finally let her smile free, which made his freeze.

Flipping her cards, she clapped and squealed, "I love this game!"

She grabbed Lucas and planted a huge kiss on his lips.

"Holy shit!" Maggie sounded delighted.

Amel's mouth dropped open. Then he asked if Harper would come with him to the casinos.

Lincoln's upper body thumped onto the table, and he was pretending to cry.

Maggie high-fived Harper before getting up. "I need a drink."

"Me too," Lincoln whimpered, his face still resting on the table.

Maggie twisted around, quirking a brow. "Have you mistaken me for your waitress?"

"Please, Maggs. Your friend cut me off at the knees. I'm going to have to mortgage my kidney on the black market to eat this week."

Harper laid a hand over his and mimicked his earlier words, "I almost feel bad taking the pot."

Sitting straight, he laughed, accepting the shot from Maggie. He took it in one swig before rubbing his hands together.

"I'm on to you now. Come on, deal another hand, Tanner," he said, without a trace of irritation.

"Just in case, shouldn't you sell your kidney first?" she teased, smitten with her new group of friends.

Chapter Seventeen

Harper floated awake, drifting from dreams to desires as Lucas's firm, warm body pressed against her backside, enticing her. She wiggled her butt. He responded by sliding his hand to her stomach, bringing her even closer.

Early June's sweltering heatwave had finally broken, allowing them to shut off the AC in Lucas's house and open the windows. They'd fallen asleep, naked and satiated, listening to the night sounds.

Now, birds chirped, and the morning sun streamed through the bedroom window, warming her skin. She stretched like a lazy cat. His hand continued its path from her belly, dipping lower, making her whole body purr.

The way he easily stroked her passion was a surprise. In the past, sex had been fun, but never compulsory. This addictive craving should worry her. What if she was coming to depend on him, to need him?

Yet, when his fingers worked their magic, and his lips trailed kisses on her neck, she didn't care. Turning, she ran a palm down his torso, and wrapping a hand around his arousal, she stroked him from base to head.

Between nibbling and kissing the light scruff on his jaw, she murmured, "Good morning."

"Indeed, it is." He hummed, playing between her legs.

They teased each other until their breaths were shallow and their bodies ached for release. When her orgasm teetered on the edge and his thrusts became more demanding, he rolled on top of her.

Nudging her thighs open with his hips, he asked, "Are you sore?"

Yesterday, they'd gone to dinner and dancing with the whole group; Maggie, Tanner, Cindy, Will, Greta, and Jacob. All evening, Harper and Lucas teased and tantalized each other on the dancefloor and in the dark corners of the nightclub.

By the time they arrived at his place, they were beyond turned on. Before the front door even closed, she was tugging on his belt, and he was under her sundress. He'd taken her against the foyer wall, with a rough urgency that matched hers.

He managed to get his jeans to his thighs before entering her. Afterward, he removed their clothes, tossing everything haphazardly into the living room. He carried her to the bedroom, teasing her until they were, again, frantic with need.

Both times were not gentle, and she was a little sore. However, with his erection sliding against her, enticing and insistent, she welcomed pain with her pleasure.

Hooking a leg around his waist, she arched. "I am, but it will hurt more if you don't finish what we've started."

He entered her with a maddening slowness, his gaze never wavering from hers. "Okay?"

"Yes," she breathed, moving under him. "More than fine. Please don't stop."

He didn't, and soon the sounds of their pleasure overrode the morning birds and the other summer sounds. She came apart, moaning his name into his mouth as he conquered her passion.

His thrusts became deeper, harder. The movement always prolonged and magnified her climax. She clutched his back, probably digging too deep. He didn't seem to care as his own orgasm claimed him, and his body shook with pleasure.

They stayed locked in each other's slick embrace until their heartbeats returned to normal. Then he asked, "Join me in the shower?"

"Can't it wait? It's Sunday. I want to be lazy all morning. Maybe drift off to sleep. Wake and do this again." She wiggled her hips.

"Woman, you are voracious."

"With you, I am."

"I like your answer." He kissed her, but before she could deepen it, he pulled away, resting on his elbows and studying her.

"What?"

"My parent's always have a Sunday dinner. Will you come with me?"

Nervousness fluttered under her breastbone, crashing into happiness, but she agreed.

His smile was warmer than the sun. "You didn't have any other plans?"

"Nope. I was going to either be lazy with you in bed all day or go to my mom's place to finish the detail work on my marble piece." She ran her thumb across his brow. "Would you ever want to go there with me?"

"To your mom's?"

She nodded.

He kissed her chin, chuckling. "Are you asking me because I invited you to my parent's house?"

"No, well sort of. I've wanted to, but assumed you wouldn't want to go."

"Why? You're important to me. I want to be around the people you care about. Besides, I like your mom. She's brazen and confident. Reminds me of her daughter."

She laughed. "I wish I had half my mom's confidence." She linked her fingers together at the base of Lucas's neck. "Plus, I'd never have the nerve to hit on one of her boyfriends."

"Well, it wasn't like I was visiting for family Christmas or something when it happened. She didn't know we were dating. And," his smile was all cocky humor, "can you blame her?"

She brought his lips to hers, murmuring, "no," before kissing him.

When heat began to seep between their kisses, he moved off her.

She reached for him. "Why'd you leave?"

He motioned to his lower half. "I'm getting hard."

"Good. Come back."

"Don't tell me you're not sore."

She couldn't deny it.

"How far is the drive to your mom's place from here or your condo?" he asked.

The one-eighty change of subject threw her. "What?"

He repeated the question.

"Both take close to an hour. Why?"

"Well, my place is much closer, and I have a spare room where I throw shit I haven't yet unpacked. Do you want to use it for your work?"

Her heart suddenly took off, as if trying to pound out of her chest. From fear or excitement, she wasn't sure.

Meeting his parents was one thing. What he was suggesting was huge.

If she moved her work studio, she'd be here all the time, practically living with him. Did he realize that? Was it what he wanted, or was he being practical, but not considering the end result?

It didn't matter because it wouldn't work.

"No, my cutting and sanding tools are loud and make a huge mess. You would *not* want either in your house."

"I want *you* in my house."

Her heart flipped. *Is he asking me to move in with him?*

He snapped his fingers as if catching a new, better idea. "The garage."

She didn't have the nerve to straight-out ask him if he wanted her to move in. Hell, she wasn't even sure if she wanted to take such a huge step.

Things were fantastic between them. Moving in together could ruin everything.

Staying safe, she asked only art studio questions. "Where would you park your car? You don't want it anywhere near where I work. I'm not talking a little dust and debris, more like mountains of it."

"It could be converted. It's big enough to divide in half. One side for a car, the other a studio." He shrugged. "We'll think of something."

Even with her emotions going off like fireworks, she was distracted by the ripple and bunch of his delectable muscles. Or maybe that was exactly what she needed, a distraction.

Either way, she propped herself onto her elbow and playfully bit his shoulder.

"You're so damn tasty." She licked where she nipped.

"You too." He nuzzled her neck. "You're a sip of warm honey."

"You're welcome to taste me any time you want." She gently pushed his head south. "Like, say right now."

He chuckled, kissing her breast. "My insatiable siren. I want to, but we should start getting ready."

He didn't leave. Instead, he nuzzled into her. She played with his hair, thinking about the previous weekend.

"You were with me last Sunday. All day and evening, why didn't you go?" she asked.

"I forgot. My mom and sister gave me hell for it." He peeked at her. "If I skip again, one of them will be after my head."

She laughed. "How could you forget? You made it sound like it's a weekly tradition."

He rolled off her, sitting on the edge of the bed. He twisted to meet her eyes, yet she got the sense he was distancing himself.

"It is, but for a while I stopped going. Lately, I've tried to be better about it."

Ah, yes. He'd mentioned pulling away from friends and family when his wife died.

Was he withdrawing from her now because of guilt at taking a different woman to meet his family? Or was it sadness at taking someone else, and not the person he truly wanted at his parent's table?

She shoved aside those painful, destructive thoughts. If she wanted to be with him, she needed to stop second-guessing his feelings for her.

"This is last minute," she said, rubbing his back. "What if they don't have room for me?"

He stood, offering her his hand and a shy smile. "After forgetting last week, my mom called yesterday to remind me. I told her I wanted to bring you. Everyone's excited to meet you."

How could she say no? Not that she'd refuse. Like him, she'd wanted to meet those who were important to him.

Nevertheless, it scared her senseless. Would they compare her to Elizabeth, as she did, and find her lacking?

Lucas tilted his head. "You okay? I swear, clouds suddenly gathered around you. If any of this makes you uncomfortable, we don't have to go. It's not a big deal."

His words were kind, but Harper caught the disappointment wrapped around them. He did want her with him, and knowing this expelled most of her worries.

"I'd love to go." She took his hand.

He brought her to him. "Okay, then let's get in the shower. Mom tries to have dinner on the table early, and I need to stop at the bakery. I'm in charge of dessert."

"We need to stop at my place. What I packed to stay here won't work for a family dinner." They linked fingers walking into the bathroom. She squeezed his hand. "You could have mentioned this when you asked me to stay the night."

"Sorry. I'd forgotten about dinner at my parents. Also, in my defense, when we talked yesterday morning, my mind was on getting you out of your clothes, not what you'd have on." He twisted the hot water knob, his gaze taking in her naked body. "This is my favorite outfit."

She skated her hands over her breasts, down her waist to rest on her hips. "Is that so?"

"Yes." He gripped her waist, fingers digging in, making her moan in anticipation.

The bathroom filled with steam as they kissed and played. Lucas brought her under the spray of water.

He poured shampoo into his palm. With his front to her back, he worked a lather into her hair. She arched into him, sliding against his arousal.

A low groan rumbled from him, and he thrust against her backside. The combination of his granite need, the warm water, and suds made her breathless with desire.

Standing on tiptoe, she bent, telling him without words what she wanted from him.

He ran a soapy hand along her spine. "No. I've been rough."

"And I like it." She rubbed against him, wiggling her bottom.

He groaned, thrusting between her legs but not entering her. "Your body needs to rest."

"I want you."

"You have all of me." He kissed her neck, coming around to face her. "Now, let me give you the satisfaction your body craves."

He went to his knees and kept his promise.

Twice

Chapter Eighteen

Lucas tapped on the steering wheel, his nerves pounding to the beat. He wasn't worried about his family loving Harper. That was a given. His worry was for her.

Pieces of his past were scattered throughout his parents' house. There was his wedding picture on the mantle. Another hanging in the upstairs hallway of him and Elizabeth when they graduated with their masters.

Right or wrong, and he had no idea which it was, Harper was bothered by his marriage. Would the many reminders create another wedge between them?

At the red light, he glanced at her. She was wrapping and unwrapping a loose thread on her linen pants. If she kept at it, she'd have them unraveled by the time they arrived at his parent's house.

He wracked his brain for a light topic to help ease her mind, coming up with his favorite summertime activity. "Did you remember to bring a swimsuit? My dad told me the boat's in the water. Do you like to water ski?"

She lifted one hand in a 'who knows gesture', while her other continued to tug at her slacks. "Not sure. I haven't done it in years."

The heavy silence returned, screaming her unease.

He took the hand unraveling at the loose thread. "Are you okay?"

"Do you think they'll hate me?"

Lucas frowned. "What? Why would they hate you? You're perfect. What's not to like?"

"I'm not Elizabeth."

He stilled, thoroughly shocked. She'd never straight out mentioned his wife by name. Plus, he hurt for Harper. She truly believed his family wouldn't adore her for the simple reason she wasn't someone else.

"So? They, and I, don't need another Elizabeth."

They arrived at his parents' subdivision. After a right, then left, he parked his car in their driveway.

He turned off the engine then shifted to bring Harper's hand to his lips. "We loved her, but she's my past. In my present, I want you."

She smiled, looping a finger between the buttons of his shirt. "I'm sorry. I'm nervous. It's making my needy side appear."

He preferred this to what she used to do—deny and run away.

Tugging on his shirt, she brought him closer. He kissed her softly, wanting to reassure her.

He ran his tongue across her bottom lip. She opened for him, tasting of cinnamon, with a bite of desire.

She slid her hand resting on his chest up and around to grip the back of his neck. A kiss meant to soothe and calm was doing the opposite.

His body exploded with need, and he slid closer to her. As he ran his palm dangerously high on her thigh, someone knocked on the driver's side window.

They sprung apart, and he jerked toward the sound. His seventeen-year-old niece stared back. Her short brown hair covered one eye. The other one sparkled with mischief.

When he rolled down the window, she said, "Mom wanted me to check on you. Make sure you're all right." She waggled her brows. "I'll tell her you're fine."

He snorted. "We'll be inside in a minute. Now, go away."

She laughed, waved at Harper, then sauntered up the walkway.

"Oh, my God." She groaned and buried her face in her hands. "I'm so embarrassed. How can I meet them now?'

"Are you kidding me? My younger sister and her husband will love this. Watch and wait for it." He pointed to the porch. "My brother-in-law will be outside in three, two—"

The front door swung open, and Austin's tall frame stepped onto the porch. With hands on hips and the biggest shit-eating grin, he shouted, "Do I need to defend this lady's honor?"

Lucas's grin widened, and he flipped off the other man.

Austin howled with laughter. Wiping at the corners of his eyes, he yelled, "See you inside in a few!"

The door closed, and Lucas took in Harper. Her face was beet-red, but her lips twitched at the corners.

"Care to explain?"

"He's my little sister's husband. Austin and Sarah are high school sweethearts. Back in the day, when they first began dating, I came outside to go somewhere. I can't even remember where. Anyway, there was this unknown car parked in the driveway with fogged windows. I went around to the passenger side door and yanked it open. I hauled Sarah out and threaten to kick Austin's ass." He shook his head, chuckling at the memory. "My sister was pissed. She might be two years younger than me, but I feared for my life. For a month, I slept with my door locked."

Harper's light laughter filled the car. "It's sweet you were worried about your sister and wanted to protect her."

Lucas grunted, opening his door. "I'm the middle child of two strong-willed, sarcastic women. They have no use or need of my, as they call it, 'caveman' ways."

They got out of the car. He tapped the hood and winked. "My dad, on the other hand, loved it. With three headstrong women under his roof, you won't be surprised to discover he has a full head of gray hair. But plenty of laugh lines too."

"I like your family already."

"They're going to love you."

"I hope so." She bit her bottom lip.

He wanted to wrap her in his arms, protecting her from her anxieties. Instead, he grabbed their dessert from the backseat and pointed with his chin toward the house. "Let's get inside so I can prove to you I'm right."

· • • ● ● • ● • • ·

"I can't believe I went to school with your older sister's husband." Harper snuggled into Lucas. "I'm pretty sure Dexter was my lab partner in science. I remember because he seemed odd. He really enjoyed dissecting animals."

Lucas chuckled. "Good thing for my sister he chose the path of a surgeon, and not a serial killer."

Harper tried not to laugh but failed. Her stomach hurt from doing so much of it throughout the day.

With an arm around her, he was drawing, slow lazy circles with his fingertip on her arm. His soft touch was soothing.

In a comfortable silence, they watched a group of kids playing on a floating dock. They were sitting in a comfy wicker loveseat on the lower deck, a few steps from the lake. The scent of summer and seaweed wafted around her, holding her in a warm embrace.

The early evening sun shimmered on the water's surface, and a light breeze ruffled Lucas's messy hair. He was the epitome of disheveled sexy in his swim trunks, and a slightly wrinkled T-shirt stretched across his broad chest.

She, on the other hand, probably resembled a sunburned, drowned rat. Her hair was a tangled mess, wrapped in an untidy bun, and a slight sunburn stung her now make-up free face. Well, hopefully. In reality, she probably had huge mascara smudges from her water adventures.

Not that she cared. She was having too much fun.

She wanted to capture this moment and somehow save it. She'd take it out on dull and debilitating days, giving her a sliver of warmth and happiness.

Earlier, they piled into the boat to go tubing and skiing. After the kids went, Lucas convinced her to try water skiing.

When she was a little kid, she tried it with her grandmother and found it impossible to get out of the water in the skis. As an adult, she had no problem and freaking loved it.

They played on the jet skis and kayaks too. It was official. She loved lake life.

Before today, she wanted to sell her trendy Ann Arbor condo for a place closer to work. Now, she needed one on the water.

Thinking about moving had her mind wandering to Lucas's idea to convert his garage into a studio for her. Was it a toss-away comment? Something he didn't mean?

As if hearing her whirling, racing mind, he asked, "What're you thinking about?"

There was no way she'd tell him the truth. The day was near perfect. She wasn't going to ruin it with serious conversation.

Also, if she saw in his face that he didn't actually want her to move in with him, it'd crush her. Better to wait for him to mention it again.

In the end, she was saved from responding. The sound of footsteps coming from behind them snagged his attention.

He twisted around and smiled. "Hey, Mom."

Harper sat straighter, putting space between her and Lucas. His mother was friendly, in a cold distant way.

When Harper and he arrived, Lucas introduced her to his parents. His dad, Grant, was a hugger, setting her at ease. His mother, Adaline, was more reserved. She'd nodded a hello, keeping a tight grip on a bowl and spoon.

Granted, at the time, both parents were busy with the finishing touches of dinner, but as the day progressed, her cool manner never thawed.

After dinner, Harper volunteered to help wash the dishes. Adaline brushed aside the offer, telling her Sarah would help, and Harper should join Lucas on the boat.

When they returned, the men stayed behind to check the motor and put away the tube and skis. She wandered into the house where she found Sarah and her mother sipping wine and deep in conversation.

Worse, when they caught sight of her, they stopped talking, and an awkward silence filled the space between them. They asked her to sit with them, but she declined, knowing the offer was good manners and not from an actual desire for her company. She made an excuse about having kayaking plans with Lucas.

They didn't, until she asked him to take her. He'd happily agreed. Once on the water again, her concern melted away with each stroke of the paddle and Lucas's comforting presence.

Now, his mother took a seat across from them, setting a tray with a pitcher of Margaritas and salted glasses on a table between them. Harper's stomach twisted, anticipating stilted pleasantries.

Instead, a warm smile was aimed at her. Harper was unsure if the open, friendliness was a show for her son or genuine. Either way, Harper returned the gesture, hoping it didn't come off as a grimace.

"Lucas dragged you off to kayak, and you missed the after-dinner wine," Adaline said. "So, I'm bringing the sunset drink to you."

Harper's cheeks warmed, and she peeked at him. Would he out her that she was the one who made the suggestion?

His brows rose, and he studied her for a moment before directing his attention at his mother. "It's only eight. We have at least another hour until the sun sets."

Adaline gave him a don't-sass-me look. "Then drink it slowly, son."

"Yes, Mother," he said, with mock seriousness, reaching for a glass.

"And," she continued, "it's my peace offering to your girlfriend."

Harper's gaze flew from the Margarita pitcher to Adaline. A small gasp escaped her lips. Lucas sat straight. "For what?"

His mother focused on Harper. "I fear I've come off cold toward you. I'm sorry. It wasn't my intent."

Wow. Guess, I know where Lucas gets his blunt, honest manners.

She tried to wave off the apology. "No. You're fine, Mrs. Genezen."

"Right there, shows me it's not okay. Please, call me Adaline."

She agreed, and Lucas's mother continued, "I like you. You're fun. My family adores you, and you make my son very happy. Those two things alone are enough to adopt you as one of mine."

"Ugh," he groaned, "Don't get all mushy. You're making it weird."

"Shush," Harper said. She was loving it and told his mother such.

Adaline smirked at her son, then said more seriously, "It's true. I'm delighted to see you happy. You were a mess after Elizabeth and the—"

"Mom," Lucas said sharply, halting whatever Adaline was about to say.

Everything in her seemed to wilt. He looked crushed, and a little panicked. Confusion and guilt flooded her. His mother had come to make amends, and now they were both suddenly and inexplicably miserable.

Harper needed to do something. "Mrs.—I mean—Adaline, when Lucas gave me a tour of the house, I noticed your academic stole framed in the office. Did you know we went to the same college?"

"Wow, what a coincidence! It's such a small school. What did you study?" his mother asked, grasping at the topic as if it were a life preserver.

"I'm an artist, mainly a sculptor. I got a Bachelor of Fine Arts."

"Ah, yes, Lucas mentioned you owned an art gallery in one of his buildings. I'll have to stop by."

"I would love that," Harper said, meaning it.

Thankfully, the tension between mother and son had disappeared. They'd both relaxed into their wicker chairs.

Adaline took a sip of her drink. "I'll bring Grant. He used to draw and adores galleries. I do too, but don't have an artistic bone in my body."

"So, your son takes after you?" she teased.

"Hey." Lucas nudged her, their laughter mixing.

She held up her index and middle finger. "Two words. Pottery class."

Adaline's smiled widened. "Oh, do tell."

She did, and by the time she finished, the sun was dipping into the horizon, and the three of them were doubled over with laughter.

Chapter Nineteen

Lucas knocked on Harper's door. Usually, he'd hear her padding footsteps on the creaking wooden stairs. Or she'd shout 'coming!' from somewhere on the main floor of her condo.

He tried again. Nothing. Her place was dead quiet.

As he pulled out his cell to call her, the lock disengaged. She stood before him with red-rimmed eyes.

"Are you okay?" he asked, alarmed.

She didn't answer, just stepped aside, motioning for him to come in.

He closed the door, his unease growing. "What's wrong?"

Handing him a stick, she bypassed the stairs directly in front of them, making a right into the living room. She slouched onto her dark blue couch, clutching one of the gray throw pillows and staring at the floor.

What in the world is wrong?

Stopping in the archway, he waited. His mild worry was morphing into a full-blown panic.

Crossing his arms over his chest, he remembered the stick in his hand.

He brought it closer to examine it. It took less than two seconds to realize what he was holding.

A pregnancy test. With two pink lines.

Holy shit.

About a million emotions slammed into him. Unable to process them all, he froze, stock-still, and stared at the test.

His rational side screamed this was too soon. The logical side said it didn't matter, what's done was done, letting his heart cry with joy.

"Lucas?" she whispered.

Shit. He shook himself. Standing motionless and mute wasn't the best response. "You're pregnant?"

"According to the three tests I took, I am," she said to the floor.

"You told me you were on birth control."

"I am."

"Will you please look at me?"

Her gaze met his, and he saw total devastation.

Damn, she wasn't happy. At all.

A chilly thought froze his blood. She might not want this baby.

He walked to the couch, and taking her hands, he brought her into his arms. "What do you want to do?" he asked, against her cheek. "The choice is yours and I'll support you, no matter your decision, but I have to tell you how I feel. I want this baby and to raise it with you.

She clung to him. A quiet sob broke from her, wounding his heart. When minutes passed and she didn't reply, panic gripped him.

He found it impossible to keep silent. "If you've never wanted to be a mother, I understand, and I'll raise the baby alone. I'd rather do it with you, but I get it might not be what you want. Just, please, please don't get rid of it." He choked on the last word, babbling, lost in his fear.

Her shoulders shook as more tears fell. He wrapped his arms tighter, bringing her impossibly closer. "Please say something. Let me know what you're thinking."

"I can't. My brain is overcrowded right now." She sniffled. "Everything is clogged in my head, wailing at me."

"Which is the strongest, yelling the loudest?"

"Relief," she said, into his shirt. "I was afraid you'd be angry and make demands I wouldn't be able to accept. Or you'd pressure me, making a difficult situation harder. Overall, I'm confused. I'm not ready for a baby. I'm not even sure I want kids, let alone with someone I'm not in a serious relationship with."

"What do you mean, not serious? We're more than some fun fling, right? I assumed after we talked that night at the bar, you felt the same."

"I meant we haven't been dating very long. I've seen you with your nieces and nephews, it's obvious you don't hate kids, but it doesn't mean you want your own."

Discomfort pinched and prickled at his skin. He wished he let his mom finish her sentence last week. She'd gotten sentimental and nearly blurted about Elizabeth's pregnancy.

He'd cut her off, wanting to be the one to tell Harper about that particular heartbreak. Although, with the way she was touchy with his marriage, he feared there'd never be a good time.

If he told her now, would it help or hurt?

She sighed. "I stared at the damn test, all my dreams fading as the pink line darkened. I pictured selling my gallery, getting a practical job, and raising this baby alone."

He tilted her chin, kissed her tear-streaked cheeks. "None of that will happen. I want to be a father. I want to be in your life."

Hell, he wanted to do more. If she'd allow it, he'd get her a twenty-four-hour on-call doctor. A bulletproof car would be nice too. Or a tank.

He learned the hard way nothing was guaranteed and wanted to stack the odds in their favor in any way possible.

Fear of losing her, losing everything again, tried to strangle him. He fought it back into the dark corners of his soul, where despair lived.

Hell, this was a sign to stop wasting time, to start their life together. He cared about her. More than that, he loved her, and now they were going to have a baby together.

Lucas kissed her cheek again, then her lips, he whispered, "Let's get married."

She jerked from his arms, disappointment clouding her beautiful face. "Lucas, I wasn't hinting for a marriage proposal."

"I know—"

She gave him an angry wave of her hand. "I get we're doing this all wrong, but hell, we haven't even said I love you to each other. I'm not getting married because I'm pregnant. My dad did that with my mom. It didn't work out well."

One. He wasn't anything like her selfish father. Two. He did love her, had for a while. He figured she knew this.

Guess I should've said the words aloud.

He couldn't now. Even he knew the timing was wrong. "Fine. I'll let it go. For now."

"Stubborn man," she said, with an annoyed huff.

"Yup, almost as stubborn as my woman."

The corners of her mouth twitched, and it eased the fist around his heart. He reached for her. Without hesitation she returned to his arms. It was even better than her almost smile.

He kissed her forehead. "You aren't in this alone."

She snuggled into his chest. "That's all I needed to hear."

Chapter Twenty

Harper made her way to Maggie's front door under the rolling clouds. The dark morning sky matched her mood. Harper's thoughts and turbulent emotions whirling and spinning through her. She was a cyclone of fear and anxiety.

Also, to her immense surprise, there was a sliver of anticipation twisting around her concerns. While the timing and circumstances were terrible, part of her was excited.

She wasn't one of those women who had to have kids, yet she wasn't against it. For her, it was if she met the right man. Lucas probably would make a wonderful father.

What was unclear was if he was the right man for *her*.

Groaning, she recalled their small quarrel. He wanted to drive her here. Run errands while she visited. Then escort her to the doctors.

Since learning she was pregnant, it was almost as if he was afraid to leave her alone. The delicate flower treatment was getting old. She'd lost it this morning, snapping at him, but at least he backed off.

His attentiveness was nice, and she was, without a doubt, relieved he wanted to be part of this scary craziness, yet it also hurt her. Maybe she was selfish that it bothered her that the doting, talk of love and marriage began after she told him she was pregnant.

Not that she'd even considered the proposal he'd thrown out last month. She was thankful he didn't mention it again.

She didn't need to get married. Nor would she ever accept when the man's reasons were clouded with uncertainty and upheaval.

He might think it was the right, noble thing to do now. However, as the years passed, he'd regret his rash decision. Perhaps abandon her as her father had done to her mother. She refused to set herself up for that sort of heartache.

She rang the doorbell, her mind far away, filled with her troubles. When the front door whipped open half a second later, she squeaked like a mouse and stumbled back.

"You okay?" Lincoln opened the screen door, stepping outside.

"Yeah, fine." She tapped her temple. "My head's in the clouds."

Lincoln glanced at the sky. "You might want to get it out of there before it gets hit by lightning."

She laughed, and it felt good. "Or so I'll notice drummers who are trying to give me a heart attack."

His eyes widened with mock seriousness. "Oh, I know, it was cruel, even wretched, of me to answer the door after you rang the doorbell."

"Good. I'm glad you understand your cruelty."

He snorted, sweeping his arm in an 'after-you' gesture.

Going in, she asked, "Are you guys still practicing? I'm early."

She and Maggie were going to try a new restaurant around the corner from her place. Unable to stay home with her thoughts and worries, Harper had taken off, arriving with more than a half-hour to spare before they were supposed to meet.

"No, Amel had to leave. There was some issue at his family's restaurant. Anyway, want a cup of coffee?" Lincoln asked.

"Do you have decaf?"

"If you don't mind instant."

"I don't."

She made sure to keep her caffeine intake low, but it was bothering her stomach. She wasn't sure if it was stress or the pregnancy.

That word and her didn't feel like they belonged together. Would they ever? Maybe after today, when they went to her first doctor's appointment and ultrasound, it would all become real.

Trailing behind Lincoln to the kitchen, she focused on his friendly chatter. He was telling her Maggie and Tanner were in the practice studio, finishing a song they've been writing and struggling with for the past week.

He was handing her the warm mug as Maggie wandered in, stopping in her tracks. "Damn, woman you look like hell. Everything okay?"

"Awe, our Mags." Lincoln snorted. "Always so gentle with her words."

She held her hands, palms up. "What did I say?"

Harper smiled, not the least bit bothered by her friend's blunt manner. "It's been a rough week."

"I'll leave you two to your lady talk." He grabbed his mug then left.

Maggie took the seat across from Harper. "Really, you seem wrecked. Are you okay?"

Unsure if she wanted to get into the pregnancy, she went with the easiest explanation. "I'm stressing about stuff to do with the gallery."

"Such as..."

"Two weeks from today, I'm hosting an art show for a prevalent local artist. The invites were sent."

Maggie nodded. "I got mine and RSVP'd."

Harper smiled. "Thank you, and so did most on the list. I'll have some big online bloggers and magazines there."

"That's great!"

"It is, *but* the artist is behind on the piece he's supposed to reveal the night of the show. We've been creating a ton of hype for the unveiling. It'll be embarrassing if he can't deliver." She drew in a breath, releasing it slowly. "Then this morning, the woman I used last time to play the piano for the gallery's opening canceled on me."

"Well, I can't help you with your artist, but I can solve your last problem."

Harper tilted her head. "Oh, yeah? How?"

"I'll play the piano at your party."

Tears of appreciation welled behind her lashes, threatening to fall. There was no way she'd accept, but gratitude flooded her. "I can't have the singer of ThreePence wasting her time at my little gallery."

"Please, you're my friend." Maggie smacked Harper's hand resting on the table. "Plus, your gallery is awesome. Be proud."

"Oh, I am. Anyway, none of this is a big deal. I'll make it work."

"Yes, and one way is with me playing that lovely, purple baby grand you have in the gallery."

She opened her mouth to protest, but her friend held up a hand. "I was going anyway. So, listen, when I arrive there better not be someone sitting on my bench. If there is, I'm knocking their ass off it."

Harper laughed, warmth expanding through her chest. She was lucky to have such a great friend. "I don't even know how to thank you."

"No need. Wait, I know." She tabbed an index finger on the table. "Since you refused to take any money for designing ThreePence's album cover *and* letting us keep the art, consider this payment."

Giving in, Harper said, "Okay. Deal."

Maggie leaned her chair on its back two legs, glancing into the living room. She was probably looking at the painting they were referring to, the one hanging proudly over the fireplace.

She did love seeing it when she visited.

Maggie's chair banged as all four legs met the tiled floor. "Are you going to tell me what else is wrong?"

Surprise made Harper's limbs tingle. "What makes you think there's more?"

"Call it a hunch."

Damn, the woman was perceptive.

"I might be pregnant," she blurted, oddly relieved to share the crazy news with a trusted friend.

Besides Lucas and her mom, she kept the news to herself, wanting to go to her doctor's first. Needing to confirm it was real before telling others.

Maggie's mouth dropped open. She snapped it shut. "Do I offer congratulations, or should I console you?"

"Got me. I'm mostly terrified." She clutched her coffee cup tighter, telling Maggie everything. How she was ambivalent about having kids, and it would depend on the man. He'd have to want a family and plan on taking part in raising his children.

"Is Lucas that man?"

"I have no idea. We're too new."

"Really? Didn't you meet him at Jacob's wedding? A year ago."

"Yes, but we didn't talk again until three months later. It had been brief and didn't end well." She remembered the elation at seeing Lucas at Greta's barbeque, followed by the crushing disappointment after they talked. "After which, another six months or something passed until we met again. We've been dating since May. So, we've actually only been together around three months."

"Do you love him? Or could you?" Maggie asked.

"Yes," she said without hesitation. "Although, I've never told him."

"Why?"

"I'm afraid he won't say it back. Or worse, he'll say it because he doesn't want to hurt me, but the truth will be in his eyes."

Like how he did when I first told him I was pregnant.

Maggie drummed her fingers on the table. "I've seen you two together. I'd be willing to bet my next royalty check he feels the same."

"More than Elizabeth?"

Maggie's brows pulled together. "It's not a competition."

Harper's shoulder slumped, ashamed. "My brain knows this, but my heart—"

"I get it," Maggie said. "Whether or not he loves you, or can't in the way you require, you're stuck with him because of the baby."

"Yup. That sums it up." Harper sighed.

When she decided to have sex for the first time, she told her mother. They'd gone to the doctor's and gotten her on birth control. After, her mom bought a box of condoms. She'd always used both, until Lucas.

What was the saying? If it wasn't for bad luck, she'd have no luck.

"So, um, are you sure? One hundred percent you're pregnant?" Maggie asked.

"I will be today. I've taken three tests. All were positive, and this afternoon, Lucas and I are going to my first ultrasound appointment."

"Seriously?" Tanner said from behind her.

Harper yelped as her heart jumped to her throat. Maggie had a similar reaction.

"Jesus, babe." She gasped. "How in the hell do you move like a freaking ghost."

"I don't. You're probably going deaf because you refuse to wear earplugs at shows." He came closer, resting his hands on his girlfriend's shoulders.

She rolled her eyes but patted his hand with affection. "I don't like how loud my voice sounds in my head when I sing."

"Stop using the cheap earplugs you get off the airplanes. Try mine."

Maggie shrugged. "Maybe."

Harper could tell this wasn't the first time they had this argument. She welcomed the distraction and watching them was amusing. They'd been together for at least two years, yet the desire and compassion radiating from them reminded her of couples in the early stages of a relationship.

She wanted the same with Lucas. So far, they had it. They respected each other, and even with the current stress, she craved him as much as the first night they met. He seemed to feel the same.

However, passion didn't mean they were destined to last. Wanting her body wasn't the same as needing her heart.

"Did I hear right? Are you pregnant?" Tanner yanked Harper from her depressing musings.

Why the hell is Tanner grinning like this is the best news he's heard all year?

"Maybe. Probably," she said. "Lucas and I are going to the doctor's today to know one-hundred percent."

"After everything he's been through." Tanner rapped his knuckles on the wood table, taking the seat next to Maggie, his smile huge as he talked fast. "Well, I'm happy for him. I bet he's thrilled."

She was confused. "Everything he's been through," she parroted. "Do you mean more than losing his wife?"

Maggie gripped Tanner's arm, and his delighted smile fell. He swallowed hard as if his previous words were trying to strangle him.

What the hell was going on?

Unease tugged on her gut. "What happened?"

"Oh, um, nothing. I meant, he cares about you. He, uh, really likes you and has always wanted to be a dad..."

Tanner's *oh-shit* face would have been comical if dread wasn't smothering her humor. Part of her whispered that she didn't want to hear the truth.

Reason screamed this was important, though, and she demanded it. "Come on, Tanner, spill."

"Harper," he said, beseechingly, "it's not my place."

She guessed, but wanted it confirmed. "Elizabeth was pregnant when she died, wasn't she?"

His shoulder slumped, and he muttered, "Yeah."

Maggie took Harper's hand. "You didn't know?"

She shook her head as her heart broke for Lucas, and herself.

The poor man had lost so much. Yet, it didn't stop the anger thrumming through her veins, settling into her heart.

It cut her to the core that he kept it from her. Especially after learning she was pregnant. How could they have any sort of future when everything kept circling around to his past, his loss?

Chapter Twenty-One

"Lucas," Harper called from the entry of his house, not sure if she wanted to shout or cry.

She settled on slamming the door, then tossed the single key to his house onto the small foyer table. He'd given it to her the day after learning she was pregnant. Insisting she take it in case she needed to rest after work, and he wasn't home to let her inside. He didn't want her driving home if she was tired.

At the time, she found it a bit excessive. Now his overprotectiveness made sense.

She called his name again, not going further into the house. She might have a key, but it didn't mean she was comfortable walking around like the place was hers.

He stuck his head out from the bedroom; his upper body was shirtless. Even in her current distress, she couldn't help admiring the view. He did have lovely shoulders and mouthwatering biceps.

"You're early. Give me five minutes." He stopped, giving her a once-over. "You look pissed. Did you and Maggie argue?"

"No. We're fine," Harper clipped.

"Hold on."

He disappeared inside his bedroom, reappearing seconds later, pulling on his T-shirt. When it fell past his belt, she met his gaze. Concern was reflected in his eyes.

"What's wrong?" he asked again.

She opened her mouth, but the words she needed to say were clogged in her throat.

Coming closer, he cupped her cheek. "Please tell me."

"Why didn't *you* tell *me*?" Her pain made her sound angrier than intended.

He stared back blankly. "Can you be more specific?"

"Why didn't you tell me Elizabeth was pregnant when she died?"

He froze, and his eyes clouded with pain. The complete devastation on his face tore at her heart.

"How? Why?" He stopped, swallowing before taking a deep breath, then continued. "What difference does it make? It's my past. Something you want to pretend doesn't exist."

"That's not true," she stuttered, not sure if she was telling a lie. "The night at the bar—"

"You promised not to run anymore. You never gave any indication you wanted to deal with my past." He whispered, yet it echoed through her like a shout. "Don't you think I wanted to tell you? I love you and want to share everything with you. From my pain and fear to happy memories, of then and now. But you treat my past as though it's a fucking infection. Something that will kill what we have."

His words gutted her. They revealed so much about him. About them.

One. He loved her and was willing to bury his pain to save her from it.

Two. She was an awful girlfriend.

Harper demanded his heart, while also punishing him for his capacity to love.

A few feet of space were between them. It felt like the Grand Canyon. She flung herself into his arms, praying he wouldn't reject her.

His arms slid around her without hesitation, and she cried into his chest, relieved. "I'm sorry. I didn't mean to make you feel that way."

"I know, and you're right. I should've told you. It's hard for me to talk about, and once you told me you were pregnant, the timing was wrong."

He stroked her hair, from the top of her head to her lower back, repeating the motion until she was soothed. Once her rioting emotions were in some semblance of order, she stepped half an inch away, needing to see his handsome face.

She took in the worry lines still etched between his brows and kissed them. "I get it. I honestly do, but it would have been nice to know. At least I'd have understood why you turned crazy, psycho protective after I showed you the pregnancy test."

His surprised laughter wiped away most of her sadness. She'd hoped her teasing would lighten the moment, and his amusement was a treasured gift.

He brought her flush against him, sliding his hands into her back pockets. "I haven't been *that* bad."

"The hell you haven't. You insisted on hovering." She grinned. "Sorry, I mean helping, whenever I was trying to work at my mom's house."

"You need a big, strong man to lift those huge pieces of marble and stone." He flexed, doing a muscleman pose making her giggle. "Seriously, you shouldn't be lifting them even if you weren't pregnant."

She snorted. "First off, I use a dolly for the big ones. Second, you were rushing to my side anytime I picked up anything weighing more than a pound."

He shrugged, not appearing the least bit sorry.

"You suggested I sell my Mercedes Roadster for a minivan?" She shuddered. "Even if I had twelve kids, I'd never get one of those."

"Fine." He chuckled. "I'll drive the minivan. However, we're going to need a bus if you plan on having a dozen kids."

She snuggled into his chest, laughing, loving his immediate assumption they'd be having this hypothetical family together. That he was perfectly happy spending the rest of his life with her.

He shifted. "It's almost four. We better get going, or we'll be late for our appointment."

She nodded but held him tighter when he started to move away. He looked at her with a question in his eyes.

"I love you too," she said.

His smile, followed by the sweetest kiss, told her all was right with the world. And them. They could handle anything as long as they were together.

· · ● · ● · ● · ● · ● · · ●

Lucas's heart was light and hopeful. He'd been positive sharing details of his marriage would send Harper running again. Instead, telling her a painful piece of his past crumbled some of the silent wall between them. He felt closer to her.

He squeezed her hand before opening the door to the waiting room. After following her inside, the scent of disinfectant and baby slammed into him.

It threw him into his past. For half a second, pain pierced him to his soul before morphing into a melancholy sadness for Elizabeth. She'd lost out on so much.

Shaking his head, he let go of the what-ifs. His time with Elizabeth was cut short; nonetheless he was grateful for the time he'd been given with her.

Changing the past was impossible, and he had plenty to be thankful for in his present. For some reason, he was lucky enough to love not one but two amazing women in his lifetime.

They took the empty seats next to a table that had been an old-fashioned dresser once. It overflowed with baby pamphlets and free samples. The mauve walls and subdued paintings murmured this was a safe haven for women and expecting parents.

Although the only other guy in the room seemed to have missed the vibe. While his partner sat calmly, flipping through a magazine, he kept taking deep breaths as if practicing his Lamaze homework. When the man began to rock in his chair, Lucas focused to the magazine rack next to the sign in window. He didn't want the dude's nervous energy to infect him.

He had enough of his own, thank you very much.

Sliding his hand through Harper's, he squeezed lightly to get her attention. "Nervous?"

She inhaled, and her shaky exhale gave him the answer. "A little."

"What has you worried? The procedure or—"

"Both. None of my close friends have been through this, so I'm not sure what to expect. But, mostly it's the *or* that scares me. After the ultrasound this will become real."

He was stuck on how to respond. He could tell her what to expect during this appointment. The next three or four as well.

However, even with the talk they just had, he worried it would hurt more than help.

As for it becoming real, it scared the shit out of him too. Part of him wanted this so bad, but he also wished it had happened a year or so later. When they were more confident in their relationship. Maybe even married.

Again, he suspected those thoughts wouldn't offer her comfort. He kept his mouth closed, wrapping an arm around her shoulder and bringing her closer. He kissed her temple, telling her without words he was there for her.

The door separating the waiting from exam rooms opened. A nurse with a no-nonsense blonde bob and purple scrubs appeared.

Scanning the clipboard in her hand, she called, "Harper."

They stood, and the nurse smiled politely at them. "Follow me, please."

With each step closer, his heart thumped faster. He didn't know if it was from panic or joy. Probably both.

After taking Harper's weight and height, the nurse led them to an exam room, telling them the doctor would be in shortly. She closed the door quietly behind her, the click of the knob settling into place the only sound in the room.

They stared at each other for half a beat before Harper said in a near whisper, "Does this feel surreal to you?"

Lucas took in the ultrasound machine, the sterile tools, and more baby samples from a variety of businesses. "Yup."

He tried to meet her gaze, but it was tripping all over the room. Patting the table, he said, "Why don't you sit?"

"Okay." She slid onto it, the paper crinkling beneath her.

The poor woman appeared ready to faint. He had to do something.

Moving closer, he tapped on one of the table's lowered stirrups. "Should I adjust these? Raise them?"

Her mouth dropped open. "What for?" she squeaked. "The ultrasound scan goes *on* the belly, right? *Right*?"

"Oh, it does, but..." He waggled his eyebrows. "I have a few fun ideas on what we can do with your legs in them."

Her lovely laughter filled the room, and she slapped his shoulder. "You're such a man."

"That I am." He ran his palms up her thighs, basking in her smile.

The door to their room opened, and a petite fortyish woman came inside. Her light brown hair was in a low bun, and she wore similar scrubs as the nurse, but the white lab coat shouted 'doctor.'

She introduced herself to him as Dr. Lafoy, then faced Harper, her smiled growing. "Let me guess, he was suggesting you try the stirrups?"

Harper laughed harder, covering her mouth and nodding. His neck and cheeks heated. He liked this doctor already.

"I swear, if I ever get tired of helping bring babies into the world, I could make a fortune selling these," she patted the exam table, "as sex props."

Lucas smirked. "Well, you'd still be helping to bring babies into the world.

The doctor full-on belly laughed. "This is true."

Walking to a small sink in the corner, Dr. Lafoy washed and dried her hands. When she turned to Harper, some of her humor was replaced with concern. "I was surprised to read you're here for an ultrasound. You've had the IUD in for almost a year. It should be good for another five. Did you have it removed by another doctor?"

Harper shook her head. "Nope. From what I learned online, it might have fallen or slipped. "

"Possibly. This has to be a huge shock. How are you handling it?" Dr. Lafoy asked.

"I'm freaking out," Harper admitted. She reached for Lucas's hand. "I'm also grateful for having a boyfriend who wants to help me raise our child. He keeps me sane."

Her declaration emptied his mind of nearly every worry and concern. They were a team, and together would be stronger.

Bringing their entwined fingers to his mouth, he kissed lightly on the pulse point of her wrist.

"You are lucky to have found each other." Lafoy placed a hand on top of the ultrasound machine and tapped it with her short fingernails. "Are you two ready?"

His pulse began to thrum as the doctor flicked on the device. Everything was about to change.

"Lie back," she told Harper. "I'm going to put some gel on your stomach. It won't hurt, but it'll be cold."

The screen was facing the doctor as the wand glided over Harper's flat belly. The eerie pulsating echo of the machine filled the room.

His heart thumped heavy and hard when a small line appeared between Dr. Lafoy's brows. She shifted closer to the screen, her lips pulling tight.

"What's wrong?" Harper's grip on his hand tightened.

The doctor didn't answer right away, all her focus on the screen. When she removed the ultrasound wand from Harper's stomach, Lucas's spirit splintered. Something wasn't right.

He tried to keep the worry from his voice. "Why can't we hear the heartbeat?"

During Elizabeth's first appointment, they heard it. Now he and Harper were met with soul-shattering silence.

He glanced at the doctor. Her earlier ease and laughter had disappeared. Panic bloomed in his chest. He repeated his questions.

"I need to do a transvaginal ultrasound," Dr. Lafoy said.

"Why?" Harper sounded defeated.

"I want to do the other ultrasound before I say anything."

Harper shifted onto her elbows. "Tammy, I've been coming to you since I was sixteen. Talk to me. Please tell us what's going on."

Dr. Lafoy's shoulders slumped, and she swiveled the screen so they could see it. "This is the embryo." She pointed to a dot on the right. "It's in the fallopian tube, instead of in the uterus. I'm sorry."

The two words hit him like a double punch. He locked his knees, afraid his legs would give out.

He didn't want to hear the rest. But since when did the universe give two shits what he needed or wanted?

"How is that possible, and what does it mean for Harper?" he asked.

"This is extremely rare, however, with IUDs, the risk is slightly higher. I'm nearly positive, but to be sure I need to do a transvaginal ultrasound." Her sympathetic gaze turned to Harper. "You have an ectopic pregnancy."

Lucas wasn't familiar with the term, but by the doctor's face, he knew it wasn't good. He swallowed the fears trying to crawl from his throat. "What happens now?"

"The pregnancy can't continue. If it doesn't end on its own, the fallopian tube will eventually rupture." She returned her attention to Harper. "You're too far along to do the wait and see method. After we do the other ultrasound, I'll give you medication to end the pregnancy. You'll have to come back at least twice a week for the next couple of weeks to decide if you'll need another injection."

Harper appeared frozen, unable to speak. Tears had gathered at the corners of her lashes before silently falling. Lucas wiped them away with his thumb, holding in the sadness threatening to obliterate him.

Facing the doctor, he asked, "What should we expect afterward?"

"She will be in some pain. How much, I'm not sure. It depends on the person. Also, getting pregnant is out of the question for the next three months."

Lucas nodded. Harper continued to stare at the screen.

He didn't ask if she was okay. How could she be?

Thankfully, she hadn't let go of his hand. He held on to it, hoping she found some comfort in it. Needing it himself.

Later, when everything was finished, he helped a silent Harper into his car. The other ultrasound and injection didn't take long but it felt like two lifetimes.

Once settled in their seats, he asked, "Will you come home with me?"

She kept her face turned to the passenger side window. "No, you have a meeting with Ben. It's close to my mom's place. Just drop me off there."

"I'm not going to 'just drop you off.' I'll call Ben and let him know I can't be there. He'll manage without me. I want to take care of you. Make sure you're okay."

She finally looked at him. The exhaustion hung from her, tearing at his heart. "I'm fine. Really. All I want is sleep. Go to your meeting. Call me after, or come back. It's up to you."

Didn't she want him there? They could comfort each other.

"I don't want to leave you alone."

"My mom will be home, if not right when I get there, shortly after." She rested a hand on his knee. "Please go. I'll feel worse if you skip the meeting. This morning you were telling me how important it was for you and Ben to impress this guy."

His brother-in-law would be pissed, but he'd get over it. And right now, Lucas didn't give a shit. Business was the last thing on his mind.

All that mattered was Harper. Of course, it meant giving her what she needed, not what he wanted.

Everything in him screamed leaving her alone was wrong. Yet it seemed sleep was what her body and mind required.

She must have sensed his inner turmoil because she whispered, "Please, Lucas, drop me off at my mom's."

His shoulders slumped. "Fine. Sleep, and I'll be there as soon as the meeting is finished."

She nodded. Her hand slipped from his leg to her lap, and her gaze returned to the side window.

His heart thudded dully. He rubbed his chest against the spreading pain. Giving up, he started the car.

They drove in a silence that screamed their loss, confusion, and agony.

Chapter Twenty-Two

Harper's cell rang as she burrowed into her old bed. She answered it without checking the caller ID, figuring her mother was calling. She knew about today's doctor appointment.

When a man's voice greeted her, she was confused. It took her a second to recognize her friend's voice. She wasn't in the mood for idle chatter. "Hey, Warren. I'm getting ready to take a nap. Can I call you back later?"

"Five in the evening seems late for a nap," he replied. "Also, why were you dropped off at your mother's to take one?"

She sat up, more awake, but muddled. "How do you know where I'm at?"

Warren laughed. "Because I'm stalking you."

After her miserable day and recalling Patricia's certainty that he wanted Harper as his backup plan, she couldn't find her humor. The phone line filled with dead air.

"I'm kidding. Relax, woman," Warren huffed. "I was driving by and saw you getting out of a car."

"Sorry. It's been a long day. I asked Lucas to drop me off on his way to a meeting."

"Do you want some company?"

It was on the tip of her tongue to refuse. She wanted sleep. To forget this awful day and the heartbroken look on Lucas's face when the doctor told them the pregnancy needed to be terminated.

However, she was starting to hurt bad and needed help. Dr. Lafoy recommended small meals and to take the prescribed meds to keep the pain under control. She'd left the pills on the counter. Plus, the idea of walking to the kitchen to make a sandwich and find her medicine made everything in her ache with exhaustion.

"Maybe for a little bit. If you'd do me a huge favor."

There was a slight pause, then he said, "Depends. If you need my kidney, I already promised it to my drunk uncle. If you want my firstborn. Fine. But," he paused, "we make it together."

She choked on a laugh that was also a sob. His timing couldn't be worse, yet somehow the joke cleared away some of her sadness.

"Nothing so drastic. All I need is my painkillers and a bowl of soup."

"Wait. Are you sick? I don't want to catch anything."

She shook her head, annoyed and amused. "No. Don't worry, you won't get a man-cold."

"Hey, those are deadly," he joked. "But if you're not sick, I'll be there in ten."

After giving him the code to the house, they hung up. She pulled the covers to her chin and closed her eyes.

She must have drifted off because when she opened them again, Warren was standing over her. His eyebrows were drawn together, and he was holding a small brown paper bag in one hand and her prescription bottle in the other. His concern chased away some of her sadness.

"Are you sure you don't have the flu or something?" he asked.

She snorted. Of course, he was worried about himself. Typical Warren. Oh well, at least he brought her food and pills.

She took the offered items. "I'm positive, but if you're concerned, feel free to leave."

"Wow, a cranky Harper. That's something I don't see often." He made a pushing motion with his hands. "Scoot. Make room for me. Tell me what happened. Was it something with *that* guy you're dating?"

Why did he insist on acting like he didn't remember Lucas's name? They met in March, and it was now the end of summer.

She shuffled to the side, and Warren stretched out next to her. Buying for time, debating if she wanted to unload on him, she took the meds and opened the soup container.

Okay, he redeemed his self-centered ways when the heavenly scent of cheddar-basil wafted from the bowl, giving her comfort. He'd remembered and brought her favorite.

She kissed his cheek. "Thank you."

"No problem," he said, sounding pleased with himself. "Now, spill. Tell me what has you upset."

She decided to tell him, giving the briefest version. After, they sat in silence. The poor guy was probably trying to figure out what the hell to say.

He plucked at a piece of non-existent lint on his jeans. Not meeting her eyes, he asked, "Are you sad or relieved?"

"A bit of both. I'm not even sure I want kids, and I most definitely didn't need one now. I would have preferred to have been married, or at least positive I wanted to spend my life with the man I'm going to have children with."

Honestly, even with the drama and complications between them, she was certain Lucas was that man for her. What she wasn't sure of was if she was the woman for him.

"Despite the stress and upheaval a baby would've caused, I'm sad." Then she admitted, "Also relieved. Which makes me feel terrible."

Truthfully, the guilt was eating her alive. Lucas lost another chance at fatherhood. He must be devastated. She hated herself for causing him pain.

She kept that part to herself. Sharing her remorse would be cathartic, but it wasn't right to share such a personal, heartbreaking story.

"How's your guy taking all of it? He's probably thrilled to have dodged the bullet."

Indignation slammed into her. "Why? Would I be such a horrible person to have a child with?"

"No," Warren stammered. "That came out wrong. It's more that I figured he didn't want to have kids."

"Shows you don't have a clue about him."

He squinted at her, brows lowering, "He does want them? Do you think he tried to get you pregnant?"

"Jesus. No. Why do you keep twisting my words to make him sound like a bad guy? What is your deal?"

She was regretting having him visit. Today, her heart was empty, and he was filling it with doubt. Maybe there was truth to what Patricia had said.

Could someone be that selfish? Was she as bad at picking friends as boyfriends? Well, besides Lucas. He was a good man.

Too good for her.

Since they began dating, she was constant drama. First running from him every chance she got, now this.

He probably wanted to break up but was too nice to do it.

Why stay with someone who might not be able to carry his kids? Sure, the doctor told them the possibility of another ectopic pregnancy was rare, but she also told them the chances of other complications were higher because of this one.

She was aware that worrying about these sorts of things was stupid. All it did was invite more pain, but her defenses were low, allowing every depressing thought to take root and bloom inside her.

Plus, she'd seen Lucas's look of absolute devastation. Being the cause of it tore at her.

Heavy pressure built behind her eyes; she was going to cry. Damn it.

From the way Warren appeared ready to bolt, he saw it. "Harper—"

Whatever else he was going to say was cut off by the ringing doorbell. It couldn't be Lucas. From the way he was talking this morning, he and Ben would be busy most of the afternoon, well into the evening. They wanted to hire a property manager and was meeting their top choice for an early dinner.

The bell rang again. "Will you hand me my phone?"

He did, and there were at least ten missed calls from Lucas. Crap.

She patted Warren lightly on the arm. "Scooch, please. I need to get the door. It's probably Lucas."

"No. Stay here. I'll answer it." He stood and walked towards the hallway. "Do you want me to tell him to go away?"

She narrowed her eyes. "No."

He held up his hands. "Fine. Fine. I'll go get him."

Misery settled into her bones. She and Warren had been friends for many years, but she feared their friendship might have to end.

• • • ● ● • ● ● • • •

Lucas swiped end call on his cell, cursing.

Why in the hell wasn't she answering her phone?

The front door swung open, and relief washed through him, followed by anger sucker-punching him in the stomach.

What the fuck is he doing here?

Warren relaxed against the frame as if he owned the place. "Yeah," he drawled.

Lucas's hands curled into fists, but he managed to keep his voice steady. "You know why I'm here. For *my* girlfriend."

He'd seen the way Warren watched Harper. His thoughts weren't always those of a friend.

The bastard continued to block the entrance.

Lucas cocked a brow as if to say, you going to move? He silently began counting. If the prick was still blocking the entrance when he reached ten, his ass was getting shoved aside. He was bigger and jealous resentment boiled his blood. Warren would go down. Hard.

At five, the other man moved aside, but not before slicing with his words. "You should let her rest. I've already taken care of food and pain meds."

The smug, accusatorial stance angered and gutted Lucas. Why had Harper let this guy, and not him, take care of her?

Lucas swallowed his pride and thanked Warren. "She told me she wanted to sleep, yet it turned out she did need someone here. I'm glad you were here to help her."

"I didn't do it for you."

"No shit. I don't care why you did it, only that it was done."

"Did you do it on purpose?"

Lucas frowned. "What are you talking about?"

"She said you wanted kids. You aren't getting any younger. Did you intentionally knock her up?"

Lucas's whole body tensed as everything in him wanted to slam the other man with his fists and anger. He barely noticed when Warren took a step back.

"None of your fucking business."

Did Harper believe the shit Warren was saying? It was a possibility. Especially after learning Elizabeth had been pregnant when she died. Through his fury and fear, Lucas tried to remember who suggested they skip using condoms.

"Yes, it is, I'm her friend," the asshole insisted, bringing Lucas back from his worries and into his rage.

He leaned in, a few inches from Warren's face. "*Her friend*. Remember, that is all you are to her. Don't try screwing with what I have with her because of your missed chances and regrets."

Warren smiled. It was cold and calculating. "Oh, you think you're permanent, do you? No, sorry. Like the others, you're merely passing through. While I'll be here, and when I'm ready, she'll be waiting for me."

If Harper weren't already dealing with a fucktastically awful day, Lucas would punch the douchebag. He wrangled in his anger. A fight in her foyer was the last thing she needed.

"I'm not going anywhere." He started for the stairs, pausing on the first one. "But you can leave. She doesn't need you."

"Yeah, being here has suddenly lost its appeal. I'll go. For now." Warren left, slamming the door.

Good.

Shaking his head, Lucas trudged up the curving stairs. Too bad he couldn't get rid of Warren's words as easily as the man.

Would Harper close him out again? Maybe. Definitely, if she believed Lucas wanted her pregnant.

Honestly, the idea of him being a father filled him with joy and terror in equal measure. The hesitation wasn't because of Harper. He'd love to spend his life raising kids with her. No, what made him break into a cold sweat was the fear of losing them.

Losing her like he lost Elizabeth and his baby. Or what happened today.

His heart could only take so much pain before it shattered, becoming impossible to repair.

He gripped the railing on the stairs so tight his knuckles were ghost-white. He refused to let his grief own him.

Pressure built in his chest, reminding him to breathe. After a few deep lungfuls of air, he continued to Harper's room.

His oxfords drummed against the mahogany floors in the wide hallway. He'd been to Victoria's house a few times when Harper was working obsessively on a project and coming here was the only way to see her. Therefore, he was familiar with the house's layout and started toward her old room at the end of the hall, on the left.

Recalling the first time he met her here, he could barely grasp the stark contrast. He'd arrived late in the evening, and she opened the door in coveralls coated in dust. They were unbuttoned to her waist, yellow tank top underneath. Without a bra.

She offered to give him a quick tour of the house. He tried to pay attention. Her childhood home was impressive but was not as intriguing as the sway of her hips or the way her nipples peaked when she caught the growing hunger in his eyes.

They'd kissed and teased each other in all the rooms on the main floor. On the vast staircase he'd just left, he removed her coveralls, finding her in hot-as-hell cotton boy-short panties. They'd barely made it to her bedroom before they were naked, and he was inside her.

A small smile tilted the corners of his mouth, and his cheeks heated. They hadn't realized her mother had returned home early from a business trip while they were upstairs. When they'd gone in search of snacks, they found Victoria at the kitchen island, eating from a takeout container.

They tried to play it off that Harper was giving him a tour of the house. Their act wasn't very convincing, given her coveralls were laying, discarded in the middle of the stairs, and she was in only those sexy boy-short panties and yellow tank top.

Victoria's grin would have made the Cheshire Cat proud. "Fantastic, I'm sure you both enjoyed the tour. Well, it sounded like you had a nice time." She'd paused, taking a delicate sip of her red wine. "It is a lovely house but has a dreadful echo. If any of the doors are left open, every sound drifts to the main floor. And I mean *every sound*."

Groaning, Harper buried her face in Lucas's shoulders. His face, neck, hell, his whole body, flamed red at Victoria's teasing.

Mercifully, she changed the subject, asking Harper about the latest piece in her studio. Then she and Lucas discussed the pros and cons of buying and renting buildings. She'd been considering trying it.

Stepping onto the second floor, the memory and his small smile faded. The house was quiet, and he swore the silence had a weight to it. It was heavy with loss, regrets, and confusion.

He entered Harper's bedroom. His family was well-off, but next to his girlfriend's childhood home, his seemed quaint. Her room was almost the same size as the main floor of his house. It sported a massive bed with a deep blue upholstered headboard and a walnut frame. Completing the opulence was a chandelier, fireplace, and matching chairs by floor-to-ceiling windows.

All of it was secondary. What held his attention was the woman under the down comforter and the rumpled area next to her. It looked as if someone had been lying next to her.

Jealousy warred with his grief. "Why did you let *him* take care of you, but not me?"

"What is with you two? I'm not helpless. I don't need either of you." She sat ramrod straight. "If he left, why don't you follow right behind him? You two can have your pissing contest outside, away from me."

Her obvious annoyance with Warren soothed some of Lucas's jealousy. He tried for a conciliatory tone. "Sorry, I was thrown and upset when he answered the door. Plus, he was giving me shit." He came closer. "I get you two have known each other for years, and I'm not trying to play the possessive lover, but Warren wants to be more than your friend."

Harper's shoulders slumped, and she dropped back into her pillows. "Yeah, I think you're right."

Her admission surprised him, and his inner caveman returned. "Did that asshole make a move on you today?"

"No, settle down, Neanderthal." She smiled, and it almost touched her eyes. "He's never liked anyone I dated, but with you, he has a *big* problem. He keeps making negative comments, trying to plant doubts, hoping to break us up. Also, Patricia has made a few passing comments that have given me pause. Combined with a few things he's said today, our friendship is probably coming to an end."

A huge chunk of tension slid from his shoulders, but he tried to hide his relief. It was obvious from the slight tremble in her voice the decision wasn't easy.

Harper's lips pressed into a thin line. "Could you at least hide your pleasure and happiness?"

So much for disguising his feelings. The corner of his mouth twitched. "Sorry, you know from our card nights with Tanner and Maggie, my poker face sucks. I can't lie, I've never cared for Warren. Today, I like him even less. Before he left, he basically said I'm on my way out, and he'll be around, ready to sweep you off your feet...when he's done screwing other women."

Her hands formed tight fists. She cursed under her breath, muttering about always being someone's second choice.

He came to the edge of the bed. "You aren't mine."

She gave in a yeah-right look, and once again, Elizabeth's ghost hung between them. He was tattered and hurting from the awful day. He didn't have it in him to fight, to make Harper understand he was able to love her and his past.

Instead, he clamped his mouth shut and took off his suit jacket. Tossing it on the nearest chair, he started on the buttons of his shirt.

"What are you doing?"

"You need to rest. I'm going to let you sleep, but I'm not leaving." He pointed to the rumpled bedcover next to her. "Or is there only room in your bed for Warren?"

"Enough." She sighed, exhaustion oozing from the one word. "Let it go."

She was right, and Lucas worked to let go of his anger. Stepping away, he placed his shirt next to his jacket. He tried to hold in the question burning in his gut.

He couldn't and blurted, "Is it true what he said? Am I on my way out?"

Her gaze dropped. His heart followed.

When she looked at him again, there were tears in her eyes.

Please don't let me lose her today too.

"I love you, Lucas." She pushed back the covers. "Will you hold me?"

Her words allowed his heart to beat again, but it wasn't lost on him that she hadn't answered his question.

"I love you too." Pulling his cell from his front pants pocket, he set it on the nightstand. Toeing off his shoes, he paused. "Will your mom come in here when she gets home?"

She offered a weak smile. "Probably. I'm sure she'll want to check on me. So get under the covers."

"Like that's going to help. You hog the blankets."

Her light laughter soothed his weeping edges. "True. I suggest you don't go nude, sailor."

"Good call." He took off everything but his T-shirt and boxer briefs. Sliding into bed, he tugged the sheet tight under his ass, making her laugh again. He gathered her in his arms, loving the way she snuggled into his chest.

With his free arm, he dug his fingers into her hair, massaging her scalp the way she loved. After a few minutes, her breathing evened and her embrace went soft, telling him she was asleep.

He wouldn't be able to follow. It was early, and his mind was complete chaos. The day started with nervous anticipation and ended in bitter, conflicting emotions.

Then Ben did a complete one-eighty, shocking Lucas. Thankfully, in a good way.

His brother-in-law had beat him to the restaurant and was sipping on a beer. The guy they hoped to hire as their property manager had texted Ben telling him he was stuck in traffic, so Lucas ordered one as well.

His rough day must've been written all over him because Ben didn't give him a hard time for his near late arrival. Instead, he asked, "Who died?"

Lucas laughed, and it sounded like he was being strangled. "With me, are you sure you want to phrase it that way?"

Ben shot forward in his seat. "Shit. What's going on?"

Lucas tried waving off Ben, saying Harper had some medical issues. He figured mentioning her would cool further inquiries. He'd been wrong.

Concern emanated from the other man, and he peppered Lucas with questions until the whole sad story spilled from him. He was surprised to find the release cathartic.

Not only did Ben understand how this was a double blow to Lucas's soul, but he was free to unload in a way he couldn't with Harper. With her, he was afraid the depth of his sadness and the underlying guilty relief would hurt her.

He'd even confessed his dark, irrational fear. His worry that everything he loved was destined to die, and maybe he should leave Harper to save her from his curse.

"That's stupid," Ben declared. "Leaving someone you care for because of fear and superstitions would make you a coward. Plus, Harper's a good woman. Without her, your life would be empty. You'd been going through the motions before meeting her."

Too surprised to be offended, he'd burst out laughing. "Who's stolen my curmudgeon brother-in-law and replaced him with Harper's advocate?"

Ben had the good grace to apologize. "Fine. I'm sorry. I've been an asshole when it comes to her." He ran a hand under his mouth and sighed. "I'm still struggling with Elizabeth's death, and I took you moving on with someone else personally. It felt like you were forgetting her, letting her go."

That last part hurt. Ben made it sound as if Lucas's marriage hadn't been important to him. Like her death hadn't nearly killed him.

"Moving on doesn't mean I've forgotten your sister. Or that I don't miss her," he'd said in a clipped tone.

"Shit, I didn't mean to make it sound as if you didn't. I know you loved her. You were a great husband, and Elizabeth adored you. It's more, watching you falling for another woman, I hurt for my sister, for all she's lost and will never experience." Ben took a healthy swallow of his drink. "I selfishly wanted you to miss out too."

Lucas had been shocked, struck speechless at Ben's honesty. Before he could think of a response, Robert, their property manager hopeful, had arrived.

The guy was exactly what they needed, and after a shortlist of questions, they offered him the job. During dinner, there was a little back and forth on the details, but it didn't take long for them to have everything settled and talking of celebrating at the popular bar next door.

Well, their new property manager and Ben were discussing it. Lucas was trying to think of a way to leave. He needed to check on Harper without, once again, appearing like he didn't care about G&D.

As he sat trying to come up with a good excuse, Ben rescued him. He told Lucas to leave, saying he'd handle the celebrating part without him.

He didn't need to be told twice. He'd taken off, heading for Harper.

He kissed the top of her head, and she snuggled closer. He closed his eyes, and somehow sleep managed to crawl into him.

He dared to dream his future held more happiness than heartache.

Chapter Twenty-Three

The heavy chords of a violin woke Lucas from a fitful sleep. He swiped his phone from the nightstand, silencing the alarm, hoping it wouldn't wake Harper.

Old, familiar depression tried to greet him with the sun and pull him back into the dark. He fought it, unwilling to give in. Not this time. Harper needed him, and he needed her.

Rolling over, wanting her against him, he was met with emptiness. Cold, wrinkled sheets lay exposed like a bad omen.

"Harper?" Met with silence, he rose from the bed.

Unease skittered along his spine. It was six in the morning, where could she be?

"Shit." He rotated his shoulders, trying to dislodge nightmares and the start of a headache.

He had an eight o'clock meeting with an important client and wasn't sure if he should reschedule. Having something to keep him busy would be nice, but he needed to find Harper first. Make sure she didn't wish him to stay.

He worried pain or something worse might have woken her.

Checking the ensuite bathroom, he found it empty. However, the shower had condensation from recent use. The sight dissipated enough of his concern that he took the time to wash his face and brush his teeth before continuing his search.

Leaving the second floor, he made a quick left, peeking inside a large, well-used study. An enormous antique desk sat in the center of the room, covered with papers and files. The bookshelves overflowing with old and tattered books called to him. He made a note to return after finding Harper.

He bypassed an ultra-fancy dining room then a stuffy, regal living room for the more comfortable and homey family room. That was where she gravitated to when needing a break from her art studio. Maybe her sleep had been as broken as his, and she'd come here to watch TV.

Nope. The screen was dark.

Making sure the room was empty, he came inside to check the sectional. The tall back faced him, making it impossible to tell if she was on the couch. He ran his palm along the cashmere throw-blanket resting along the top, bending and finding it empty.

Why in the hell did the house have to be so flipping big? The environmentalist in him balked at the waste. The boyfriend in him bellowed in frustration.

Worry made his pulse pound, and all this square footage was aggravating the shit out of him.

Right as he opened his mouth to shout for Harper, a cupboard slammed from the kitchen. *Fucking finally.*

Spinning around, he headed in that direction, calling, "Why didn't you wake me?"

Entering the kitchen, he skidded to a stop. Victoria, not Harper, sat at the delicate circular table next to the bay window.

"Given I hit on you the first time we met, my daughter probably wouldn't appreciate me waking you," Victoria teased.

Her small smile was a little worn around the edges. He opened his mouth but didn't know what to say.

Was he supposed to apologize? He was sorry.

Not for getting her daughter pregnant. He loved Harper and would have been the man she needed, the father their child deserved. Together, they'd have given their child infinite love and a happy home.

He'd have made her see he wasn't anything like her father. He would stay by her side for as long as she wanted him. She was his heart.

No, his regrets lay in the physical and emotional pain the pregnancy was causing her.

Victoria walked to the cupboard next to the double sink. Grabbing a mug, she handed it to him. "Have some coffee. You look as tired and beat as my daughter."

"Where is she?"

"In her art studio."

He set the empty cup on the counter, turning to leave. All his worry slammed back into him. "She's supposed to be resting, not lifting freaking heavy stones and marble."

"Stop," Victoria commanded.

He stilled immediately.

Shit. No wonder this woman was such a success in her male-dominated job.

It didn't mean he was happy she was stalling him. The need to find Harper was damn near a compulsion.

"Do you know what happened yesterday?" he asked tersely.

"Yes."

His anger surged, and keeping his voice calm was difficult. "Then why did you let her go in there? She needs to rest."

Victoria cocked a brow. "Last time I checked, she's a grown woman. She doesn't have to listen to her mom. Or her domineering boyfriend."

"I'm not domineering," he huffed. "I'm concerned. The doctor said Harper needed to rest."

"Listen." She reached for the coffee pot and filled his discarded mug. "You go barging in there making demands, telling her what to do, it won't end well. She has enough of me in her that she'll tell you to piss off. Then to prove a point, she'll start messing around with the heavy stuff. Right now, she's hand sanding the delicate part of her sculpture. Nothing taxing. She needs her art. It's soothes her mind."

"Maybe I should give it a try." He nodded thanks when Victoria handed him the steaming cup.

She rested her hand on his shoulder. "How are you doing?"

The kindness and understanding in her voice nearly broke him. He dropped his gaze to his coffee. "I'll be fine," he muttered into his mug.

What could he say? That the heavy clouds of despair were trying to gather around him again. Or how he feared Harper was pushing him away, and this time it'd be for good.

Instead, he changed the subject. "At least I found her. This place is worse than Daedalus's labyrinth."

Victoria chuckled. "Yeah, this house is a monster. It's way too much for me. Hell, it was even before Harper moved out. Now it feels like a mausoleum."

"Why stay?"

"Originally, I bought it with my ex-husband planning to fill it with children. He made other plans and left. After that, I figured one kid was enough for me, but Harper struggled with her father walking out. I didn't want to uproot her by moving. Then I had the art studio made for her when she was a teenager. She still uses it, so I'm staying."

He was impressed. On the outside, Victoria came across as ruthless, even a dash heartless, yet her actions spoke volumes. Her heart would match his mother's.

"Harper's lucky to have you."

"I'm the lucky one. She keeps me grounded. Reminds me what's important." She rested against the counter and grinned. "On that note, she's fortunate to have you. You might have noticed, I don't hold men in high regard, but Lucas, you deserve it. I'm happy she found you."

His mouth fell open. Damn. She'd made him speechless. Something that *never* happened.

"Aw, you're flummoxed." She took a sip of coffee, her eyes sparkling with mischief. "It's a cute look on you."

He laughed, finding his voice. "Why do I suspect you love making men tongue-tied?"

Winking, she twisted around to refill her mug. She held the pot higher, silently asking if he wanted a refill. He did and gave her his cup.

After she filled it, he took a healthy sip, loving the deep roast.

Tipping his cup toward her, he said, "Thanks. I'm going to check on Harper." He laid a hand over his heart and grinned. "I solemnly swear not to be a Neanderthal."

"Smart man. Oh." She opened the cupboard, getting another cup and filling it with coffee. "This will help." She handed it to him. "Please try to be patient with her. She's sensitive and tends to ignore or run from her pain."

He was well aware of the way she handled her troubles. The problem was, with his current mindset, he might not have the motivation to keep chasing her.

"Thanks." He gave a half smile. "For the coffee and laughs. I needed both."

"Me too." She patted his arm before returning to her seat by the bay window.

He dipped his head in goodbye before making his way to Harper's studio. Since her tools were noisy and the dust terrible, the workshop was in the farthest corner of the house.

His brisk strides carried him down a massive hallway, through a gigantic mudroom. Looping the coffee mugs through one finger, he used the other hand to open the solid, heavy door of the studio.

She sat at an enormous metal table in the center of the room. Behind her were rows of industrial shelves, each filled with slabs of marble and different stones of all shapes and sizes. In front of her was the bust of a woman.

Harper peered around the statue, offering a tired smile. When her gaze landed on the mugs of coffee, it became more genuine. He tried not to let it bother him.

"You read my mind." She set a sheet of sandpaper on the table before wiping dust-covered hands on her thick apron. "I was about ready to take a break to get some coffee and toast."

"I don't have any food." He pointed with his thumb over his shoulder. "Do you want to go to the kitchen?"

"Is my mom still there?"

"Yeah."

She shook her head. "Then, no, I'm good staying here."

Lucas rubbed his forehead with his free hand. In the past, she always seemed to treasure time with her mother. "You two okay?"

She waved a hand. "We're fine, but she keeps hovering and asking if I need anything. Mom isn't the mothering type. It's weird having her doing it now."

He grinned, making a mental note not to linger and coddle. Coming to stand behind her, he set their mugs on the table. "If it makes you feel better, she gave me a hard time."

"Oh, about what?" There was a smile in her voice that lightened his heart.

"I heard someone in the kitchen and thought it was you. I came barreling in there. She told me you were here, working." He ran a thumb along a brow. "I might have pissily asked why she let you come in here to lift heavy shit when you're supposed to be resting."

She snorted, muttering, "Let me."

"Yeah, that's what she said. Oh, and called me a Neanderthal."

He took a sip of coffee, drinking in Harper's laughter. Her hair was in a messy bun, and she wore a loose T-shirt, exposing her graceful spine. He bent, kissing her neck.

Normally, she'd have turned and deepened the kiss. Instead, she leaned forward, taking a sip of her coffee. It might have been unintentional, her moving away from him, but he suspected his touch was the cause. It bothered her.

The quiet rejection cut him.

"Grab a chair, sit with me," she said.

Shoving aside his hurt, he pulled over a stool. After dusting it off, he sat, reminding himself just because he yearned for her touch to comfort him, didn't mean she needed or wanted the same.

Handing him the other coffee, she asked why he was up so early.

"I forgot I set my phone's alarm. Originally, I planned on going to the gym before my eight o'clock meeting." He checked the Shinola wall clock. "I should call and cancel before it gets too late."

She frowned. "Why would you? If you skip the gym, you'd have plenty of time to get home, shower, and make it to your meeting."

"Because I want to stay with you," he nearly growled. His injured pride leaked into his words, making him sound harsh and angry.

He took her hand, hoping it'd gentle his tone. He hadn't meant to sound angry, but her easy dismissal of him hurt.

Setting her mug on the table, she cupped his cheek. "I'm fine, I just need a distraction."

"We could distract each other."

She quirked a brow. "The doctor said no sex for at least two weeks."

He snorted, tapping the tip of her nose. "I was thinking of binge-watching TV or lying around and reading, you nympho."

"Oh." She laughed, her hand falling from his face. "That does sound nice, and we can do it when you don't have meetings and work."

He started to protest, but she kept talking. "Really, Lucas, I'm good. What I need right now is to lose myself in my art. I promise I won't overdo it. If I need anything, I have my mom, or I'll call you."

He wanted to stay. For her and himself. He was afraid to be alone with his thoughts.

However, he didn't want to be accused of 'hovering'. It might push her away more, so he gave in. "You won't go home?"

"No. I want to stay and work on this." She indicated the bust.

"Okay," he said with a sigh. "I'll get out of your way."

"You aren't in my way."

Her words rang false, and he did his best to pretend they didn't, kissing her. He'd intended to leave, but doubt kept him in his seat. "Are we good?"

"Of course." Her gaze dropped, speaking louder than her words.

She was shutting him out.

"Harper. Don't."

"I'm not *doing* anything." She selected a square of sandpaper. "You better get moving, or you'll be late for your meeting."

He stood. He couldn't fight for them. Not when his heart was battered and bruised from yesterday. Not when she was stepping on it now.

"Fine. I'll call you tonight." He kissed the top of her head and left, not bothering to look back.

· · · ● · ● · ● · · ·

The door clicked closed as Lucas left. Harper squeezed her eyes shut and took a calming breath.

It didn't help.

She dropped the sandpaper, inspecting her chisels. Selecting one, she returned to the delicate bust.

The light tapping of the tool and the piano from her favorite band played softly in the background. The combination somewhat soothed her heavy heart.

Her psyche was exhausted, yet her body demanded this soothing ritual. She needed something solid in her hands because her mind was stable as quicksand.

Last night, in Lucas's arms, she'd fallen into a deep sleep only to wake a few hours later with cramping. After, she couldn't do more than doze on and off. The pain and her sadness made it impossible.

She didn't get why ending the pregnancy hurt so much. Not the physical part, but emotionally.

When she'd taken the test and saw the pink lines, she'd been devastated, picturing her gallery and dreams disappearing. Envisioning Lucas either leaving her or trying to bury his resigned disappointment.

When none of those worries came to fruition, his unexpected happiness at her pregnancy bothered her. It made everything between them more complicated. Then, after learning of Elizabeth's pregnancy, difficult didn't even begin to describe Harper's emotional state.

Maybe she was one of those women who was never satisfied. Someone who waited for rain and clouds even on the sunniest of days.

All that was certain was the loss of the baby shredded her heart.

The worst was she couldn't talk with Lucas about it. Every time she tried, his devastated face at the doctor's, flashed in front of her.

She refused to pile more hurt on him.

Even if it left her lost and incredibly lonely. It would pass, and she'd find her way to him.

Or she wouldn't.

A sharp pain sliced through her. With him, she hadn't given him only her love, but her whole heart. How could she live without it?

The statue in front of her blurred, and she blinked, confused. When light splashes of wetness hit her cheeks, she realized she was crying.

"Shit." She threw the chisel on the table, giving in and letting the tears fall.

Chapter Twenty-Four

Lucas's cellphone vibrated on the couch. Setting aside his book, he checked the caller ID. Tanner's name flashed across the screen.

Lucas considered ignoring it. Lately, he preferred being alone. However, he couldn't keep avoiding people. Plus, this particular friend wasn't one to give up.

Answering, he tried to sound enthusiastic. Tanner didn't seem to notice and got right to the point.

"I'm getting the tickets for Arts, Beats, and Eats. The Grimms and their women are coming, but you never told me if you and Harper are going. Have you decided?"

With a deluge of new contracts for Energy Solutions jobs and his avoidance of all things social, Lucas had forgotten about the festival. Tanner and Maggie planned on checking out the local talent, hoping to find a band to open for them when they went on tour this fall. Everyone else wanted to stuff themselves with good food while listening to live music and perusing the art for sale.

Lucas also wasn't sure if Harper would want to go with him. She'd thrown herself into her work as well, and they hadn't seen much of each other in the last couple of weeks.

He should make an effort. It might be fun. Maybe it'd help remind him what that even meant. He'd forgotten. "Let me try to get a hold of Harper. See if she's interested."

"Try?" Tanner's confusion carried over the phone.

"She's been busy," Lucas said flatly.

"Busy, or keeping her distance from you?"

He and Tanner had talked shortly after the doctor's appointment. The poor guy called, riddled with guilt and apologizing for blurting to Harper about Elizabeth's pregnancy.

Lucas hadn't been angry. It was his fault for not telling her, and he said as much to Tanner. Then he told his friend about the awful doctor appointment. Later that night, Will called.

His friends were worse than gossiping teenagers. Lucas loved them for it. Talking helped, especially since he couldn't discuss it with Harper. Every time he tried, she changed the subject. It seemed she wanted to forget it ever happened.

He shook himself, returning to the call. "Hell if I know, Tanner. She's not easy to read."

"I get that. Maggie's the same. Man, in the beginning... Fort Knox had nothing on her."

Lucas laughed. "No wonder our women get along so well."

Is she still mine?

"Truth," Tanner agreed. "Anyway, sorry I've been MIA. This last tour was a killer. You doing any better?"

"I'm dealing. What else can I do?" Wanting to change the depressing topic, he asked, "Anyway, how was it having your mom on tour with you?"

"She wasn't there for the whole thing. Thank Christ. She and Roger met us in California." Tanner grumbled. "I'd hung out enough with her as a teen doing the roadie gig with her various boyfriends. Now it's plain weird having Mr. Grimm there. He might be a retired cop, but he carries the vibe like a damn badge. He made some of the less law-abiding on the tour nervous."

Lucas laughed, slapping his book lightly against his thigh. "I can't get over Jacob and Will's dad with your mom—"

"Yeah, they're even more of opposites than you and Harper."

"Or you and Maggie."

"Touché."

His phone vibrated against his ear. "Hold on. Someone's texting me."

It was Harper, telling him Cindy was visiting and asking if they were going to Arts, Beats, and Eats. He messaged back, telling her Tanner was asking the same. Told her he was game if she wanted to go.

She did, and he passed along the message to Tanner.

Her response was a smiley emoji. *No, call you later. No, I can't wait to see you.* He didn't bother replying to her and told Tanner to get the tickets before hanging up with him. Lucas wasn't in the mood to talk to anyone.

Why did love have to be so damn hard?

Back when he met and fallen for Elizabeth, he couldn't grasp why his friends complained relationships were equal amounts of pain and pleasure.

Everything with her had been easy. Their friendship turned to passion without any upheaval. He proposed, and they married shortly after their college graduation. She wanted to start a family right away, as did he. She was pregnant a few months later.

Everything was smooth, his life spread before him. He wanted for nothing.

Then, bam, everything he loved was torn from him. Gone. One day was a dream, the next a nightmare.

Years later, he meets a woman who makes his scarred heart beat again.

Simple and easy? No, Harper wasn't smooth. She was sharp edges and jagged lines. A force as passionate as her art and just as beautiful.

He'd fallen for her, hard and fast.

However, the naïve boy in college was long gone. The man he was today understood the pain of love. What he didn't know was if he was strong enough for it.

· · · ● ● · ● ● · · ·

Harper set her cellphone on the end table next to the couch, worry niggling at her. Lucas hadn't responded. Again.

More and more of her calls and texts were going unanswered.

It hurt even if she wasn't sure what she needed him to say.

That was a lie. She wanted to hear; *I miss you. I love you. Come over.*

Yes, she wanted to hear those words, but she didn't expect them. Something changed between them since the pregnancy.

Before all this, he told her he wanted more than her body. Yet he was more than willing to let her decide on how much they were committed. Almost as if he feared it as much as her.

The only time he'd given any real indication he wanted long-term with her was his half-hearted suggestion she move her work studio to his house. Something he never suggested again, until she was pregnant.

After which, he'd come on way too strong. Saying he loved her, asking her to marry him.

She believed he was more in love with the baby than her. It hadn't made her jealous, but it did hurt. Her insecurities festered, whispering he was staying with her for their child and not out of love for her.

Now she was left wondering, especially with his recent absence, if he no longer wanted her. Perhaps he was hoping they'd eventually drift apart completely.

"What did he say?" Cindy asked, tugging Harper from her unhappy musings.

She smiled, though it sat plastic and false on her. "He wants to go. In fact, he was getting ready to call me. He's on the phone with Tanner, who was getting a count, ready to order the tickets."

Cindy clapped her hands. "Yes! It's been forever since we all went out together. It'll be fun." She stopped, her grin fading. "Um, why do you look miserable? Don't you want to go?"

"No. I do." Harper chewed the inside of her cheek, running a finger along the rim of her wine glass.

Cindy had arrived unannounced with a bottle of her favorite wine. Talking with her cousin did lift her spirits, but the reminder of her disintegrating relationship with Lucas popped her good mood like a fragile bubble. After his curt text, the shards dug into her heart.

"Then what gives? Five minutes ago, you were happily chatting away about the gallery and now... Oh." She took one of Harper's hands in both of hers. "Are things not good between you and Lucas? What happened with the pregnancy has to be hitting you both hard. Also, Will mentioned Lucas suffered from depression after Elizabeth died. He isolated himself from work, friends, and family. Eventually, he started seeing a doctor. Is he struggling again?"

Cindy's words might have meant to offer comfort. Instead, they were a kick in the gut.

He told Harper he'd struggled, but she didn't know the severity. Had he been afraid to tell her or was he waiting for her to ask?

Either way, she'd failed him.

"I'm not sure if he and I are good," she said with an honesty she found difficult to share. Even with her cousin. "We're polite and kind to each other, but something is off, and I'm not sure if it's him or me."

"What do you mean?"

"Well, I have this habit of running when things get difficult—"

"You don't say?" Cindy's eyes widened in mock disbelief.

Harper laughed. "Nice to meet you, Pot."

"Yeah, well, Kettle, we do have that in common," Cindy quipped. "Remember, back in February, we both took off to Spain together? Me, trying to get away from Will, and you pretending like you weren't running from Lucas."

"Seems we weren't fast enough. We were caught."

"I, for one, am glad I lost that game of chase." Cindy smiled.

The contentment radiating from her made Harper a tiny bit jealous. She was happy for her cousin but wanted the same with Lucas so badly it was a physical ache. Why were they continuously pursued by heartache and complications?

Instead of agreeing or disagreeing with her cousin, she ignored the comment. She took a sip of her wine and stared, unseeing, at the TV across from them. Her mind was a million miles away, simultaneously replaying the trip to Spain and worrying about what was happening between her and Lucas.

Cindy cleared her throat, shifting sideways on the couch. She settled one slim leg under her bottom, her attention one-hundred percent on Harper.

"What about you?" she asked.

"What about me, what?" Harper finished off her wine and stared at her empty glass. Her eyes burned, but she refused to let the tears fall.

Cindy scoffed. "Don't play dumb. It doesn't suit you. Are you glad you were caught?"

Holding in her tears was impossible, and a few escaped down her cheeks. "Honestly. I don't know. I can't tell if Lucas and I have hit a rough patch, or if it's something else. Something irrevocable. I don't want to drag out the inevitable. I stayed with Edward for so long—"

"Lucas is nothing like that ass-hat."

"True. I do tend to repeat my mistakes, but thankfully not that one. Although, he has the power to hurt me in a way Edward never could. I didn't love him enough. Ending it with him had been difficult because I was forced to face the humiliation of the way he'd used me, but there was no true love lost. With Lucas, there is, and it scares me."

"Honey, face it, you're already in deep. If you run, you'll only cause yourself unnecessary pain."

"Staying hurts too." She slumped into the couch. "Anyway, I'm not sure if it's him or me walking away. The only thing I know for sure is day by day, the gulf between us is widening. I have no idea how to stop it."

Cindy set her wine on a silver tray resting on the ottoman. She brought Harper into her arms, hugging her. "I wish I had the answer, but as you know, I'm terrible at relationships."

She laughed, and it came out a little choked. "Whatever. You and Will are doing great."

"It's all him. He's the adult. I'm a toddler when it comes to emotions. Ask him, he'll tell you."

Laughing lightly, Harper broke the embrace. She set her empty glass on the tray to refill it. "He would, hoping to get a rise from you. I know how you two," she made air quotes, "like to fight."

Cindy gave a wicked smile. "This is true. Poking my bear does usually end in fun times." Her smile turned soft. "Anyway, come with us this weekend. You *and* Lucas. I bet it's what you two need. A fun day with excellent friends, leaving behind all the pressure and worries."

It did sound lovely. Even the idea of it boosted her spirits.

She filled Cindy's wine glass, offering it to her, then, lifted her own. "Cheers to that."

Chapter Twenty-Five

Harper stood with Cindy in Maggie's driveway next to what her band nicknamed the 'mugger van.' Made sense. The white paint and lack of windows did scream *stranger danger*.

"When are Will and Lucas supposed to get here?" Harper asked no one in particular.

Maggie shrugged, pulling out what appeared to be a guitar case. "Got me, but the van is ready.

They decided to meet at Maggie and Tanner's house. The Arts, Beats, and Eats brought in a big crowd, and parking would be a mess. Plus, most of them wanted to have a few drinks. Will was happy to be the designated driver.

Cindy glanced at her phone. "Will messaged me when they left, nearly half an hour ago. I'm guessing they'll be here any minute."

Harper nodded, messing with the sleeve of her white linen shirt. Moving to the seam of her skirt, she made sure the front slit was perfect.

When she began to play with her fishtail braid, Cindy snatched her hand. "Stop fidgeting. You're making me antsy."

Her cheeks warmed. "Sorry."

"I take it things are still off between you and Lucas?"

"Yup." She popped the p, trying to sound as though it didn't matter. "We've talked twice since last week. All polite and mundane."

"That will change today," Cindy promised. "You both need this. Time with friends, to relax and let go."

"Yeah, maybe." Harper didn't believe it, but what else could she say?

Luckily, Will's car pulled into the driveway, ending the conversation. Lucas sat in the passenger seat, and she feasted on him like a starving woman.

Taking in his full, tasty lips, edible jawline, and candy green eyes. Ones that were watching her with equal amounts of hunger.

"Damn," Cindy breathed, fanning herself. "Nothing mundane about the way your eyes were eating each other up."

Harper licked her lips and smiled. "We have all sorts of issues and problems, but it doesn't change the fact he's yummy."

"Maybe that's what you two need." Her cousin waggled her brows. "To get laid."

The image of Lucas naked, stretched above, buried deep inside Harper, shot through her mind and straight between her legs, warming and chilling her. They hadn't been together since the day before the awful doctor's appointment.

She had the IUD removed and switched to the birth control shot. Dr. Lafoy told her weeks ago everything was fine. It didn't matter. Harper wasn't ready.

She craved his touch and comfort, while simultaneously fearing the vulnerability of needing him so much. Even more now, with the distance between them.

The men got out at the same time, Will's gaze jumping between her and Cindy. "Judging by your expressions, you two were having an interesting conversation. Care to share?"

Cindy's grin widened. "We were talking about sex. Want to know the details?"

He shook his head. "I swear, woman, you're always talking about sex. You're worse than a man."

"Are you complaining?"

"Nope." He brought her into his arms.

Harper envied their easy love. They had their issues in the past, but they had it now, and she wanted it with Lucas.

He stopped in front of her, the complete opposite of ease. His hands were shoved into his pockets, and a tight smile was on his lips.

After a few awkward seconds, he stepped closer and wrapped her in a loose, stiff hug before kissing her cheek.

Her cheek? What the hell?

She'd love to be ballsy like Maggie. She'd grab her man's face and kiss him as Harper wanted.

Trying to be bold, she took a deep breath and entwined her fingers with his. The simple gesture made her heart pound.

She was such a wimp.

"About time you guys arrived. Weren't you supposed to be here a half-hour ago," Jacob hollered, striding toward them from the backdoor, holding Greta's hand. "I bet it's my brother's fault you're late."

"Yeah, yeah," Will drawled, shrugging. "There was a slight problem at the restaurant. I got home late and needed to shower. Believe me, no one here would have wanted me to skip it."

"I appreciate it, babe." Cindy ran her nose along the back of his ear.

"Come on," Tanner called, next to the driver's side door. "The later we go, the busier it gets."

"Hey," Will said. "I thought I was driving."

"Only if I drink," Tanner replied.

"It's for the best," Maggie cut in. "Even with this short, twenty-minute drive, you put Tanner in the back, he'll be green by the time we arrive."

"You still get carsick?" the Grimm brothers asked in unison.

Tanner snorted. "It's not something you outgrow."

"Remember the time Dad let him come camping with us to Pictured Rocks?" Jacob asked his brother.

Will groaned. "How could I forget? Thank God you shoved his head out the window in time."

"Um," Harper interrupted, facing Tanner. "So, if you drink, you don't get motion sickness?"

She'd never heard of such a thing.

Maggie laughed. "I wish. No, but we'll give him shotgun and hope he naps on the ride home."

Harper leaned closer to Lucas. "Let's make sure we sit in the last row of the van on the trip back."

He laughed, and the sound eased the tension in her shoulders. Maybe Cindy was right, this was exactly what they needed. A pressure-free evening with friends.

Harper looped an arm around his side, inhaling his heady scent of masculine spice, eager for the night ahead.

• • • ● ● • ● ● • • •

Lucas sat in a folding chair, ignoring the outdoor stage and band. He studied the darkening sky, watching the last vestiges of day fading on the horizon.

The hours seemed to have slipped away from him. It had been an odd, yet good day.

Strange because he wasn't sure how to act around Harper. She seemed as unsure. There was a definite divide between them. He wanted to bridge it, but self-preservation held him back. He couldn't keep giving to a woman who had one foot in the relationship and the other ready to jet at the first sign of trouble.

The band switched songs, dragging him back with a slow, bluesy melody that was somehow both sad and seductive. It entranced the audience and had people crowding the makeshift dancefloor.

Harper was one of those dancers, swaying to the music with her friends. She was hot.

From the way his friends were eyeing their wives and girlfriends, he wasn't the only one captivated with the scene.

Jacob set his beer next to his chair. "I'm going to see if my wife wants a dance partner."

"Good idea." Will stood.

Jacob's brows furrowed in obvious confusion. "What?"

Will slapped his brother's shoulder. "Not Greta, you idiot. I meant I want to dance with her sister."

Lucas laughed, but it shriveled and died when some asshole moved behind Harper, putting a hand on her waist. She kept right on dancing.

Jealous fury coated his skin.

She had a few drinks and wore one of those easy, buzzed smiles. Her eyes were closed, her hands above her head as she moved to the music.

He hoped either she didn't notice her new dance partner or assumed it was him. Leaving his chair, he went to find out.

He was in front of her in less than a minute. Her lids fluttered open, and when she saw him in from of her, she swiveled, taking in the man behind. She whipped back around to face Lucas.

Her tipsy confusion mixed with the man's slightly panicked one almost made him smile. He held it in, glaring at Harper's dance partner.

Raising his hands, the guy backed away, mouthing, "My bad."

Lucas gave him a curt tilt of his chin, bringing Harper into his arms. On tiptoes, she said into his ear, "I thought he was you."

Now he did smile. Laughed too. "Yeah, I gathered as much, when you tried to figure out how I was in front and behind you."

They gave up talking. They were close to the speakers, making it difficult to hear.

He was glad. They got to enjoy each other's touch while ignoring their problems. It let them put off the conversation that needed to take place.

The fast-paced song switched to a ballad. Her arms encircled his waist, resting her head against his chest. He settled his chin on her silky hair, loving how she'd come closer without hesitation.

He wasn't sure if it was the ever-darkening sky, the music, or the strong drinks she'd had earlier that made her freer with him. He didn't care. He'd take it.

All too soon, the song ended. When the band announced their last song of the evening, Harper ran her palms up the front of his body, clutching his shoulders, bringing him to her.

His mouth crashed against hers with a near desperate need, devouring her desires. Her lips tasted of lust and longing. Her hands slid to the back of his neck, burying in his hair and gripping him tightly. A groan of relief and hunger escaped from him.

He should slow down before they were kicked out for indecency. Should, but couldn't. Not when she wasn't showing any signs of hesitation.

A needy whimper fell from her lips to his, hotter than a demand for sex. His hand slipped from her lower back to her ass, bringing her against him and grinding.

Without warning, the stage lights flashed bright, startling them apart. Her swollen lips and the desire burning in her eyes made everything in him tighten and harden.

From the side of his vision he saw Maggie and Tanner make a bee-line for the band. It appeared they'd found their opening act.

Lucas had no idea if they'd been great or terrible. Once Harper was in his arms, the music faded away as he concentrated on her soft lips and supple curves pressing against him.

Someone tapped his shoulder, and Will asked, "Ready?"

Lucas nodded, his gaze never leaving Harper.

Cindy whispered something to Harper. She blushed, glancing at Lucas then quickly away.

What in the hell had Cindy said?

Whatever it was pissed him off. He could damn near feel Harper's walls rising around her again.

Hell no.

Refusing to let the distance return, he brought her back to his side, wrapping an arm around her waist. She stiffened slightly but didn't put space between them.

As they walked to the parking lot, chatting, joking, and teasing with their friends she relaxed again. He could almost pretend everything was fine between them.

By the time they piled in the van, she was laughing and clutching him for support. They, along with Maggie, took the bench seat in the back. The second row was Cindy, Greta, and Jacob, with Will driving and Tanner in shotgun.

Harper snuggled into him, talking with Maggie and unconsciously playing with the inside seam of his jeans. He closed his eyes, letting his head fall against the headrest. He solved math problems and thought about global warming—anything but Harper's hand roaming higher up his thigh, and how much it was turning him on.

He thanked all that was holy and unholy that the drive was short. In under a half-hour, they were pulling into Tanner and Maggie's driveway.

"Harper, I'm going to go home with Will. You should come with us since you've been drinking," Cindy said, her voice sounding robotic and rehearsed.

"Or you can stay here," Maggie suggested. "We have a spare bedroom."

Cindy gave a sharp shake of her head, her gaze darting between him and Harper. Was she trying to get them in the car together? Maybe that was what she was whispering with Cindy right before they left the festival.

He felt like an ass for being pissed at her. He was going to ask Will what his girlfriend's favorite wine was, and he was getting her a bottle. Maybe two.

"Oh," Maggie stuttered. "I mean...maybe not. Yeah, um, never mind. The bed is broken."

"No, it—" Tanner started, but Maggie elbowed him in the ribs.

Before the moment turned any more awkward, Lucas said, "*Or* I could drive you home. I only drank two beers, and it was hours ago. I'm good. Ben lives outside of Ann Arbor. If you can't take me home in the morning, he will. I'm sure even on a Sunday he'll be going into the office."

His heart pounded, waiting to see if she rejected his offer. The last time they spent a night together was right after the doctor's appointment at her mom's house.

Harper tapped her foot as if deciding. Then she peeked shyly between lowered lashes. "If you don't mind, I'd like that."

He exhaled a slow, relieved breath. "Not at all."

Chapter Twenty-Six

Harper slid into the passenger seat of her Mercedes, giddy excitement thrumming through her blood. Dancing in Lucas's arms had been bliss. His kisses, ecstasy.

Things weren't perfect, not by a longshot, but maybe this was a start.

"Do you mind if we go to your condo?" he asked, while adjusting the seat and mirror. "I'm doing a remodeling project. My place is a mess."

The kitchen and bathroom were new. He hadn't mentioned any recent projects. Did he not want her at his place?

"Nope, that's fine." She tried for carefree, but sounded tense.

He sucked in his lips, biting on them as if trying to keep his aggravation inside. She tried to think of something to say. To bring back the light mood.

In the silence, he started the car. It wasn't until they almost reached the main road when he finally spoke.

"Listen, if you're uncomfortable around me, I won't stay the night. I'll drop you off and bring your car back tomorrow."

No. No. That isn't what I want at all.

She covered his hand on the gear shift with hers, snagging his attention. He turned briefly from the road.

"It's not you. It's us. Does that make sense?"

"No." The hard line of his lips matched the weary slump of his shoulders.

She tried to explain herself better. "We need to talk, but I don't want to tonight. I want us to ignore whatever is going on between us. For now, tonight, let's lose ourselves in each other."

Braking at a stop sign, he stared at her. Not saying a word.

Panic seized her. She was ruining everything.

Removing her hand from his, she stared at her lap. "Okay, fine. Bad idea. I'll—"

He slammed the car into park. Reaching past the console, he took her face into his palms. "No, it's not. I need to get lost." Grazing this tongue along her ear he hummed, "In you."

A shiver pebbled her skin, reigniting her desires. "Good."

• • ● ● • ● ● • • ·

Lucas kept having to remind himself not to speed, but his foot was lead.

The rest of the drive was filled with inane talk while bursting with physical, tantalizing teasing. A lingering hand on the thigh, a finger tracing a bottom lip, and whispered, naughty words that touched everywhere.

By the time they were in Harper's living room, he was ready to bend her over the damn couch. Instead, he somehow managed to rein in his hunger and still his exploring hands and mouth.

He wanted her to take the lead. Since the doctor's appointment, she'd been skittish about sex.

Thankfully, tonight, her hesitation seemed to have vanished. She tossed her purse on an armchair before tugging on the hem of his T-shirt.

He took the hint and yanked it off. Bringing her into his arms, he claimed her mouth with his lips. Between kisses, he removed her shirt and skirt. She relieved him of his jeans and boxer-briefs. Each item of clothing dropped on their path to her bedroom.

Once there, he laid her gently on top of the comforter, taking in her beauty. Her rose-colored silk bra and panties showcased her flawless skin to perfection. Her nipples strained against the expensive fabric, begging for his attention.

He was happy to oblige. With the predatory need, he crawled onto the bed, hovering above her.

Kissing her shoulder, he grabbed her bra strap with his teeth, dragging it down her arm. With his lips, he worked his way to her exposed breast. He toyed and teased her with his tongue, teeth, and mouth until she was whimpering his name.

He stopped, smiling wickedly before flicking the tip of her nipple with his tongue. Moving to the other breast, he played until she was begging for more.

"Please, Lucas," she panted.

He did as she demanded, skating a hand to her stomach before dipping into her panties. She rocked into his palm. Watching her chase her pleasure made him impossibly harder.

Wanting to make sure she was ready, he worked her into a near frenzy with his fingers. Right before she crashed over the edge, he stopped, moving between her legs, he gently nudged them farther apart.

She gasped, and her whole body stiffened.

He froze. "What's wrong? Did I hurt you?"

"No, but..." she trailed off, her gaze fixed on his shoulder.

She had him damn near close to panic levels. He scooted off her, resting on an elbow and gripping her chin softly, making her meet his eyes. "What? Tell me."

"Would you mind wearing a condom?"

Surprise shot through him, and his hand fell away. "Didn't you switch to the shot after having the IUD removed?"

"Yes, but I don't want to take any chances."

He understood, yet a numb sadness sank into him. "Okay."

She twisted around, opening her nightstand. He was glad to have a second without her focus on him. He needed to get his shit together.

Part of him, hell most of him, got where she was coming from. Getting pregnant on birth control, and the way things unfolded was a special kind of hell for them both.

He'd rather cut off his dick then have her go through that again. However, this felt more like she was pulling away from him, building another barrier between them. Her way of keeping him at a distance.

Things were rough between them, but he wanted to work through them. Get married, be together.

Did she want the same?

His churning thoughts were unfair. It didn't stop his unreasonable heart from aching.

"Found them," she said triumphantly, then her shoulders slumped. "Damn it. I ruined the mood."

He looked at his lap. Yup, he was half hard.

"No. You surprised me is all, and I got lost in my head." He tapped his temple. "This one. The wrong one," he joked.

She laughed, lightening some of the encroaching darkness.

"Come here," he said.

Her smile fell away. "Lucas—"

Before she could say anything, he kissed her quiet. "Remember, tonight's about getting lost in each other."

It might be a mistake, but he was tired of the foggy glum covering him. He *needed* to get lost in her pleasure. To forget. Just for one night.

Kissing and teasing her body, the only talk was him telling her everything he was going to do to make her tremble and moan. Soon, he'd distracted her with enough pleasure she seemed to have forgotten how to speak.

Perfect. His undivided attention was on their mounting desires and sweet gratification.

Chapter Twenty-Seven

Lucas stepped from the shower and wiped off, before wrapping the towel around his waist. He put on a pair of jeans and a T-shirt he'd left at Harper's place, while listening to her side of a conversation filtering from somewhere on the main floor.

Following her voice, he found her in the kitchen already dressed, sipping coffee and talking on the phone. From what he caught, she was talking to an artist. They were going to meet and see if his work was a good fit for her gallery.

It filled him with pride that her business was thriving. He wanted her to succeed, whether or not he was a part of it.

She ended her call. Her gaze ran over him with a mixture of weariness and affection.

"Will you be ready to leave soon?" she asked.

"Do you have time for breakfast? There's a great place by my house. Or I could cook."

They needed to talk. His need to ignore their problems disappeared with the moon.

She glanced at her watch. "Not really. I'm meeting with the guy who I was on the phone with in a little more than an hour. Plus, we're meeting for brunch to discuss his portfolio."

He set aside the mug he'd taken from the cupboard. "Fine. Do you want to leave now?"

He tried to keep the annoyance from his voice, but the way her lips pressed into a white slash, told him it came through.

Oh well. She might be content to keep running, avoiding what was breaking between them. He wasn't. One way or another, he'd have his say. This odd limbo was killing him.

Yet, as they drove to his house, he said nothing. Everything was clogged in his throat, and as each mile passed, the silence grew heavier between them. By the time she parked in his driveway, it was nearly solid as concrete.

Forcing his way through it, he said, "Come inside."

"I can't."

"Why? Your meeting isn't for at least another half-hour."

She didn't answer. Just kept staring out the windshield.

His patience snapped. "Harper, look at me."

When she did, his stomach lurched. Tears were pooled at the corners of her eyes.

"Talk to me," he begged. "Tell me what you're thinking."

"I'm not sure if we should be together."

Fuck.

A tightness wrapped around his chest. "Why? What did I do wrong?"

"Nothing."

She was speaking in riddles, driving him crazy. "I'm so fucking confused. Come inside. Let's talk. Figure us out."

Her hands gripped the steering wheel tight, making her knuckles pop. "I can't. I need space. From you."

"What the hell has this last month been?" he nearly shouted. Shutting his mouth, he took a deep breath to calm himself. "This push and pull is wearing thin. I can't keep doing it."

"I'm a burden to you, too much to handle. I need to let you go."

"Where the hell is this coming from?" He threw up his hands, exasperated. "Did I give that impression last night? This morning? Hell, anytime since I've met you!"

She slumped in her seat, her head falling against the rest. A single tear rolled down her cheek, falling from her jaw. "You've been through enough. I don't want to cause you any more pain."

He wiped the wetness from her cheek with his thumb. "You're worth the pain and the pleasure. When will you believe this?" His anger drained away.

"I don't know, Lucas. Maybe that's what I need to decide. If I'm worthy of your love. I fear I'm like my parents. Not cut out for commitment." She twisted to face him. "I'm scared of *everything* when it comes to you. When things are perfect, I'm on edge convinced it won't last. When it's difficult every fiber in my body wants to bolt."

Defeat settled into his bones, but he tried one more time. "You aren't your parents. You make your own path. Don't choose this one."

"I have to do this. I'm sorry." The hollowness in her voice told him there'd be no changing her mind.

"So am I." He dropped his hand from her cheek and kissed her.

It tasted like goodbye. He opened the door of her car and walked numbly into his house.

Chapter Twenty-Eight

Harper caught sight of her mom hovering in the door of her studio. After cutting the power on her rotary tool, she removed her goggles and smiled. It felt stiff and false.

She did enjoy visiting with her mother, but a melancholy sadness had settled into Harper's bones, making it difficult to enjoy any company. Laughter and genuine smiles seemed to have abandoned her.

Her mom crossed her arms, tapping her nails. "You're here again?"

Harper shrugged. "I want this finished by next week."

Plus, her sole comfort was in creating. It quieted her turbulent mind while also allowing it to wander. The statue was coming along nicely, even if everything else in her life sucked.

She missed Lucas so much, she swore her heart had an actual dripping, bleeding wound. Yet, she wasn't going to call him. She'd done the right thing. Maybe.

"I get that, but you have damn near barricaded yourself in here." Then as if sensing the source of Harper's pain, asked, "Doesn't Lucas miss you?"

Harper had wondered when her mom would ask about him. She hated answering it. Each time it made it more real. More permanent.

Grabbing a small chisel, Harper began gently scraping the ear of the statue. "We're taking a break."

Her mother came all the way inside. "You broke up?"

"I'm not sure. I told him I needed space. We haven't talked since."

Harper blew fallen dust from the earlobe before starting on the hairline. The quiet tapping and scraping filled the room. She gave off the illusion of being busy. In reality, every bit of her concentration was on not falling apart.

Her mother took the chisel from Harper. She huffed but didn't demand it back.

"You're okay with that?"

Harper shrugged, swallowing her sadness.

I won't cry. I've done enough to fill all five of the damn Great Lakes.

"I don't believe you. The two of you are good together. Happy."

"Maybe I'm like you and Dad. Not great with relationships. I spent two years with that asshole, Edward. Now I've been dating Lucas on and off for almost a year. It's been nothing but complications and difficulties. I'm better off alone."

Harper held out her hand, silently asking for the chisel. Her mother shook her head.

"One." She held up a finger. "Your father has been married close to twenty years, proving he's fine with commitment. Just not with me," she said, before lifting another digit. "Two, love is messy and difficult. Deal with it."

Harper's brows pulled together. "What, like you?"

"You aren't me."

"Maybe I should be," she shot back.

"My life and choices are different than yours."

"How so?"

"My heart was brutally torn apart by two men who I adored and loved. They treated the treasure I offered them like a cheap trinket—"

"Twice?" That reveal completely sidetracked Harper.

Her mom shook her head. "It's a story for another time. For now, let me say, I'm too jaded to risk love again. I have you for my heart. I don't need or want it from my lovers." She ran a hand through Harper's hair before resting it on her shoulder. "You, my daughter, need it."

She wanted to argue. Found she couldn't, not when her mother's words rang true. "Okay, fine, you might be right. But it doesn't mean Lucas is the man for me."

"Why not? He loves you and you him. Or did I read you two wrong?"

"He does, but maybe not enough. What if he's like my father?"

"What do you mean?"

"Loves me, but loves someone else more."

"Are you referring to his wife?"

She nodded. "I swore I'd never be a man's consolation prize."

"And you shouldn't be. However, are you sure you are to Lucas? Did he ever make you feel that way? I've seen only adoration from him when it comes to you."

"I told you about the first night we met, right?"

"Yes, but that was a long time ago, well past a year. Also, that wasn't him wanting one woman over another, like your father. It was a man blindsided by grief. Something he believed he'd laid to rest."

Again, her words spoke the truth. It healed something within Harper she hadn't realized was broken, although it didn't vanquish every doubt.

"It wasn't the only time he was hot and cold with me. It happened again when I found out I was pregnant. Sure, before he cared, had even made an ambiguous suggestion about me moving in with him. Then, bam." She slammed her shaking hands together. "I show him the test and suddenly he loves me and wants to get married. Don't get me wrong. I respected and appreciated that he wanted to be a part of everything. At the same time, it felt like being loved for what I could give him, not who I am to him. Does that make sense?"

Her mother blinked a few times. "Whoa. And yes."

Being understood loosened the knot in her stomach. "Yeah. I was pissed, reamed him out."

"How'd he take it?"

"Said he did love me and had for a while. He figured I knew without him having to say it."

They looked at each other and muttered, "Men."

Harper smirked, the comradery did wonders for the gloom trying to suffocate her.

If only it lasted. Recalling her current situation with Lucas and the weeks that followed had her misery returning, crashing into her, tenfold.

"Anyway." She sighed. "He probably said it because he's a nice guy and was trying to do the right thing."

Her mother took Harper's hand in hers. "Honey, you are kind, talented, and gorgeous. You are a gift for any man. Why in the world do you believe otherwise?"

"Because he pulled away after I was no longer pregnant."

"Maybe he was hurting and needed time to regroup. Did he stay away? Tell or show you he didn't want to be with you?"

"Well, no." She crossed her arms over her chest. "He also never mentioned marriage or moving in together again."

Her mother's stare said are-you-kidding-me? "Didn't you tell me not even five minutes ago that you gave him hell for even suggesting it?"

"Well, yeah. He asked right after I told him I was pregnant. That screams responsibility, not love."

Her mom held up her palms in surrender. "Hey, I'd have responded the same way, but you have to consider, it might be the reason he didn't ask again. Plus, don't forget you're not the only one who lost that baby. As I said, he's probably hurting as well. Marriage and the future might not be on his mind at this particular moment."

"He never invites me to his house anymore. To stay at his place." She was beginning to wonder if she was grasping for excuses. Fearing she made a colossal mistake.

Her mom's brow scrunched together. "He doesn't stay the night, or want to spend time alone with you?"

"No. He doesn't invite me to his home."

Why was it, the more she talked, the more ridiculous her fears and worries sounded? Taking in the pity on her mother's face, she was thinking the same thing.

"I failed you."

Shock and disbelief slammed into her. "What? You're a fantastic mom and a great role model."

"Sure, I've taught you how to be a strong woman. It seems I didn't do so good on the love and relationship part. You believe either men will fail you or that you aren't worthy of love. Which is it?"

"Maybe a little of both," Harper admitted. "However, Dad taught me that. Not you."

"I raised you, not him."

"His actions affected and shaped me."

"Perhaps, but we're getting off-topic. I want to focus on you, not your father's or my failings." She grasped Harper's shoulders. "Now, pay attention, daughter. Are you listening?"

She nodded.

"You are worth any man's heart. If you truly believe Lucas can't love you the way you want, let him go. But I'd make damn sure it isn't because of fears and what-ifs. You'll regret it. Believe me, good men aren't easy to come by. Don't wait for him, or things, to be perfect. It'll never happen."

"I don't want perfection. But I do need all of him."

"You're positive you don't have him?"

"I don't know. Maybe." She clutched her head. "Damn, I'm such a mess."

"No, you're afraid. Too many people give their hearts to those unworthy. There's nothing wrong with looking before leaping." She hugged Harper. "Although to keep with my metaphor, you've been circling Lucas for a while, it's time to decide to jump or walk away."

As if a switch was flipped, her turbulent mind quieted. Harper stood. "I need to go."

Her mother gaped. "Where?"

"To Lucas's house."

"Wow. Just like that," she snapped her fingers, "decision made."

"What can I say, Mom? If you ever get tired of conquering the business world, you'd make a great therapist."

Her mother's laughter filled the studio. "Hardly. I'm much too self-centered to listen to people's problems all day. Only yours, my love. Anyway, you knew, you'd only needed someone to untangle your thoughts."

"Maybe." She started for the door but when her mother called to her, Harper turned. "What?"

"Um, you might want to take a shower first."

She removed her safety goggles, letting them hang from her neck. She took in her arms covered with dust, then patted her messy bun. More filth and grime fell from there.

"Good call." She laughed, nearly skipping toward the bathroom.

Lucas's possible rejection scared her, but she was done running from her fears.

Chapter Twenty-Nine

Harper took a deep breath and rang Lucas's doorbell. Before she even exhaled, it swung open.

Yelping, she stumbled, nearly falling off the porch.

What the hell is with me and porches?

Lucas caught her, his eyes wide with shock. "What the hell? Where'd you come from?"

His warm touch was potent, and his intoxicating scent invaded her. She drank him in, her longing making it difficult to speak.

He let go, stepping away. "What are you doing here?"

Not the greeting she was hoping for, but at least he didn't tell her to leave. Well, not yet, anyway.

"You have such a nice front yard, I decided to visit it." The lame joke withered and died between them. She tried again. "I wanted to talk. Do you have time?"

"I'm meeting Will. We're going to a Tigers game."

"Ten minutes. Please."

Lucas stared past her, focusing on something in the distance. Time stopped as she waited for his answer.

"Fine." He opened the door, moving aside to let her go in first.

Once inside, he led her past the living room and into the kitchen. Did he not want to settle in and get comfortable with her on the couch?

He leaned on the counter, crossing his arms over his chest, waiting. She sat at the table. Fidgeting, her hand hit a file.

She read the tab: art studio.

"What's this?" She opened the folder.

"Your studio." His voice was flat. "Remember, in the summer when I suggested it? I'd gone ahead with the project. My plan was to surprise you. Instead, I lost my garage, but got a really fancy storage room-slash-workshop I'll probably never use."

She checked the start date. Mid-June. Shortly after they had the conversation. Before the pregnancy. The reason he hadn't wanted her over became clear. Self-loathing filled her.

During her drive here, she considered herself magnanimous. Willing to risk her heart on a man who might not be ready for love.

It turns out, she was the one who wasn't ready.

She started with the most important first. "I'm sorry for all my running, insecurities, and fragile confidence in us."

Hope might have flickered in his eyes. It vanished before she even blinked, making her wonder if it was her imagination. He tilted his head as if studying her. "What is it you want from me, exactly. Forgiveness? Absolution?"

"I want you. I want to go back to the way things were."

"I don't."

Her heart cracked and wept. She'd let too much time pass. It made him realize she wasn't worth the trouble.

Her initial instinct was to leave. To find a quiet place to fall apart.

This time she'd stay and fight for them. "Did I kill the love you had for me?"

"No. You left three weeks ago. It's going to take a hell of a lot more time than that to lose what I feel for you." He didn't sound happy about it.

She rose from the table to stand in front of him. "Do you want it to go away?"

"I'm not sure. I love you and wanted to spend the rest of my life with you, but the way you keep leaving is murder. You keep shutting me out every time we have a problem or if there's even a hint of one. It's killing me. I can't constantly worry I'll say or do something that'll send you running. Again."

"In my defense, I told you when we last talked, I wasn't running. That I needed to pause, to take some time to think."

"I haven't heard from you in nearly a month," he growled. "Which tells me you're pretty damn uncertain. Or done with me."

"No." She shook her head venomously. "It was my insecurities getting the best of me."

"And, now, what? Poof." He made an exploding gesture. "They're gone?"

"Of course not, but I want to face them for you. For us." She stared into his angry eyes. "Are you willing to do the same for me?"

"I'm not the one who keeps walking away."

She could accept most of the blame. But not its entirety.

"Don't tell me you didn't pull away from me as well. Remember our first night together? That was a messy starting point for us."

"I agree." His hands fell to his sides before he shoved them into his pockets. "Are you going to hold it against me forever? I never said I didn't have my scars. I accept yours, will you shoulder mine? Or run every time I expose them to you?"

"No, I'm not punishing you for our first night together, merely trying to get you to see what's going on in my head. Yes, I was unfair when it came to your past. I'm truly sorry, and I promise to do better." She came closer, resting a hand on his arm. "But we both put up walls."

The stubborn set of his jaw told her he wasn't going to give an inch. His words confirmed it. "When did I do this?"

Was he serious? She breathed in patience. "The only time you've said you loved me was the day we found out I was pregnant."

He leaned heavily on the nearest wall as if he was tired. Hopefully it wasn't of her. "I told you, I felt it before."

"Yes, but you didn't *tell* me until after. It came off as duty, not love. Then after everything fell apart, you retreated into yourself."

"Can you blame me?" His voice was shaking with fury or sadness. "This was the second time my chance at fatherhood slipped through my fingers. And like last time, I lost two people I loved."

Her chest tightened, her heart squeezing her. "What do you mean?"

"Before, I lost Elizabeth and my daughter. This time the baby and you. You shut me out. Both times I was alone to deal with my grief." His Adam's apple bobbed a few times as he seemed to be gathering himself under control. "I dealt with it because I love you and was willing to wait for you to come back to me. I thought you returned when we went out with our friends. Instead, you gave me one night before leaving. Fucking again."

"I was hurting, positive you blamed me for ruining your chance at being a father."

His head jerked as if she slapped him. Before he could confirm or deny it, she wrapped her arms around him. Her whole body shook, fearing his rejection.

"All I can say is I'm sorry, and my days of running from you are over. I'm yours forever. If you want me."

He stood stock-still, neither returning her embrace or speaking, until his cell dinged. She let go, and he fished his phone from his pocket. He typed something before meeting her gaze.

Her heart thrummed in her chest, racing beside her hopes and fears, waiting for his verdict.

"I have to go."

That's it?

"Um, who's running now?"

He smiled. It was a little worn around the edges but genuine. "Maybe. This is a lot to process. Plus, I'm meeting Will at a diner before the game. He's already there." He held his phone to her, Will's text on display. "Could we talk later?"

"Are we okay?" she asked.

"Harper, I swear, I'm not playing hard to get, but I thought we were done. I was trying to come to terms with it. Learning to readjust to life without you. Then I step outside and there you are, like a damn mirage, saying you want me back. I need to process everything you've said. I can't do it with you right here, and Will blowing up my phone." To drive the point home, his cell chimed again.

She stepped aside, her heart hurting. "Fine, go. I'll wait for you."

It seemed like he wanted to kiss her. She wished he would.

He didn't. After an unsure nod, he left.

Hearing the door click closed behind him, she listened to the creaks of his old house settling, deciding what to do next.

• • • ● • ● • ● • • •

"Sorry, man." Lucas slid into the booth across from Will.

"About damn time. You're almost forty minutes late," his friend complained. "What the hell happened?"

"Harper stopped by as I was leaving."

Will's eyes widened briefly. "Really. What did she want?"

"To talk." Lucas slumped into his seat. "To get back together."

"Um, isn't that what you wanted?"

"Yeah, but we've been through this before. A few times. I'm not sure I want to get back on that ride. I'm tired of how it ends."

"You're positive it will end, and the same way?"

"Well, no."

"Is it easier being without her?"

"No."

"Do you love her?"

"Yes. Are we playing Twenty Questions?" Lucas drawled.

Will smirked. "If you want. I've got plenty more."

"No. Get to the point."

"This reminds me of a conversation we had a few years ago, right after Elizabeth's funeral. You told me your biggest regret wasn't the pain of loving and losing her, but the time you wasted not being with her."

"That's different. I kept things casual because knew I'd fall hard and fast with her. Which I did, I might add. I was convinced I needed to finish college before getting serious with anyone. I didn't want to get married or have kids until I had a good job. With Harper, it's totally different."

"How so?" Will asked.

"I'm afraid she'll take off every time things aren't perfect." He ran a finger around the top of his water glass. "You and I both know, life rarely goes as planned and rushes by much too quickly. I don't want to spend mine chasing someone who might never stop running."

"Might," Will repeated. "Are you willing to let her go on a might?"

"I'm not sure."

The waitress stopped at their table, asking what they wanted to eat.

After she left, Lucas said, "Damn, did you miss your calling as a therapist?"

Will snorted. "Ha, I was thinking bartender. People would come from all around for my killer cocktails and advice." He shrugged. "Too bad for the whole recovering addict thing."

"Dude, I remember the drinks you made the few times we partied together. They were awful. Stick to the chef spiel. It's your calling." He glanced around the small bistro. "Which reminds me. Why are we eating at a restaurant a block from yours?"

"I'm afraid if we met at mine, someone would drag me into the kitchen with some issue or another." He propped his elbows on the table and lowered his voice. "Also, I'm checking out the competition."

The waitress returned with their drinks. Once she was gone, Will pushed Lucas's tea toward him.

"Drink this, son. Tell me your problems." He squinted at the tall glass. "What the hell is this?"

Lucas grabbed his drink. "Fresh peach tea. Don't judge. It sounded good."

"Oh, I'm definitely silently judging you, but let's get back to your therapy session."

"Um, what's this," he made air quotes, "session going to cost me?"

"Not much. Just dinner."

"Okay, Dr. Grimm—that is such a shitty therapist name, by the way."

"Bad as your girly tea?"

Lucas laughed, throwing his unopened straw at Will. "Excuse me, I didn't realize your orange Faygo was manly."

"Well, now you know. Knowledge is power and some other crap." He took a drink, then set his glass aside. "I have one more question."

Lucas made a get-on-with-it gesture, taking a sip of his drink. To hell with Will's teasing, the tea was freaking good.

"All the times before, when she took off, who came back to who? Did you pursue her, or the other way around?"

"I went after her. Why?"

"This time, she went to you." Will relaxed into his bench seat, resting his arms across the top back. "Wouldn't you say that's proof she's ready to stop running?"

Good point. In the past, she gave excuses for her actions. Today, she was straightforward with her mistakes and difficulties. There was a determination in her he'd never seen before.

This time she was serious. He knew it then, and now. So, was he the one running this time?

Maybe.

The waitress dropped off their food, saving him from answering. At the moment, Will's attention was on his food.

"This is my competition?" He poked at his pasta.

"You haven't even taken a bite. It might be perfection on a plate." Lucas jumped on the topic change. He checked his watch. "Anyway, eat fast. The first batter's up in less than an hour."

"Remind me again. Whose fault is it we're late?"

"Yeah, yeah…"

They did make it to the baseball game on time. Once there, the innings dragged on forever, even went into overtime. By the time Lucas slid his key into his front door, it was nearly midnight.

Indecision crawled over him. Should he call Harper or wait until the morning?

He wanted to try again. And again, if necessary. As many times as needed. She was the woman for him. He was willing to convince her of this, no matter how long it took. Plus, she was right. They'd both been holding back. He wanted that to change. Starting tonight.

He hung his keys on a hook inside the closet foyer. Walking into the living room, he removed his cell from his pocket and bounced it in his hand. The debate to call her continued to rage in him.

Until the quiet sound of leather shifting sent his heart racing. He swiveled around to face the couch. Someone was rising from it.

Swearing, he flipped on the light.

Harper stood before him, hair tousled, her eyes blurry from sleep. She looked like a dream.

"Shit, woman, that's the second time today you've made my heart jump in my throat." He couldn't help smiling.

She returned it, shy and sexy. "I told you, I'd wait for you."

He twisted at the waist, glancing out his front window. Yup. There was her Roadster parked at the curb.

Really observant, dude.

"I didn't think you meant it literally." Uncertainty flashed across her face, so he quickly added, "I don't mind. At all."

"Good. After you left, I couldn't go. I've spent the last year running from you. I'm done." She searched his face. "Unless you need more time. I did spring this on you."

"Yeah, you did, but I don't need more time." He came closer, brushing his lips across hers. "All I need is you."

Her mouth met his, and the demon sitting on his chest evaporated. His tongue teased her lips, craving more. She opened for him with a soft moan.

When they broke apart to catch their breath, she asked, "What changed? You were uncertain when you left."

"I talked with Will." He tickled her waist, making her squirm. "Don't ever tell him I admitted he was helpful. Plus, something you said rang true."

"Oh, yeah, what?" She ran her hands along his arms as if needing to touch him.

It suited him. His body was starving for her touch.

"I didn't realize at the time, but part of me was okay with the constant threat of you leaving. It allowed me to hold back. Not give you all of me. I'm terrified of loving and losing you." He kissed her temple. "Whether it's you walking away or something more tragic. And, you're right, I did pull away from you after the pregnancy."

He gently kissed her forehead and cheek. "They weren't for the reasons you said earlier. I never blamed you. But it had given me another awful taste of bitter loss. Deep down, I wasn't sure if I wanted to put myself in the path of that kind of debilitating pain again. Loving you would. It took time for me to understand it didn't matter. I was already in too deep. I'd take any agony life threw at me for even a sliver of time with you. You're worth it. Anyway, when I finally yanked myself from my pain and doubts, things were already broken between us. Guilt ate at me for not being there when you needed me. Then I lashed out when you asked for time. I'm sorry."

"So am I. My insecurities didn't allow for you to be open with me. Honestly, I didn't believe in love until I met you. It took a while for my head to accept what my heart had been telling it for months. I'm sorry you were the one to suffer through my growing pains."

"Arriving here made it worth it."

She took his hand, leading him toward his bedroom. "With you is where I'm staying. Forever and always."

Epilogue

Four Years Later.

"You almost ready?" Lucas strode into the living room.

Harper finished sticking the last piece of tape on the final birthday gift. Setting it aside, she took in her handsome husband. They'd been married three years, yet every time he walked into a room it still made her heart flutter. This feeling, she was sure it'd last well past their fiftieth anniversary.

She was sitting cross-legged in the middle of the living room floor, surrounded by wrapping paper. He took her hand, lifting her into his arms. She rested her head on his chest, loving how they fit together perfectly.

"I am," she told him. "But let's give Lily a little longer."

"If we do, there's a good chance we'll be late for the party."

"If anyone understands it'll be Greta and Jacob. They have two-year-old twins, so I'm sure they get it's a sin to wake a sleeping baby."

"True." He ran a palm along her spine. "What do you want to do while we wait?"

"Sleep," Harper moaned. Even saying the word made her eyelids heavier. "Your wonderful daughter woke me four times to nurse last night."

"And twice more for the hell of it," he added.

"Yeah." She hugged him tighter. "Thanks for taking her."

"Anytime. Once she's done nursing, I can do it more often."

A comfortable silence filled the room as Harper snuggled more into him, enjoying the lavender fragrance of detergent on his cotton button-up and the underlaying earthy spice of male. He ran his fingertips over her thin cashmere sweater, then along her spine.

He probably meant the movement to be relaxing, but heat was beginning to pool between her legs. She couldn't help it. Her husband was sexy and had a magic touch. He made her feel safe, cherished, and desirable.

Sliding her hands into the back pockets of his jeans, she brought him flush against her.

Tipping her face to him, he shifted to kiss her gently. She teased him with her tongue, turning it erotic.

Desire burned away any trace of sleepiness as he gathered her wool skirt in his hands, and she walked him backward toward the couch. They fell on to it, all frantic hands and lips.

She straddled his hips, rocking against him, and working on his shirt buttons. With a groan, he gripped the hem of her sweater.

A knock on the front door echoed through the house. Lucas cursed as Lily's startled grunt sounded from the baby monitor. Then, thankfully, went silent.

Quickly standing, Harper said, "We better see who it is before they wake her." She pointed at Lily's nursery.

Lucas snorted, pointing to his lap. "Babe, you better do it. I'm not really up for answering the door."

"Well, it looks to me like you're *up* for something." She giggled.

He rose and gripped her hips. "Yeah, and it isn't answering the door."

She'd gotten curvier since the pregnancy and birth of their daughter nine months ago. Sometimes it bothered her, but Lucas liked the change.

He kneaded her ass, eliciting a moan from her kiss-swollen lips. "Get rid of whoever's there, and I'll show you what I'm good for," he growled against her mouth.

There was another light knock. He slapped her butt. "Hurry."

She sprinted away, tempted to push off whoever was on her porch. Swinging open the door, she froze.

"Surprise," Cindy sang. Her gaze traveled from Harper's toes to her hopefully non-make-out tasseled hair. Her cousin smirked. "Oh. Did we interrupt some important *adult* time?"

"No." Heat crawled up Harper's neck, making its way to her cheeks.

"Um, is wearing your skirt sideways the new fashion?" Will asked, the humor spilling from his voice.

Harper's flush deepened, and she fixed her skirt. "Oh, shut-up, you two." She laughed. "Come inside. You weren't due in until around five. What changed? You guys are supposed to be closing out the party, not be the first arrivals."

"We checked the flights last night, and if we were willing to do a short layover in Chicago, we'd make it in time for the twin's party," Cindy told Harper on the way to the living room.

Lucas was putting away the wrapping paper, acting cool and unaffected. However, his rumpled hair, untucked shirt, with the top four buttons undone, gave away they hadn't been wrapping presents.

Will smirked at Lucas. "Sorry, man. Didn't mean to be a cockblocker."

"Will," Cindy admonished her husband, although her impish smile said she didn't care in the least.

Lucas laughed. "We have an infant. I'm used to it." He came around, giving them both a hug. "How was the restaurant opening? How's New York?"

"Smooth as these sorts of things can go," Will replied. "The head chef is extremely talented, and the staff is top-notch. Still, I'm nervous. It's our first bistro outside of Michigan."

Cindy patted his chest. "I have a good feeling. It will be the top eatery on the East Coast."

"And if not, I have my hot-shot travel journalist wife to keep me in pretty clothes." Will kissed Cindy, light and quick on the lips.

She snorted. "Oh! That reminds me. I got to visit the headquarters of *Travel and Leisure*. It was nice putting a face to the place that has accepted so many of my articles."

Harper placed her hands on her hips. "I hope you didn't have too much fun in New York. Don't get any ideas about moving there. My two best friends travel all the time. During your downtime, I want you here," she complained good-naturedly.

"Don't worry, cousin. Will and I have no plans to move. Plus, I sure as hell wouldn't go somewhere colder than here." Cindy pointed at the living room's window. It faced the backyard. The trees were bare, and the grass was covered with a thick layer of snow. Turning back to them, her eyes were shining, and a nervous smile pulled at the corner of her mouth. "Also, I'm going to need you and Greta nearby for the ten million questions I'm sure to ask."

She placed a hand on her flat stomach. Joy leaped in Harper's heart. "You're pregnant?"

Cindy nodded, and Harper ran to her cousin, wrapping her in a tight hug. "I'm so happy for you!"

She heard Lucas congratulating Will as she squeezed Cindy tighter, asking, "When are you due?"

"Early fall."

As the four of them talked, Lucas's cellphone rang. He told them it was Tanner before answering and stepping away.

"Is ThreePence done with their latest tour?" Cindy asked.

"Yup, finished last week. That's it until after the wedding." Harper rocked on the heels of her feet. "Can you believe Maggie and Tanner are finally tying the knot?"

Not because they didn't love each other. They did, profoundly and deeply. Harper learned during their years of friendship, Maggie bucked anything traditional.

Cindy squealed. "I can't wait to party with my girls. While my favorite will always be Greta and Jacob's combo Bachelor/Bachelorette party," she winked at her husband, "your girl's weekend in Chicago for shopping, museums, and clubbing was a blast. Now we get a week in Vegas! It will probably be my last big party before the baby."

Mentioning infants made a nervous tremor flutter in her stomach.

It must have run through Lucas as well, because he said, "I wish we could bring Lily."

"Dude." Will laughed. "Vegas and babies don't mix. Although, I can totally picture you at the Poker table with your Baby Bjorn."

Lucas shrugged. It was true. He'd do it. They took Lily nearly everywhere with them. They were lucky their careers allowed it. Although, Harper suspected it might change when Lily began to crawl. Art galleries and offices weren't the best places for an inquisitive kid.

Then again, maybe not. To Harper's complete surprise, Ben adored Lily and loved entertaining her when she visited the Salvador Building. He'd swoop her into his arms, carrying her off with cuddles and baby-talk.

Harper bumped her husband with her hip. "You better not try to bring Lily. Your parents would be devastated if they didn't get their one-on-one time with their newest granddaughter." She leaned closer and said, "I'm very excited to have your delicious body all to myself without any interruptions."

He kissed the side of her head. "That, and a few nights of unbroken sleep."

She relaxed into him, sighing, "Oh my god, yesss..."

As if sensing she was the topic of discussion, Lily's happy squeal sang through the baby monitor.

Lucas chuckled. "It's because we were talking about sleep—something she forbids us to do."

"Oh! Let me get her. I want the first person she sees to be her Auntie Cindy."

"No." Will speed walked down the hall toward the nursery. "You got her last time. It's my turn."

The two took off for the nursery, Cindy playfully shoving and trying to trip Will. He was complaining it wasn't fair because he couldn't retaliate against his pregnant wife.

"Should we be worried?" Lucas laughed.

"Nah, they'll wear each other out before reaching Lily." Harper smiled wide enough for her face to hurt. It felt wonderful.

That happened a lot since letting go of her fears and giving Lucas her heart. She'd never met someone with so much love to give. It now seemed silly she'd once believed he couldn't give her all she needed. He did and so much more.

She entwined her fingers behind his neck and whispered, "I love you."

"Always, my wife." He kissed her. "Yesterday, today, and tomorrow. Forever."

Bonus Story

Welcome, I love that we are meeting here, at Lucas and Harper's happily ever after! If you're not ready to leave the feel-good world of romance, I have a treat for you- a FREE novella.

Sign up for her newsletter at DKMARIE.COM, and you'll receive a story from the Lake House Love series along with my monthly newsletter!

Visit DKMARIE.COM and sign up for the newsletter, and the FREE novella below will be delivered to your inbox.

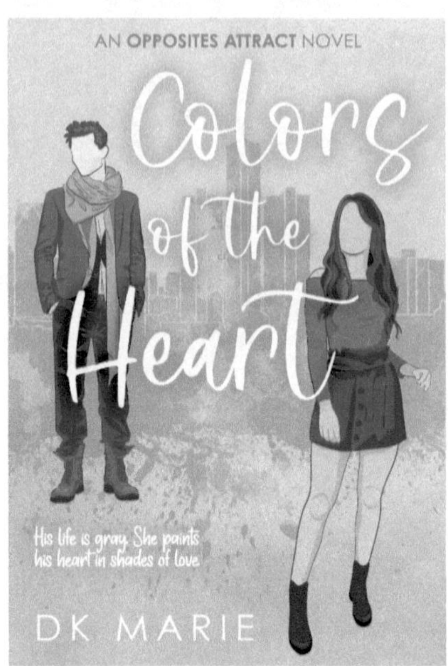

AN OPPOSITES ATTRACT NOVEL
Colors
of the
Heart
His life is gray. She paints
his heart in shades of love.
DK MARIE

Dear Reader

Whether you're a returning reader or new, thank you. It is wonderful to write, but a dream to share my stories with others.

Lucas and Harper are my heart, and it's a joy to share them with you. I hope you love reading their story as much as I did writing it.

Also, if you're not ready to let them go, talk to others about them —by leaving a review on Goodreads or whatever site you love. Even a simple sentence would mean the world to me and will keep the vibrant colors of Harper and Lucas's love in others' minds and hearts.

Last, you can visit them as secondary characters in most other Opposites Attract books.

Keep reading for an excerpt of Fairy Tale Lies.

Thank you!
DK Marie

Chapter One

Greta Meier dashed down the carpeted hallway of Swift Financial, ignoring the agony of power walking in three-inch heels. That pain was minuscule compared to the dread pooling in her stomach. She'd lost track of time. Again.

Sure, she'd managed to fix the in-house software issue but, meanwhile, had forgotten the new client meeting. Glancing at her tiny gold Rolex, she groaned. Less than five minutes to make it to the other end of the building.

She could picture her boss's disappointed face, made all the more stressful because it was her father. The image had Greta quickening her pace to a near sprint.

Rounding the final corner, she sighed. The large glass doors were propped open. Relief calmed some of her anxiety. She wasn't late.

Inside the conference room, her assistant Rae motioned to the empty seat next to her. Greta nodded and skated alongside the outermost edges of the table, wishing she were smaller, invisible. She hoped no one would notice her near tardy arrival. The last thing she wanted was to come across as the empty-headed daughter of the boss. Someone who'd gotten the internship through nepotism. Therefore, any misstep ate at her confidence like termites to wood.

She took her seat next to Rae and tried to squash her rampant doubts. Running a shaky hand over her chignon, she made sure every hair was in place.

"Where's Allen?" Greta glanced around the table while needlessly straightening the collar of her pale, pink blouse. Realizing she was fidgeting, putting her anxiety on full display, she stilled and met Rae's gaze.

She handed the client folder Greta hadn't had time to open and sighed. "Another virus was detected on Blake's computer. He demanded we fix it, like yesterday. Allen's working on it."

Greta accepted the portfolio, her worry shifting to annoyance. She didn't want to talk about her ex-fiancé, much less be reminded he was in-house counsel. Before their breakup, they hardly ran into each other at work. Now Blake kept inventing problems with his PC and contacting the IT department. Rae and Allen found it hilarious, but Greta despised the drama. It made her and Blake appear unprofessional.

Refusing to meet Rae's playful smile, Greta peered down the table at her father. His back was to a large window with its blinds pulled. The leaves from the giant elm and oak trees swayed in a lazy breeze, helping to block Michigan's hot summer sun from the room. She'd love to be out there, relaxing in the shade, enjoying her summer and free of stress.

Her gaze zeroed back in on her father, and the usual mixture of pride and discontent filled her. She understood he only wanted the best for her, but sometimes his rigidness was stifling. Carrying her father's expectations, and his disappointment of her, was a heavy burden to shoulder.

Thankfully, he hadn't noticed her near-late arrival time. There'd be no displeased glances, no lectures concerning punctuality. He appeared distracted, deep in conversation with a man she assumed was a new client.

She gave an inward sigh of relief, allowing some of her distress to dissolve. Father's career talks turned back the clock, and suddenly she was closer to seven than twenty-seven. Enjoying the reprieve, she relaxed into her seat and studied the client. He sat sideways, elbow propped on the table, large hand covering most of his face as he talked with her father. There was something familiar in the set of the client's broad shoulders and his inky black hair.

Inexplicably, her heart began to race. Watching him filled her with trepidation and an unexpected yearning.

Her father faced the room, pulling her gaze from the stranger to the wall clock. Yup, ten on the dot. A meeting never started late.

She glanced back at the client and choked on an exhale, her heart plummeting. He'd dropped his hand and was facing forward.

It can't be him.

Her heart skipped with joy. Then promptly flooded with dread.

"You okay?" Rae whispered. Her voice sounded far away, wrapped in fog.

Greta couldn't answer because the client's familiar icy-blue gaze had locked on hers. His eyes widened in recognition.

He was clean-shaven, and today his hair was neat and combed back, but there was no mistaking him. *Jacob.* He had one of those striking faces, impossible to forget. The memories of the way those bedroom eyes had heated as he'd taken in her naked body, or how those full lips had ravished her, made him unforgettable.

However, she wished he'd slip from her memory and the conference room. Whatever his reason for being here wouldn't be good for her.

"Good morning. Let me introduce Mr. Jacob Grimm."

Hearing his name, he turned toward her father, allowing her to breathe.

Rae nudged Greta, probably waiting for an answer. Too bad. She was admitting nothing.

"He runs Rework, a business repairing and refurbishing antiques. We're taking it to the next level," continued her father. "He plans on opening a brick-and-mortar shop in Detroit and developing a better online presence."

Business owner? No, no, no.

There had been some mistake. He wasn't supposed to be sitting at her father's conference table. Jacob was a deliveryman. He worked for his uncle. It's what he told her at her mother and stepfather's home. So, why wasn't he lifting heavy things and breaking promises?

Greta flipped through the file Rae had given her. Successful was an understatement. His client base was impressive, as were the big names in the dossier. Stapled to the back of the folder was a copy of Jacob's license.

Foolish woman. Hadn't her father always told her to come to a meeting prepared? Had she even glanced at the file, she'd have recognized Jacob in an instant. Weeks had passed, but that foolish, impulsive afternoon was far from forgotten.

As her father addressed the room, Greta focused on Jacob's picture. She found it safer than facing the actual man.

They'd only spent a couple of hours together, but his wicked full mouth and penetrating gaze had been impossible to forget. Along with his magical ability to destroy all her restraints. Greta still couldn't quite believe how easily her inhibitions had fled in the company of a perfect stranger.

She closed the folder and rubbed her sweaty palms on her pleated linen skirt. She stared at her father and tried to concentrate on his words, though he could've been speaking another language and she wouldn't have noticed.

There was no way she could swallow her embarrassment and work with Jacob. Not even for a day, let alone a week or more.

Her pulse thudded in her ears. What if he bragged about his one-night-stand with the boss's daughter? Father would kill her. Not literally, but professionally. He wouldn't want the family name smeared with tawdry office gossip.

He'd promised, after she graduated with her Master's in Web Development, she'd take over Swift's websites and handle the clients needing web development help. Would the offer still stand if he learned of her history with Jacob?

So much for proving herself with a summer internship. Greta wanted to weep at the disappearance of her imagined stellar portfolio. Swift Financial would have been wonderful on her resume.

Focus. I need to focus and get control of the situation.

Leaning in, she whispered to Rae, "I need to go. Would you and Allen mind handling this account? I'll owe you one."

"What's wrong?" Rae's forehead furrowed in concern.

That question was too big to answer now. Later. "Will you do this for me?"

Rae bit her lip. "I'll try, but you know your father wants you in charge of web designing."

Yes, I know. Hopefully I'll come up with a stellar excuse to wiggle out of the Rework contract.

She'd worry about it later and mouthed a thank you and gathered her papers. When there was a pause in the main conversation, she addressed the room. "I'm sorry. There's been a mistake. Allen Carnaby will handle this account with Mrs. Caitlin." She stood. "I'll find him."

Her father's stern voice stopped her. "No, Ms. Meier, the account is yours and Mrs. Caitlin's. I have another project in mind for Mr. Carnaby." His tone brooked no argument.

Darn it. There went her quick and painless getaway.

She nodded. To argue was pointless and would only anger her father. Returning to her seat, she glanced covertly at Jacob. He'd lost most of his color and looked like he'd been poked with a cattle prod.

Replaying the exchange, she realized she'd been addressed by her last name. Jacob must have caught it, grasped its significance. He appeared rattled.

Good.

Maybe he didn't want to share their secret any more than she did. Thank goodness. It would save her from her father's wrath.

Next challenge—squashing her lingering thrill at seeing Jacob again.

Chapter Two

Her, of all people!

Jacob blinked. Nope, she hadn't disappeared back into his fantasies. Her!

He tried not to stare but found it difficult to accept the rapid-fire shocks. The most nerve-racking item of the day was supposed to be signing his financial dream on the dotted line. Instead, he sat face to face with the woman who haunted an entirely different set of dreams.

He'd strived to banish the memory of their spring afternoon together. He wanted to forget the way her laughter had made him lighter, more alive. He'd tried to forget those soulful hazel eyes and sexy, full lips. Lips made for kissing.

He sure as hell hadn't forgotten the way she'd barely given him time to dress before shoving him out the back door. Confused and insulted, he'd returned to the grand salon, or whatever rich people called those extra useless rooms, to help his uncle finish the job. She'd disappeared, obviously embarrassed by him and what they'd done.

Going by her current reaction, things hadn't changed. She still saw him as a weed in her impeccably manicured life.

Not that he wanted to make their past known. A Meier, not a Silverstone!

The delivery order had clearly stated the items were for a Silverstone residence. Hadn't she made the comment the home was her parents'?

Shit. Was she Charles Meier's niece, daughter, or young wife? Each one of those options landed like a brick in his gut.

Seriously, of all the women in the world, why did it have to be her? Here? Now?

His life revolved around building Rework. His focus so complete, he couldn't remember the last time he'd been on a date or even noticed a pretty woman.

Then two months ago, his uncle Marty called, asking if he'd help deliver and install an antique chandelier. Jacob agreed, expecting nothing more than a little extra cash.

Instead, he'd been knocked on his ass at the mere sight of the woman who answered the door. Her jewel-like amber eyes, accented with those full lips, was captivating. What's more, after they'd left for lunch and talked, her confident reserve and quiet ferocity seduced him. To his surprise, she was as drawn to him as he to her. Watching her struggle between virtue and wickedness, and letting her wild side win, had been the hottest thing he'd ever experienced.

"Mr. Grimm?"

He gave a mental shake and focused on Charles. Freaking Charles *Meier*. "Sorry, what did you say?" Jacob was proud at how calm he sounded.

A Meier, not a Silverstone...

"Would you please accompany Mrs. Caitlin and Ms. Meier to their office," her father or uncle or husband repeated.

Jacob suspected Charles made this request a few times.

"They'll need your insight for the new webpage and additional information to upgrade your accounts."

"Okay. No problem," Jacob replied.

The two men stood and shook hands. Jacob's was trembling, but at least he'd been able to talk past the anxiety trying to claw its way out of his throat.

He followed the two women from the conference room, wondering if he'd jeopardized years of hard work with one impulsive and incredibly hot afternoon. He couldn't lose his contract with Swift Financial. Every bank had turned him down, said his company was 'too niche', this was his last chance.

What was she to Charles Meier? Would she tell him how'd they met and what they'd done?

Sleeping with his wife or daughter might be enough to have the man searching for loopholes in the contract and dumping Rework.

Once in the corridor, Jacob moved next to the women. His focus shifted from the woman who used and dumped him, to the pretty African-American. She was watching him with open curiosity.

He didn't want to have this conversation with an audience. "Greta, can we talk... alone?"

She didn't even bother looking in his direction, answering in an imperious tone and sounding like the princess she thought she was. "No. There's no need, and please address me as Ms. Meier."

The other woman gasped, her gaze jumping between him and Greta. "You two know each other?"

"Yes," Jacob replied.

Greta spoke over him. "Not really."

The hell she didn't. Was she going to pretend they were complete strangers?

"Mr. Grimm," came a man's voice from the conference room.

All three swung around at the unexpected interruption.

The guy stumbled back. Jacob could only imagine the expressions on their faces.

"We forgot to have you sign a couple of things. Will you please come back? I'll show you to the IT office after."

Jacob ran a hand down his face, peering at Greta. From the hard set of her jaw and defensive posture, her talking probably wasn't going to happen. He nodded to the man, moving away from the two women.

Before returning to the conference room, he stopped and faced Greta. "We aren't finished. We have to talk."

The prospect didn't seem to please her but screw it, he needed answers. And to set things straight. There was no way she was going to ruin this for him. After years at a standstill, his business was moving forward.

Want to keep reading? Click on the book cover!

Also by DK Marie

LOVE SONGS

She sings to the wild side of his heart, strumming his needs against his desires, disrupting his harmony.

Maggie Preswyck carries music in her soul; she lives and breathes melody. Nothing and no one can get in the way of her band's success. Including Tanner Reid— her sexy, temporary guitarist. His talent and quiet humor are irresistible. But mixing business with pleasure could destroy her heart and career.

Every time they rehearse, the chords of passion between them deepen. But Maggie will never give up on her music, and Tanner doesn't want the life of a musician—Her dream is his nightmare. With no middle ground, all that waits for them at the end of his time with the band is heartbreak.

Can Maggie and Tanner adjust their dreams, or will they become another sad love song?

Love Songs is the second book in the standalone, steamy Opposites Attract contemporary romance series. If you like strong characters, intense and swoon-worthy scenes, then you'll adore DK Marie's passionate friends-to-lovers tale.

Get a Love Songs for a story that'll sing to your heart!

TASTE OF PASSON

She has a taste for trouble. He craves more than her body. Together they could be a recipe for love or disaster...

Opposites, Cindy Meier and Will Grimm, have two things in common. They love to annoy each other, and their siblings are getting married. *That's it.*

Oh, and they have to plan the weekend wedding party. Will doesn't want to put up with the spoiled socialite who lives in a fantasy world. And Cindy could think of better ways to spend her free time with her hot but grumpy brother-in-law. The only way to survive the awful chore is with snips, sarcasm, and sparring.

When they're forced together on the sunny beaches of Lake Michigan, their annoyance and amusement morph into something neither expected nor wanted—desire. They give in, agreeing it won't extend past the weekend. *It can't.* Will had finally crawled out of the hell he'd created, and someone like Cindy would send him back into it. And while she might enjoy Will's body and what he does with it, she won't change to fit into his life.

As they struggle to keep their attraction and deepening feelings at bay, they'll have to decide if overcoming their differences is worth the passion they've tasted...

Taste of Passion is the third book in the stand-alone steamy *Opposites Attract* contemporary romance series. If you like vulnerable, real characters who'll make you laugh, lust, and fall in love, you'll adore DK Marie's friends-to-lovers romance.

Buy *Taste of Passion* for a delicious story that'll fill your heart!

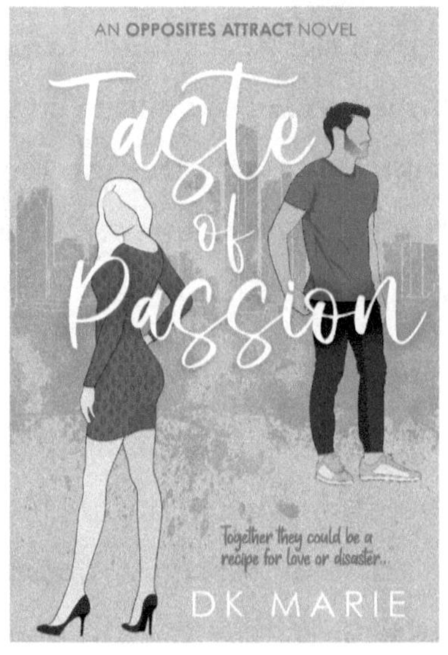

New Series! Lake House Love

A small-town romance series with heart, heat, and a splash of humor.

About Author

DK Marie loves to indulge in all things hot. Men, writing, reading, and coffee. The order of importance depends on the day.

Like characters in her books, she lives in Michigan, enjoying her happily ever after with her husband and kids. When not writing, she loves the heater, concerts, and traveling.

Talking to readers is jelly jam! Click on the tree to find her on your favorite social media!

Acknowledgments

There are so many people to thank. First, my family, who've supported and understood my need to disappear into my stories for weeks on end. My wonderful editor, Jodi. My talent cover designer, Avery.

And I definitely can't leave out my writer friends on social media and real life. Writing is an isolating career, and having other authors to lean on is a lifejacket when the waters get rough.

I have to give a shout-out to Shanna and Rowena. Thank you for beta reading this story and all the other help you've provided along the way. I'd be lost without you ladies.

And to you. With readers, these stories would be only musing in my mind. Thank you for let me share them with you.